Trauma's Worth

By

Heather Jessica Sieben Bell

ISBN:

Dedication

This book is dedicated to my amazing children:

Isaac, Emmitt, Kilie, and Jaycee

You are my world, my purpose, and my heart.

I love you unconditionally.

You are all worth it!

Acknowledgments

I have been told, nearly all of my life, that I needed to write a book/memoir. The older I've gotten, the more urgent that need has become, and it was finally time. So many people throughout my life should be thanked for helping this book become my reality, several for choosing to be there when they didn't have to be, Ron and Nancy and Frank and Lee, and several for helping to create the trauma that inspired the book in the first place (but can I really thank them?).

For the actual production of the book, and, more importantly, for the growth and evolution into who I am now, a person I am very proud to be, there are some people who must be thanked personally, for without them, I am not quite sure I would have survived the last several years, let alone had gotten to where I am now.

To my amazing kids Isaac, Emmitt, Kilie, and Jaycee, thank you for being the definition of love and showing me that I am enough as just me. Thank you for giving me a purpose and a reason to endure. (And for Marcy, my sweet labradoodle born the day after my free-fall started… you always just know.)

To Marge for always knowing where I stood (even more than I understood at times) and for supporting me at each step, for believing in me and my purpose, and for encouraging me to own my mess with pride.

Mike, thank you for answering all of the hard questions, even the ones without answers, for being my friend and mentor on my faith journey, and for accepting where I came from, what faults I have, and who I am underneath it all.

To Lisa, thank you for staying my friend through the worst years, for supporting me as I found my way, for the many miles of therapy runs, and for having such an amazing son!

BreeAnn, my blessed angel of a friend, your soul and heart are unmatched. Your encouragement and nonjudgemental support have helped me accept myself and have the confidence to know I'm worth it.

To Bobee, Jen, and Michelle, the Grand Canyon crew, for the hours of conversations while tackling Rim2Rim, the most amazing, exhausting, and motivating event ever. Thank you for being there for those final steps during that pivotal experience and moment in my journey to being a better me, my reset.

To the crew at Hazelden, especially Bruce, Tammi, Nyk, Steve, and Luther, you all helped me heal in more ways than I can count. You allowed me to trust colleagues again by being such genuine and honest people. You helped me find the joy in medicine again, and the hours of commute to the greatest colleagues, allowed for my dictating this book!

To Jillian, Misty, and Teresa, without you all, clearly, I wouldn't be here. You know who you are and what you all did—I am indebted to you forever!

Steve and Margie, thank you for not only your support and encouragement for this project but also for your kindness, love, acceptance, grace, generosity, and forgiveness. Thank you for giving me a place to live at times and for being a sounding board on so many things. For being an example of unconditional.

And to you, Josh. Although you're not in this book, not really anyway (wait for the next one), without you and our story, I would never have become the better, more authentic version of me, the real me. Thank you for taking down all of my walls and for trying so hard not to fight me back when I got triggered. I am a work in progress. Thank you for loving me anyway. Thank you for tolerating my hours of writing, editing, and mental blocks, and, more importantly, thank you for doing the laundry, dishes, 'boy jobs' and painting while you waited. Thank you for loving my kids as your own and for sharing Ben and Graham with me, too.

To my main editor, Ava, you are a rockstar, and I appreciate everything you have done to make this book even better than I could have imagined. Thank you for being sensitive to the hard parts, understanding my greater purpose, and highlighting what mattered most.

To June and Alice, thank you for coordinating the entire team for this project as well as for the screenplay project. And June, additionally, thank you for tolerating my paranoia and irritability throughout this more than two-year process and for somehow managing to still encourage and support me anyway. I am so sorry!

To Waseem, thank you for truly seeing my story and the greater impact it can have on so many people. For the hours of work put in to build a team to help get the book and my story out to so many more people than I could ever have dreamed. If this story has the impact you promised it can, then I owe you that dinner I promised you!

About the Author

Heather Sieben Bell is a dedicated author, physician, and mother whose life experiences have shaped her compassionate outlook. Through her writing, Heather shares her reflections on resilience, personal growth, and the power of self-awareness.

Heather's professional background in medicine has given her a unique perspective on life's challenges and the strength required to overcome them. Coupled with her personal experiences, she offers a voice that connects deeply with readers, encouraging them to confront struggles with courage and honesty.

As a mother of four, Heather draws inspiration from her family, which she describes as her greatest source of pride and purpose. Her children have profoundly influenced her understanding of perseverance and grace, themes that are reflected throughout her work.

Heather's ability to communicate her thoughts with clarity and warmth allows her readers to feel both understood and motivated. She writes with authenticity, sharing insights into how challenges can teach us valuable lessons and shape our sense of purpose.

When she is not writing or practicing medicine, Heather enjoys finding ways to nurture meaningful connections and continue learning from life's experiences. Her dedication to helping others find strength through her work has made her a trusted and relatable voice for many.

Through *Trauma's Worth* and her future projects, Heather aims to inspire readers to reflect on their own lives and find strength in their unique paths.

Table of Contents

Purpose: My Heart

My purpose in writing this book is to show my kids and others that it is okay to struggle, it is okay to fail, and it is ok to be sad and to need. I want to show that it is okay to admit your mistakes and own them. It is okay to have guilt and maybe even shame, but it is important always to be honest and true to yourself. Even more importantly, I want to show that, no matter what has happened and no matter what was done or why, we all deserve forgiveness and grace, and are worth another chance to try to get it right. Even if that doesn't go well either, it's important to continue to keep trying!

My greatest accomplishment, pride, joy, heart, soul, and purpose is my four kids. To respect their privacy, this will be brief.

I found out I was pregnant for the first time on Mother's Day, 2009. A week prior, Carson, my ex-husband, and I graduated from Medical School. To say we were shocked is an understatement. We had literally just graduated from medical school, had a 2.5-month-old yellow lab puppy (Ripley), we were moving 5 hours away from anyone we knew for residency, and we were buying our first house. It's the whole "don't make a lot of life changes all at once" thing. I do wonder what would have happened to our marriage had we just been married for a while, just lived as the two of us, really got to know each other, traveled together, and just been together to establish the ebb and flow of a life-long partnership… hmm, well, maybe we should have done those things BEFORE we got married, but still, I wouldn't change a thing because we have the most amazing kids in the world.

I do wonder if there were too many firsts and stress and not enough happiness and contentment. Maybe our timing was wrong. But is timing ever truly wrong, or do all things happen the way they are supposed to? The entire flow of my life, it seems, is all based on timing. So many things happened too soon, and it seems I learned all my lessons too late. So maybe that's not actually a thing then, either.

Did the too-soons need to happen when they did so I would learn the lessons that came too late, or did I just rush so many things that I never had a chance to learn the things that would have helped and prepared me for when the too-soons came? It's an interesting idea, really. I will say, however, that some of my too-soons were impossible to prep for, and as a result, the trauma that followed delayed the lessons, or, rather, the lessons were just confused or lost in translation, overshadowed by the innate need just to survive. This, then, resulted in reality, wisdom, self-awareness, self-worth, and understanding, as opposed to just survival, being way too late.

So why, then, when I loved Carson so much, did it not work and why couldn't we figure it out regardless of the timing? Did the timing actually play in, or was it never a good match anyway? I could argue both sides of this argument myself. I think if we had more 'time' either we would have found that perfect flow and connection with each other, that very important marriage foundation, or we would have realized we were never a good match at all anyway.

I'm not sure I would have gotten to that place of seeing how poorly matched we were at that point in my life, especially while so entranced by his outward perfect-to-the-world charisma and where I was at with my trauma therapy. It doesn't matter now, I suppose, and what is important at this moment is that there will always be love there because of our kids. In that sense, one could argue that the timing was perfect because had it not been what it was, these amazing 4 kids wouldn't be, and the world clearly needed them to be!

The deepest love of all, beyond imagination, is the love I have for my kids. Even thinking about them, I can feel my heart burst with joy every time, it never fades and, if anything, just grows more each day. Throughout my kids' lives thus far, I have experienced many highs and many lows; I've made some of the greatest choices, and I've made some of the absolute worst choices. I have been a person I am proud of, and I have been a person I am so very ashamed of; I have been an amazing example and I have been the absolute worst example. It is a Jekyll and Hyde situation that I wish I could redo parts of.

I do believe that I am an absolutely amazing mom, much like my mom was. Ironically, I didn't 'see' or 'know' or, rather, appreciate how amazing my mom was until it was way too late... again, the timing thing. I suppose this is more common than not for all parent-kid situations. I just wish I could personally tell her that.

At times, with my kids, I feel like I am trying too hard or that I am always falling too short. It's like the insecurities I have related to so much abandonment and so much just always trying to prove myself worthy of one true person who will always choose me, somehow, perhaps, makes me try too hard with them. I just do not have that innate feeling of what 'home' feels like and I just question if I am good enough for them all the time.

But then, if I step back and look at me through their eyes, and I acknowledge how in tune and attuned I am with all of them, and I just feel what I feel with them whether we are 'home' or not, I know, and I believe, that they are the very purpose I live for, and that I am enough. I know that one day they will all leave and be adults and possibly parents and have their own lives, but I also know, okay, I hope, that I will always be home for them. I know that I don't have to be perfect for them.

When they inevitably know my mistakes and all the things I've not done right, they will probably have questions, and they may be mad and hurt and other things, but more than anything, I hope they will come to me directly to ask the questions. I hope they will understand how I got to my bad parts, how I got to my good parts, and how I owned it all and found the strength to stand up and try again and fight to be even better. I hope they know that they don't have to be perfect; I hope they know I will be there always, no matter what and no matter where, regardless of the circumstances.

My kids know what love and home feel like and, one may argue even more importantly, what safety feels like. I hope and pray that they never feel the need to prove themselves, that they can always be their authentic selves no matter where they are, that they can walk away when they aren't being respected, that they can dream and hope and stumble and fail and restart and struggle and know that they are never alone. I hope they learn from my mistakes.

Preface: This is My Story

This is the truth from my perspective. This is my recall of events, situations, traumas, and feelings. I will not, and cannot, speak to the intent or the mindset of others; I am only able to give my internalized feelings, and they should be interpreted that way. Many may argue or try to, but that can be their truth. This is mine. There is nothing in this book that is meant to defame anyone, for the events described are meant only to lay out my experiences and how they all shaped, molded, and helped me grow in my resilience and strength. My story will show my traumas and patterns of my past to hopefully help others find revelations in their own experiences.

No one knows why certain situations become traumas that we carry with us, but, in reality, it is no one else's place to judge how anyone experiences any given situation. I wouldn't choose my triggered reactions to the traumas of my past, but I wouldn't have chosen to be treated the way I was, either. Although many situations, especially into my adulthood, look like I chose the situation, 'choices' are not that simple. When we are trained to accept being treated a certain way, and our normal comfort mistakenly grows from being manipulated or love-bombed, the patterns are not actually that difficult to understand. Even I question 'what was I thinking,' but hindsight is, by nature and definition, too late.

The underlying tone and message of this book is meant to show resilience in the face of direct 'capital T' traumas, situational traumas, and traumas I essentially brought on myself, driven all from the same place of just wanting to be enough, chosen, and loved. Humans are, after all, meant to have connection and live in community. I have no intention of presenting myself as a hero or as a victim. I am simply attempting to demonstrate resilience from the perspective of a repetitively abandoned and unchosen female in a predominately male-dominated world and how, as such, at times, I was preyed upon, how I felt that I needed to behave and act, and how it all fell apart, and then was brought back together. I am not perfect, nor have I ever, nor will I ever claim to be. I will, with full sincerity, own each mistake and role I played.

Please, if you know me or the others in the book (names have been changed), understand this is my story, and I do acknowledge there are multiple interpretations of each situation. Again, I do not intend to cast blame, give excuses, or rationalize my contributions and actions in these situations. I hope, throughout the reading, you, the reader, will understand the growth, self-awareness, and journey that I took and use the example not for any other reason than to give possible light and inspiration to your life so your fall won't perhaps, need to be as far.

Prologue: Know Thyself

My sister Anna died on September 2, 2021. She had a tattoo just under her collarbone, in Greek letters (no idea why), that said, "Know Thyself." When I was asked to write the obituary and subsequent eulogy, this phrase wouldn't leave my mind and, as such, had to be part of the narrative. (Two days before the funeral, I got a replica of her tattoo on my wrist.) Over the time since her passing, however, this phrase has gained even more meaning.

In my field of practice, addiction medicine, I have the honor and privilege of meeting the very best people this world has to offer. People who have literally seen Hell, people who have experienced an entire world of torture, some self-created yet mostly not, and people who, unlike those far more fortunate for a multitude of reasons, are the strongest, bravest, most resilient, humble, gracious, forgiving, compassionate, and kind people that exist (there are so many other words I could list, but you get the point—they are the best).

They own their 'ugly' and, on top of that, they typically also got and/or get to own it in public where everyone else, clearly far too bored in their own stark white lives, get to, for some reason, have an opinion. (Honestly, I believe they feel they get an opinion for the sole purpose of masking their own issues they are not strong enough to tackle.)

I'm not even talking about the 'ugly' that is in the court system where, yes, strangers do 'get' to have an opinion. I'm referring to the gossip and ridicule and public shunning that occurs because everyone else seems to think they know 'the whole story and truth' and therefore feels it is their place to divide the 'them' out (like addiction or, frankly, being human and making any type of mistake, somehow may become some communicable disease and all of those who are not living in sparkling glass houses and displaying their, hypocritically, publicly perceived perfection each Sunday in the church is not worthy of, well, anything—let alone grace, love and, my favorite, the very forgiveness their 'Sunday perfection' is supposed to be about.)

But I digress...my patients, whether in long-term recovery, still actively using but wanting to stop but feel so hopeless and helpless they have no idea where even to begin, or who are caught in the disease cycle, are the most beautiful humans. But here's the thing: many of my colleagues and friends have also been through the same Hell and live with the same disease, so how can society so easily 'other' one from another? Why do some with the genetics and disease of addiction get chosen to be the 'better' even if they have the "worse" addictions or more "dirty" addictions? We don't divide breast cancer patients based on anything else but severity and need, so why does this disease get treated so differently? I will never understand.

One of my colleagues, when discussing Alcoholics Anonymous (AA) as a concept and then in relation to other spiritual ideas, told me about a book, "*The Spirituality of Imperfection. Storytelling and the Search for Meaning*" by Ernest Kurtz and Katherine Ketcham. This 'enlightenment' of a recommendation was made at the very beginning of my orientation with him. I wonder how, exactly, we got to such an in-depth place while discussing such a long-accepted concept so fast. And that, my dear readers, is the beauty of the disease, the beauty of the broken, the beauty of the shunned or outcast or ridiculed or questioned or the 'less than' or the mistake makers… they get it. They just know, they feel, and they, like my colleague, welcome, embrace, and give grace and support. They understand. He saw right through me that day.

Nearly 30 years my senior, this 'old, white male' was the first of his kind in my entire career to see me as his equal. All others before him judged, questioned, minimized, harassed, and so many other disgusting things, and got away with it because of the business of medicine and the 'good old boys club' which, by its very definition, was intended to 'less than' anyone not like them.

Let me digress further and add that just before this encounter with this new colleague, I got to experience three white men in recovery from this same exact disease who had also been seen as less than in their lives treat me the same way the good old boys club had. There are those in recovery who, upon gaining this magical perceived 'power,' feel the need to repay the hell to someone else in order to sleep better at night because, by acting in the way they had been treated, they somehow just 'made it.' They, however, it must be said, are the extreme minority of those in recovery.

Anyway, there I was, with a brand-new colleague who had himself visited the depths of hell, who, even later, upon learning some of my story, still accepted me and extended grace. Not only that, he brought up so many thought-provoking concepts, actually cared about my ideas, and then pushed them further with this small yet significant book.

This book recommendation, in true fate of nature, tied back to my sister and her 'Know Thyself' tattoo and was just the sign I needed to tell me I was where I belonged. It pushed me down the path of self-forgiveness, self-acceptance, and self-love to a place where everything you are about to read can, at least in one big wave, also start to be forgiven.

On page 19 of "*The Spirituality of Imperfection*," the authors start by saying, "The search for spirituality is, first of all, a search for reality, for honesty, for true speaking and true thinking." (Spirituality in this context does not mean religion or even God necessarily, but, rather, is a greater concept of self and sense.) They then comment on the Delphic oracle's first admonition, *Know Thyself,* for denial, i.e., self-deception, is the very paradox of knowing oneself. So, to these authors, "Know Thyself" as a spirituality of imperfection is:

A spirituality of imperfection suggests that spirituality's first step involves facing self squarely, seeing one's self as one is: mixed-up, paradoxical, incomplete, and imperfect. Flawedness is the first fact about human beings. And paradoxically, in that imperfect foundation we find not despair but joy. For it is only within the reality of our imperfection that we can find the peace and serenity we crave.

I'll let that sink in for a minute. You may, like I did, need to read that over a few times.

My story is not 'fun.' I wouldn't want to relive most of it (except, if I could, while re-living it, make different choices which would, however, then change where I am at today...

something I'm not sure I would actually want in the greater purpose of things). Still, in the re-living that happened while writing, I have learned so much. I accept that I am nowhere near perfect. I accept that much of what you will read are things that I didn't have control over. I accept that when I did have 'control,' I also made some very bad choices. I accept and acknowledge that for so long, I did live in a state of self-deception, and so this is my story and my journey to *Know Thyself* and understand my Trauma's Worth.

Chapter 1: Heathen

Yes, that's right, heathen. (*Heathen, per the Merriam-Webster dictionary, is a nonreligious or uncultured person.* Not, in itself, bad, but I was told by my Catholic family that it meant a "devil-like" person.) Maybe that should have been a clue or foreshadowing of what was to come. Who in their right mind gives the nickname "heathen" to an elementary school girl? I, the precocious, way-too-talkative, FOMO (fear of missing out) child, never cared what the word meant. What I did know is that HE had given it to me, and that was all that mattered.

Who is this "he," you may ask? Looking back now, that answer feels blurred, as there have been many "Hes." To give just one man ownership of that beloved title—He (capital H and all)—seems anticlimactic, even unjust. It fails to acknowledge the near-mirror-image shadows of the original He, whose followers, as you will see, far surpassed the faults of the original. Yet, forty years later, the original He managed something his followers never could: humility.

So, my accepting and even embracing ownership of this nickname—a nickname, mind you, that only one person actually called me directly—does it represent my taking ownership of all my own trauma, whether I directly or indirectly created it? Is it my self-imposed label as the "common denominator" of the trauma, as if by my mere existence I manifested these hardships just to prove I could survive them? Or is it that I was gaslit to believe I was the problem and the cause of it all?

Does it even matter? It all happened, and I survived. But let's be honest: "survive" can have many interpretations. Will I always feel as if I am wandering, just waiting to live out my self-fulfilling prophecy as the common denominator? When things go wrong, we typically look for the one factor they all share—the common denominator. Or, as the many shadows of the original He led me to believe, am I simply choosing to be unhappy, choosing chaos, bringing it all upon myself? Or, more likely, is it far more complicated? I clearly wasn't the cause of many of the traumas, but as a victim of them, I chose the chaos of other traumas because they were, in the true PTSD lens I lived behind, more comfortable and felt safer than what was actually the safer option.

My dad was my first He. I don't remember much from those early years when, as is common, he, my mom, and I had the perfect in-photo family situation. This "picture-perfect" family almost didn't exist at all, for on the day I was born, my mom nearly died. Yes, this heathen child started life with chaos. I was "stuck" so I was delivered via a rare procedure known as the Zavanelli Maneuver. The only way to get me out was to push me back in and perform an emergency C-section. Thankfully, I don't remember it, as it sounds horrifying.

But it pales in comparison to the trauma my mom endured just to have her already-a-week-late firstborn child. She almost bled to death. Luckily, she didn't, but that whole day led to significant anxiety and, according to the annulment papers that would come after their marriage ended three years later, PTSD, and a seeming shift in her whole personality. (*This was successfully argued as the basis for their marriage's annulment, finalized when my dad remarried.*)

I should probably have neurological damage or worse. Still, I was lucky, from a medical perspective. Instead of physical trauma from lack of oxygen or other complications, I began life, instead, with unrecognized psychological trauma, I began without human attachment. According to the medical records, after I was deemed physically okay, I wasn't held by anyone for several hours. - Maybe surviving my birth was a sign, or simply practice, for everything that was to come.

Coming to terms with this trauma has been one of the hardest things to comprehend, process, and find peace with. The lack of human connection in those first few hours set the foundation for my lifelong struggle to form—or maybe better stated, to find—true and healthy attachments. This became the undercurrent of my life: the pursuit of this elusive concept of attachment. It seemed so innate and natural when I had my own kids, yet it evaded me in romantic relationships.

In other words, this initial trauma of abandonment—even though it was unintentional and medically necessary from my mom's perspective—led me to seek attachment from individuals who were completely incapable of forming a healthy bond. An oxymoron, if you will. The one thing I sought was the very thing I subconsciously chose to avoid.

My working theory is that I subconsciously seek out people who lack the capacity for attunement and attachment, so when the inevitable abandonment happens, as is my pattern, it hurts less. It reinforces the midbrain's fight-or-flight response. The problem is clear: if one never experiences true attunement and attachment, how long can one survive? We, as humans, need connection for survival.

One difficulty in understanding trauma lies in the inability to identify the "who," or rather, the one who caused it. The realization that the mental and emotional trauma of abandonment can be just as devastating as physical or sexual trauma complicates this further. And when you layer additional traumas on top of that, it creates a chaotic mess of fight/flight/freeze/fawn responses.

If we cannot identify the source of the trauma, how can we break the pattern? The "He" pattern became easy to recognize only decades later, in retrospect. But with the trauma of my birth preceding even that, the original baseline was worse than I could ever comprehend, making this realization nearly impossible to process.

Dissecting this concept even further: how can someone feel abandoned by something they never had? How can one experience a sense of loss without ever having felt possession? How does one even process and heal from this when, to some, this entire concept may seem dramatic or ridiculous because, let's face it, the importance of attachment at birth is just now starting to be accepted medical knowledge? Seeking this unknown and unrecognized attachment has become my greatest challenge and the underlying theme of my life. The moment I realized this, however, was the moment everything changed.

It was the moment I began to "Know Thyself," embracing all my messy, chaotic, and beautiful pieces. It was the moment I found my worth, my value, when I began to understand the "why" of me and the gifts I gained from it all—the moment I chose myself.

Chapter 2: Pedestals and Sisters and a Disney Princess

My first memory of abandonment is quite vivid. I was 3 years old, sitting on a snowbank, watching my dad move out. Little did I know I wouldn't see him again for two years. I'm not sure if the divorce itself felt like abandonment, but his complete disappearance certainly did. This became a recurring habit of his.

I don't remember his return, why he came back, or even the moment I saw him again. I don't recall what he said or why he left, nor what compelled him to come back. I do wonder, though: if he had never returned, would I have the same abandonment issues? When he left, I was left behind, but perhaps his return made the leaving real. I'm sure at some point in my life, I would have felt the impact of his departure and questioned why he chose to leave me. But would that realization have been delayed? And if so, would it have softened the trauma of the abandonment?

In my work on ACEs (Adverse Childhood Experiences), it seems that the earlier in life trauma occurs, the greater its negative impact. Since I cannot actually remember many details of the situation, some might question why it even matters. But those would be people with no concept of trauma—people who cannot take the time to understand from someone else's perspective. Ironically, these are often the very people I chose to chase. Maybe I did so out of shame, feeling different and easily abandoned, believing I wasn't worth anything more. Perhaps I gravitated toward those who were like my dad, needing to prove something. More likely, it was a complex combination of both.

Regardless of why, I chased them. And despite everything, my dad did come back, and I chased after him first. I started this unhealthy pattern of chasing the unattainable. I was 5-years-old.

So, where did he go and why? I would only learn the answer many years later, long after it was too late to salvage the decades of chaos I had created. That answer brought more self-doubt and questions about who I was in the "nature" sense, and, unfortunately, I actually cannot share the answer, just that his disappearance was to "protect me." *(Of course, the not sharing of the reason is also to 'protect me'. As, decades later, it could still matter.)*

Somewhere around the age of 5, he came back, and I became your typical child of divorced parents in the 1980s. I lived with my mom most of the time and visited my dad every other weekend. Unfortunately, like I'm sure happened to many others, my dad was placed on a pedestal. Perhaps it was the complete lack of rules and the focus on having fun, though I couldn't tell you what we actually did that was so fun. Or maybe he was pedestalized simply because he had left—the whole "you want what you can't have" thing. It was what it was, and aside from a few scattered memories, most of which don't even include him, I really don't remember much. This lack of memories is more significant than it might seem, as it mirrors the "lack of" memories from the time I spent with my mom.

After years of therapy, the "lack of" now makes complete sense. Memories are formed when the brain processes events as significant or important, often tied to survival, learning, or validating connection with others. At this point, there weren't, outwardly at least, any devastating traumas to imprint on my memory—except for sitting on that snowbank at age 3 (an age where I shouldn't even have such vivid memories). But the absence of genuine, true attachment to either parent meant my memories and the events didn't register as relevant for survival or connection. So, instead, I remember these moments as if flipping through a photo album—completely emotionless. For emotional memories to form, one needs to be intentionally present and feel connected, something I wasn't. I was living in a state of fight-or-flight, unsure of what healthy attachment looked or felt like.

My lack of attachment to my mom, my first trauma (which I wouldn't even recognize as trauma until decades later), meant I couldn't be emotionally present or connected with her. You don't need to consciously remember a trauma for it to affect your midbrain and register it as such. The trauma of my dad leaving made it equally hard to connect with him, no matter how hard I tried. I was, in essence, living in a state of limbo that I was too young to understand. My mom did try, but, for some reason, my brain didn't register her efforts as safe. My dad didn't know any better—how could he? My brain didn't feel safe enough to be emotionally present in a vulnerable way, which meant I didn't have the positive experiences needed to form lasting emotional memories.

Oddly enough, my parents got along just fine, and I was like every other child of divorce I knew—I wanted nothing more than for my mom and dad to get remarried to each other. But, like most children of divorce, as I grew into a teenager and then an adult, I became glad that never happened. When I was around six, both of my parents remarried—not to each other, but to other people.

Let's start with what happened at my pedestalized dad's house when he married an amazing woman named Mary. Mary was, without a doubt, one of the most beautiful women in the world. She had thick, shiny black hair and wore makeup like the people on TV or in magazines—the kind that looked natural but definitely wasn't. She was loud and unapologetic about it (which fit me perfectly because, well, I've never been accused of being quiet), and she loved to sing—all the time, loudly, and without worrying about the key. I was completely in awe of Mary. To me, she was a Disney Princess, which only elevated my dad's pedestal even higher—he had to be the Prince.

My mom, on the other hand, was very down-to-earth and simple in her appearance. Her naturally curly hair was often pulled back with a small clip or cut short, and I don't think I ever saw her with a blow dryer or curling iron. She wore very pale pink lipstick and blush, and maybe a swipe of mascara. Her daily uniform was either her nursing scrubs or a jogging suit. She was so *mom*, while Mary embodied the image of what little girls looked up to with awe and wonder.

I don't remember the first time I met Mary, but I do recall being at her parents' house, surrounded by her many siblings, feeling both overwhelmed by the sheer number of people and embraced by the love and connection they shared. They welcomed me with open arms. At my dad and Mary's wedding, I had the honor of being a junior bridesmaid and even got my ballet shoes dyed blue to match my very 1990s-style dress. (No, I don't remember the wedding itself, but I definitely remember those shoes!) I lived in a princess world of shiny, pretty things for four days a month. In other words, I *lived* for those four days; nothing else mattered.

Looking back, it's almost funny how few specific memories I have of what made those weekends so wonderful. I really should ask Mary how she managed to make cleaning seem like such a blast because, oddly enough, cleaning with Mary is one of the clearest memories I have from that time. It's bizarre that when I think back on those six years, cleaning with her stands out so vividly, as if it's one of the only memories I have. It's typical, I suppose—research shows that when a child goes to the non-primary parent's home (especially on the every-other-weekend schedule like I had), there aren't many rules, so naturally the child prefers that home. Did I have more freedom there? Absolutely. But I also had Mary.

Somehow, Mary convinced me that cleaning was fun, or maybe I just bought into it because she made everything fun. We would clean the duplex top to bottom every time I visited, with "Jeremiah Was a Bullfrog" *blaring* on the stereo system. I'm sure there were other songs, but in my mind, it was this one on repeat. So there we were—the "we" in my memory is just Mary and me—scream-singing and cleaning together. Where was my dad, you might ask? Who knows—you'd have to ask Mary.

Thinking back on this, it does seem a bit strange—my near-obsession with Mary. Most children of divorced parents don't typically form such a strong bond with the new person, the 'step' parent. Perhaps it was because Mary's personality was the one I envisioned for myself in 20 years, in contrast to my quiet and reserved mom. Or maybe it was because she was part of *His* house—my first "He." Everything that belonged to that house was going to be the best, no matter what. Or maybe, just maybe, it all goes back to the very day I was born—the same day my actual mom almost died. I didn't have that innate attachment to my mom that nearly all babies have. From day one, we shared trauma—mine, deeper than conscious memory, etched into the literal first moments of my existence, and hers, a vivid, PTSD-inducing reality.

Mary wasn't the first non-mom female presence in my life, so it wasn't just that I clung to her out of some desperate, primal need for connectedness. It was more than that: Mary was married to my first "He." My six-year-old self found 'home' for five years.

Not long after my dad and Mary got married, my sister Anna was born. Anna was adorable—photos confirm that. Even as she grew into an adult, she had the benefit of Mary's genetics but the drawback of also having our dad's influence. Honestly, my childhood memories of Anna mostly consist of photo ops, because I didn't see her very often. The key thing is, I don't remember disliking her.

Looking back, you'd think I might have struggled with Anna's arrival—suddenly I had to share my dad and my new 'mom.' But, in reality, it wasn't like that. Anna simply existed, and my dad remained on a pedestal.

It would be many years later—Anna was 29, and I was nearly 37—when Mary and I exchanged Facebook messages (below are our exact words) about the connectedness between Anna and me. I hadn't seen Anna or Mary in over 20 years, as my dad and Mary divorced when Anna was just four. This exchange took place the day after I saw them both for the first time after all those years. It was at our cousin's wedding where we discovered this sense of connection.

Mary: It warmed my heart to see you again.

Me: I cannot agree more! I have missed you so much, and although I can't change the past or the guilt, seeing you all—especially Anna—makes me so grateful and happy! I hope our relationship continues, and that excites me bunches!

Mary: I agree. I have missed you too. I think about you often… shamefully, I never reached out. We can't change the past, but we can move forward and form a revitalized relationship. I'm so happy we found this opportunity to begin again! I'm thankful.

Me: On Saturday, when I got so overwhelmed at that table, it was an overwhelmingly amazing feeling—just a sense of home. For the first time in I don't know how long,

I felt comfortable being myself with people like me. I know that sounds absolutely ridiculous, but I think you saw the effect it had on me! I am so excited!

Mary: Sitting at that table and listening to you and 'your kind' (lol)… it was an absolutely amazing experience. Watching it all unfold, I could feel everything align, and it felt *right.* I just couldn't believe what I was seeing and hearing—*family.* My heart soared knowing that you all really belong. I don't even know if that makes sense, but I think you understand. Yes, I saw you grasp the situation. It was exciting, comical, and surreal. It was your flock of family finally coming together, and *you belong.* Anna belongs. You are all connected, and you didn't even realize how disconnected you had been. I wanted to laugh and cry at the same time. I was so happy for all of you. I watched and listened to the spicy, sassy, opinionated, and loud Sieben ladies—I loved every minute of it.

One would think that, finally, at age 37, I truly did find home after that… but you'd be mostly wrong. My life doesn't quite go like that… to be continued.

Anyway, during our drives back and forth from his house to my mom's, from ages 5 to 11, Dad and I would talk about school, dance, and my goal of being able to live with him someday. When it came to school, any grade less than an "A" was met with a question: why wasn't it an "A"? "You're a Sieben, you're the best, so be the best." All very matter-of-fact. So then, guess what? I *was* the best. I had to be the best so that my dad could brag, so that he'd be proud, so that I was good enough, so that he would, for sure, want me to live with him when I turned 12, like he said I could. Were these direct "if this, then that" statements? Did I really need to be perfect? Likely not, but to a child, when this God-like figure says something, it gets internalized as reality.

During this time—this living for my 12th birthday—I did, of course, have to *survive* living at my mom's. This concept of surviving at her house makes me so mad and sad. At the time, I truly saw it as a survival situation, as if I was enduring until I turned 12. In reality, my mom was everything I was trying to manifest in my dad; I just didn't see it. Some might say I chose to be difficult and created a much harder situation for myself. They're probably not wrong, but like in addiction, the choice isn't intentional. It's the subconscious survival mechanism of the brain, choosing what it was trained to need. My midbrain was trained to believe, from my first seconds, that my mom wasn't a connected being, despite all her actions that showed she was the most connected. Choosing this true connection was far too scary to my fight-or-flight self because if I were to lose it, the devastation would be unbearable. My midbrain, however, chose to chase the one it knew it couldn't fully reach. There was safety in knowing the potential for loss had already been survived once.

Ironically, my mom also got married when I was around age 6. My stepdad—well, I have exactly zero memories of him. They went to the courthouse, and the next thing you know, he wasn't even allowed in the hospital when my sister was born. In other words, I do not remember this marriage at all. What I do remember is Molly's arrival, one month and six days before Anna, to be exact. Molly was not the sister I 'wanted' (yes, this has changed), because her arrival marked the beginning of what felt like the world realizing how difficult I was and, to a 7-year-old, that I wasn't worth it. Molly's birth singlehandedly took away my "only child" status and the attention I did get. Even though I didn't have a deep connection, I did have superficial attention, and now most of it was gone and shifted to her. I was jealous, and it felt like another abandonment.

Even the day she was born, my aunt Candy—my mom's sister and my Godmother—found out she wasn't going to be Molly's Godmother. This wasn't acceptable to Candy; she needed more. She didn't speak to my mom or us for several years because being just my Godmother wasn't good enough. I'm sure there was more to it, but at age 7, this was my truth, and that's why I remember it.

From the day she was born, Molly was happy, content, and "the cutest baby on the planet," as our grandpa declared. He had previously said I was his favorite. I felt completely replaced. All the trauma my mom associated with my birthday, it seemed, was lessened by this perfect delivery and bonding experience. Mom and Molly connected, and connect they did. Some of this played well into my grand scheme of leaving to live with my dad when I turned 12, but since I spent most of my life at my mom's with Molly there too, I didn't know how to handle it.

Over the next few years, I tried to get attention by 'being perfect.' I mowed the lawn, cleaned the house, babysat my very happy sister, and even had my mom order weekly educational and arts-and-crafts activities for me to do with her. Did I resent Molly at this point? I don't think so. I did what I could to be the perfect daughter and sister, and I had the escape of going to my dad's every other weekend. My mom appreciated my 'perfection.' I'd get little notes, surprise Snickers bars, or other "just because" treats. This reinforced (in my child's mind) that I had to be perfect to feel loved.

My mom was a great mom, although at the time, I was too focused on turning 12 to appreciate it. I was a competitive dancer, which occupied 3-4 nights a week for practice and most weekends during competition season. My mom never missed a minute. She wasn't a "dance mom," but she stayed quietly in the background, making sure I had everything I needed in my full drama-queen mode. For three years in a row, she took me to the National Competition, which included fun road trips with just us. When it was just Mom and me, things were great, but when Molly was around, I felt different. This wasn't true, I see now, but to my constant fear-of-abandonment brain, it was overwhelming, so I kept some walls up.

In my mind, when Molly was around, she was even more obviously the favorite because she was so happy and so cute, while I was hard and difficult. There always seemed to be a disconnect. Now, decades later, I see it so clearly that it makes me very sad. What I would have described at ten years old as "You hate me," or "Molly is your favorite," I now understand differently: my mom was in tune with both of us, but the early bonding that's supposed to happen at birth didn't occur with me. That primal connection never formed, but it did with Molly. They, together, felt that connection. My mom tried so hard to form that with me, but I was too triggered to let it happen.

Research shows that direct skin-to-skin contact at birth and immediately after is crucial for this connection. Honestly, I'm not sure how to feel about this research. Does it help explain why I never felt like I fit in? Sure, but it also brings a sense of sadness and, in a way, hopelessness. Subconsciously, in my 'reptilian' brain, I must have sensed that difference, that trauma. To protect myself, I enforced the disconnect, fearing that if I didn't, I'd get hurt or abandoned. My mom, on the other hand, chose to keep her walls down and remained emotionally attuned to me, recognizing that the trauma of that day wasn't my fault. She tried to connect with me, but my traumatized, abandoned brain couldn't reciprocate. (The age where trauma happens, again matters. The trauma she experienced at my birth happened to a fully developed adult brain, it knew how to process and heal. My brain, on the other hand, was far from developed and knew only abandonment.)

The one person who saw through my 'un-happiness' and attitude was my grandma, my mom's mom. Of course, she loved and adored Molly, but she also seemed to understand me. When I stayed at her house, I would follow her around constantly, afraid of missing something or worried that someone would say something negative about me behind my back. I almost needed the literal glued-to-her-side physical attachment. We used to stay up late playing cards and talking. We even had a system—a full Grandma-Heather notebook documenting which card game we'd play and every score we ever had. This went on for years—so many card games, so many late nights, and so much talking. I shared everything with her; I was never afraid to tell her anything. She was my safe place.

During that same period of my life, I talked and walked in my sleep. My grandma would apparently stay up for hours at night, sitting by my bed and listening to my ramblings. She never woke me or interrupted but would ask me about what I'd said the next day. For some reason, my midnight sleep-talking always had a deeper meaning, uncovering feelings I didn't even know I had. This led to even more conversations between us. My grandma never questioned me or pushed me to be happy; she just listened. She was safe—or so it seemed.

Chapter 3: Broken Pedestals

February 1994 changed everything. I was 11 years and 4 months old, eagerly counting down to my 12th birthday. October couldn't come fast enough. That day, the day everything shifted, was a Saturday—my dad's weekend. I had dance practice for three hours, and he dropped me off around noon, nothing unusual.

When 3 o'clock rolled around, I went out to the lobby and saw my mom waiting for me instead of my dad. I wasn't happy. Even now, I vividly remember saying to her, *"Why are you here?"*

She looked at me with a seriousness that immediately unsettled me. "I have some news," she said. "You're not going back to your dad's."

I froze, trying to process her words. Then she added, "Your grandma, your dad's mom, is in the hospital, and it's not going to end well."

My mom, a nurse, never sugarcoated anything. She explained that after dropping me off at dance, my dad had gone to his parents' house to visit. When he got there, he found his mom lying on the kitchen floor, unresponsive. As I later learned, she had suffered a significant heart attack—her diabetes, as I've since understood, was poorly controlled. While she was in the hospital, her lung collapsed. She didn't survive.

There must have been a funeral. I must have been there. It must have been sad. But that's all I know—a lot of *"must have beens."* The memories are vague, blurry, and incomplete. The next time I *think* I saw my dad was nine months later, in November, a month after I turned 12. That's when my grandpa—his dad—got remarried. Yes, that quickly. (For what it's worth, they've now been married longer than my grandparents ever were.)

Do I remember the situation? No. Do I even recall seeing my dad at the wedding? Not really. The only thing etched in my memory is my new step-grandma's fancy shoes. Funny, the things we hold on to.

My grandma dying was when my life fell apart for what I consider the first time. Maybe my dad driving away when I was three, only to reappear when I was five, should count as the first. But this—this apex of a birthday that didn't happen like it was supposed to—marks the moment I first consciously felt abandoned. Lost. Insignificant. Completely unworthy.

All the promises? Gone.

Not only did my dad disappear from my life when his mom died, but he also turned several other lives upside down. You see, he had met my now-second stepmom. This led to another divorce for him—this time from Mary—and left another one of his daughters, Anna, in the aftermath. I lost my dad again, and I lost Mary. Now, I was left with a mom I had never taken the time to truly know or invest in, a woman with whom it seemed the only thing we shared was a single, horrible, traumatizing day.

This man, my dad, whom I had pedestalized, just left. When I say I pedestalized him, I mean I spent all my childhood energy, time, and thoughts dreaming of the day I could walk into the 'perfect' world I had fantastically created in my mind—a world where living with him would be everything I imagined it could be. Looking back now, I see how unrealistic and heartbreaking that was. I feel so much sadness for the 11-year-old me who missed out on so much because of those dreams. I wish I could go back to that younger version of myself, to that 5-to-11-year-old child, and understand how it all unfolded the way it did. How did the pedestal get built? What happened when he reappeared after being gone for two years that made me so completely invest all my time and energy in him?

I can't remember, of course. But what I've come to learn through therapy is that those six years or so of putting him on a pedestal—a choice that, looking back, seems like such an obvious mistake—set the foundation for my future. A future where I would repeat the same pattern with several other "Hes." "He's" painted with red flags. And, as is often the case with repeated patterns, they became more exaggerated, and dramatic, over time.

For instance, I don't recall my dad badmouthing my mom. I don't remember my mom being a terrible parent—quite the opposite, actually. I don't even remember the specifics of the whys or hows that led to my fixation. Yet, as I grew, the pattern grew with me. The red flags got bigger, but my choices in "Hes" stayed the same. Maybe a part of me keeps chasing the "He's" hoping to change their minds, trying to convince them to choose me for once, and not themselves like each one of them has. Maybe chasing the "He's" is trying to heal my hurt inner child, like trying to make my dad not leave. Maybe, however, to heal that child, what I should have done all of these years is chase the opposite of the "He."

I vividly remember the sense of isolation, rejection, and abandonment when my 12th birthday came and went—along with several more after that. Those memories stayed with me because they seemed to confirm my deepest anxieties about abandonment. They reinforced the belief that I wasn't worth it, despite all the promises.

Looking back now, I see that the biggest issue with those insecurities was that they were misdirected—aimed at the wrong parent. I would sit in my room, consumed by the question of what I had done to cause this, to make him leave again. I'd sit there, wondering, *Now what?* In my pre-teen mind, I felt it was already too late to fit in where I was, and I felt utterly alone. (Yes, yes, I know now it was a gross over-exaggeration, but at the time, that was my reality. And no matter how irrational someone's perceived reality might seem, it's real to them. Dismissing it as ridiculous or trying to convince them it's 'wrong' only makes things worse.)

Meanwhile, my sister Molly had completely taken over everyone's attention and affection. I was too difficult, too unhappy—too *everything*. In a moment of desperation, my mom once said to me, "Heather, you are the most unhappy kid in the world." It was an unfortunate statement—one that still haunts me to this day. It's not just an internal haunting, either. I've shared this moment with several people who claimed to love me, only to have them throw those exact words back in my face later.

Still, I can't blame her. She wasn't wrong. I was unhappy—and, in hindsight, I probably would have been unhappy anywhere except with my dad. But instead of directing that unhappiness toward him, the one who had actually left, I took it out on my mom, the one person who stayed. It makes sense, in a way. My pattern of choosing chaos is predictable. My fight-or-flight brain clung to the chaos I knew—the one where abandonment was expected and happened—rather than risking the safe, loving space that could devastate me if it were taken away.

The fear of losing something truly safe, of being truly loved, prevented me from ever fully embracing it.

I see now that the trouble is—and always was—that my dad's actions were never about me. He didn't choose to leave me with the intent of making me feel abandoned. It wasn't about me; it was about him. Yes, I understand he was a parent, and maybe it *should* have been more about me. So, in a way, I get the argument about his choices. But what I've grown to realize is that he just did the best he could with what he had at the time. He didn't have the capacity to stay, and he knew I was safe and cared for by my mom.

When his own mother died, he was in crisis. He reacted and fled. I was an innocent bystander in his world. I had put him on a pedestal for reasons I don't fully understand, but the truth is, he never chose to be up there.

The next few years were a blur. I felt lost and deeply alone. I lived in a house full of love, but I couldn't feel it because I didn't feel like I belonged. I was appreciated for what I did, acknowledged in every way that mattered, and wanting for nothing. Yet something was always missing. There was a constant sense of disconnect.

Over time, all my differences became glaringly apparent—both the good and the bad. Not only was I unhappy, but I also started to notice another truth: I was "too big." At dance, we were weighed weekly. My therapist says this was the start of my eating disorder because, for the first time, I had something tangible—something measurable—that I could control. But we'll get to that.

During those years, I did whatever I could to avoid being at home. I joined every extracurricular activity I could find. I spent as much time as possible at my friends' houses. I just didn't "fit" at home. I felt lost because everything I had planned for my life seemed to disappear overnight.

My mom handled this "backlash" in a way that only she could have—probably the only way that would have worked for me. Things got bad several times. I would spiral almost like clockwork. On the surface, things would seem fine, calm even. But inside, my turmoil would build and build. Then, inevitably, something would trigger me—an obscure "travesty," a casual "Molly is just so happy" comment about my sister, or, in true cliché fashion, someone simply looking at me the wrong way—and I would combust.

I became irrational and emotional. My sense of "nothing is good enough" would reach a fever pitch, and there was nothing anyone could do to stop it. Deep down, I just needed to be held. I needed to be told I was enough, to feel connected, safe, and chosen. I didn't want anyone to explain my behavior to me, least of all my irrational outbursts. I just wanted to be wanted.

And my mom *did* want me. She *did* love me. She *did* provide in every way. But the reality was, I was so terrified of being wanted—of being chosen—and then abandoned again, that nothing could break through.

At my worst, I was suicidal. On two separate occasions, I attempted to overdose on handfuls of acetaminophen and ibuprofen. Nothing happened—I remained healthy and fine. A blessing, yes, but at the time, it just felt like torture.

The first time went something like this: there was a brand-new bottle of acetaminophen in the cabinet and a half-full bottle of ibuprofen (the big ones). I took them *all*. The next day, my mom went to grab acetaminophen for a headache, and, well, they were gone. Of course, my 14-year-old self thought I was so clever for leaving the empty bottles right there in the cabinet.

When my mom grabbed the empty bottles and asked me about it, I lied. I mean, what else was I going to do?

"That's so strange," she said, "I just bought a brand-new bottle of acetaminophen, and I'm sure the ibuprofen was at least half full."

My response? "Why are you blaming me? I didn't do anything."

That was followed by my usual attitude and irritability, and yet another day when everyone had to walk on eggshells around me.

She simply said, "Guess I'll have to go buy more."

Both bottles were replaced later that day. She never said another word about it. Neither did I—until the next time, a year later. That second attempt looked nearly identical to the first.

Looking back, I wonder what on Earth kept her so calm. She took care of me, health-wise, like she needed to. But whatever grand gesture I thought I was aiming for turned out to be... anticlimactic. My mom knew me so well. She understood exactly what I was "needing" and "wanting" and how to approach me in the best way possible. She chose not to give attention to the "bad" behavior. It was a risky gamble, but one she won both times—no questions asked.

After both incidents, I was "good" for a while. Strangely, it was her lack of reaction, her refusal to give me the attention I thought I was seeking, that comforted me the most.

This is the magic of my childhood.

Although my mom and I never had instant bonding or attachment—although it often felt like our only connection was our shared trauma, and though we struggled to communicate about almost everything—she was *so* in tune with me. My mom *knew* me. She understood what I needed, how I needed it, and when I needed it.

The one thing missing, however, was my ability to know, feel, and truly believe it at the time. Unfortunately, the thing that *fixed* me, was, arguably, the worst-case scenario.

Chapter 4: The Collapse, The Diagnosis, and The Daughter

May 15, 1998, was my first formal dance: the 9th-grade Flower Ball. It was everything I had hoped for. I wore a crushed black velvet, full-length dress, and my hair was styled in an elegant, fancy updo. My "date" was Mark—my first boyfriend. You know, the kind of middle school boyfriend where holding hands in the hallway was the pinnacle of romance. (And yes, this was pre-cell phone days, so at 15, that was how I rolled.)

Before the dance, we went out for a fun dinner with our moms, who played chauffeur and chaperone, and everything seemed perfect. For that night, all was right in my little corner of the world.

But then, Saturday, May 16, 1998, happened.

Each memory from the following year is so deeply etched in my mind that it feels like it all happened yesterday. Gotta love trauma, right? Looking back, I often wonder if my mom ever thought about the cruel irony of it all. One of the rare days when everything in our mother-daughter world felt harmonious and joyful, only to have it all come crashing down the next day.

Mom, an RN, was working her usual every-other-weekend shift on the med-surg floor at the hospital. Nothing about the day seemed out of the ordinary—Molly and I were likely at home, doing whatever it was we usually did. Then came the phone call.

Somehow, Mom managed to power through an entire shift on a busy med-surg floor, caring for patients like always. But as she was getting ready to leave, standing in the locker room with her coworkers, dressed in her white uniform and her likely Looney Tunes lab coat, she collapsed. As in, ghostly pale, hit-the-deck collapsed.

If you have to collapse, there's probably no better place to do it than a hospital.

Her coworkers immediately sprang into action. When they ran her bloodwork, the results were shocking:

- **Hemoglobin**: 5g/dL (Normal for a woman: 11.5–15.5g/dL)
- **White Blood Cell Count**: 500/mL (Normal: 5,000–10,000/mL)
- **Platelets**: 50,000/mL (Normal: 150,000–400,000/mL)

For anyone unfamiliar with medical terms, those numbers are *horrible*. How she had managed to function with those levels for so long is a mystery—a miracle, really. Her body must have been in a slow, silent decline for months, adapting and compensating until it simply couldn't anymore.

She was admitted to the hospital immediately. They gave her several units of blood, performed a bone marrow biopsy, and ran a battery of other tests. (She kept a wallet-sized record of her counts—most of them, anyway. At some point, there were so many blood draws that she stopped writing them all down. I wonder what went through her mind the day she stopped.)

Within two days, she was sent home and discharged with no real answers but plenty of questions.

The following Thursday, May 21, 1998, was a day I'll never forget—the most non-subtle day of my life. I stepped off the school bus that afternoon, and the sight in our cul-de-sac hit me like a punch to the gut. Both sets of grandparents' cars were there. Both of Mom's sisters' cars were parked in front of the house, too.

Even at 15, I knew this was bad—like, *really bad*. I'd already seen the numbers from the hospital, so I had a sinking feeling about what was coming. But seeing all those cars parked together—knowing that this group of *family* members never assembled in one place unless something was serious—I just *knew*.

I knew things were bad, but at that moment, "bad" took on the full weight of "worst-case scenario." (I've always been fatalistic and prone to extremes a trait that only deepened after this, as you'll soon understand). My fear wasn't for me—it was for Molly, who was only eight, for my grandpa, who had never been shy about declaring my mom his favorite daughter, for my grandma, who, in her own martyrdom-laced way, managed to act relatively normal around her, for her patients and colleagues, and for everyone else. My mom was the glue holding everything together. I couldn't imagine the world maintaining any sense of balance without her running it.

Interestingly, I wasn't worried about myself—not even a little. My brain decided to cling to the absurd Hallmark fantasy where my absentee prince of a dad would magically reappear and rescue me. Even after not seeing him for four years (and counting), that was my default assumption.

When I walked into the house, it felt like stepping into a made-for-TV drama where no one knows how to turn on a light switch. Despite it being 3:30 p.m., the house was dark as night, filled only with muffled sniffs and sobs. My grandma looked up at me, her face streaked with tears and said, "Go talk to your mom. She's in her room."

I found my mom sitting on the edge of her bed in another inexplicably dark room. She was crying quietly—much quieter than everyone else. She didn't look surprised or even shocked. Looking back, I think she must have known something was wrong long before she collapsed. She had recently returned from a cruise, and I imagine she didn't want to ruin the trip by acknowledging whatever warning signs she might have noticed.

She told me she had "myelodysplasia" (MDS) and that it was the worst kind.

An aside—what is MDS? MDS, or myelodysplastic syndromes, is rare. Current data (as of 2024) says it affects about 4 in 100,000 people in the U.S. Back in 1998, when my mom was diagnosed, her doctor said she was the youngest case they'd seen—just 39 years old and with no previous cancer history. Most people who develop MDS are older or have undergone chemotherapy or other cancer treatments. Robin Roberts from *Good Morning America* was diagnosed years later with a similar condition several years after her breast cancer treatment.

MDS can affect any combination of the three main blood cell lines—red blood cells (hemoglobin), white blood cells, or platelets. The more cell lines affected, the worse the prognosis. My mom, of course, had all three. The "hope," if you can call it that, was for the condition to worsen into acute myelogenous leukemia (AML), which could then be treated with chemotherapy and a bone marrow transplant.

MDS can sometimes be genetic, but my mom didn't have that gene. She also had no risk factors. So why her? That's a question I've been asking myself for most of my life.

In 1998, treatments to help the body produce missing blood cells were either not available or not widely used. Essentially, she lived on transfusions, hoping for an "official" cancer diagnosis so she could start treatment. The prognosis at the time was grim. Most people died from infections due to low white blood cells or from hemorrhages caused by low platelets.

When she told me all this, I didn't react. At all. I stood there in the dark, frozen. Was it shock? A lack of emotion? Or was my brain trying to form a plan of action? I couldn't tell. What I did know was that I had perfected compartmentalizing everything, even at 15, and in that moment, I believed something was deeply wrong with me.

I had spent years living in a holding pattern, waiting for life to "start" with my dad. That limbo had numbed me to all the good things about my mom and my actual life. Standing there with no tears, no words, and no reaction was so uncomfortable that I fled. I bolted out of the house, jumped on my bike, and rode the four miles to my best friend Kendra's house.

When I told Kendra and her mom, they both broke down in tears.

But maybe it wasn't just compartmentalizing that made me react—or fail to react—the way I did. Maybe my brain, already traumatized by multiple abandonments, went into survival mode. Maybe, deep down, I had connected so strongly with my mom that the mere suggestion of losing her triggered my instinct to flee. If I didn't feel the pain, if I physically distanced myself, I couldn't be hurt by it. Maybe that's how my mind, trained to protect itself, coped with the unthinkable.

Kendra and I went to her room, and for the first time, I fully owned my feelings. I had to change. I had to let go of my imagined, idealized "future life" with my dad. I had to love my mom and be the daughter she deserved. More importantly, I now realize, I had to stop running from being loved—even if it meant risking the possibility of being hurt again. I had to recognize that she was safe, that she was home, and that I was safe and home, too. I belonged. I was loved simply for being me.

These attachment "issues" of mine, rooted from the moment I was born, left me stuck in a constant state of flight, fight, freeze, or fawn—primarily flight, especially when it came to attachment. This was no one's fault. The human brain, as complex and remarkable as it is, operates in fascinating ways. Even my seconds-old, primitive brain—still locked in its reptilian, all-species-survival mode—registered trauma. Perhaps the simple act of being whisked away to a silent nursery, alone except for a nurse who was not my mom, left an imprint. That imprint may have taught my brain to equate healthy attachment with pain and aloneness with safety, creating a distorted version of comfort. Somehow, my brain guided me to run from healthy attachment (my mom) and instead fawn over unattainable, idealized attachments (my dad). Many of the "Hes" to come in my life would reflect this pattern. I see it now, in hindsight—a pattern as predictable as it is misleading. And what is predictable often feels safe, even when it isn't.

This idea of "unattainable in a healthy way" fascinates me. My dad, you see, simply didn't have the capacity to attach at the time. Today, decades later, I no longer see this as his fault. I no longer believe he chose to leave me. To truly attach to someone, there must be attunement—a quality my dad lacked. Attunement, the ability to deeply connect and respond to another's emotional needs, is essential for attachment. Without it, attachment isn't possible. But rather than digress too far from my mom's diagnosis, I'll return to attunement later. I'll also dedicate parts of many chapters to this recurring theme of fawning over those who lack the capacity to attune. I believe there's a spectrum of capacity, and my subconscious habit of fleeing from true attachment to seek out chaos was my version of safety. Chaos felt familiar, and I excelled in it. Fleeing also meant I never had to be vulnerable, which felt safer—but it was a lonely safety.

And then, on that otherwise random May day, I made a *choice* to attach to my mom. Such a strange concept! Can one truly choose who to attach to? I think so. After all, we choose the Hes—partners to date, marry, or build lives with. But, at an emotional level, I believe that our brains only allow so much choice. What this decision "looked like" to me was striving for perfection. I decided that attaching to my mom meant I had to be perfect for her to reciprocate. Again, that was my subconscious assumption and not based at all on how my mom had acted my entire childhood. Part of this stemmed from the need to make up for lost years, but it was also because I didn't believe I was worthy of being chosen or loved unless I was flawless. In May 1998, I re-learned what I thought was the secret to being accepted, wanted, needed, and loved: be perfect. I didn't, for a second, believe I was enough just as I was. I became perfect for my dad after all, and he still left, so I just had to try harder.

Of course, this idea had its roots earlier, in my longing for my dad to want me—to feel I was good enough for him or what I imagined he wanted. But in May 1998, that belief crystallized. It became both my ultimate survival mechanism and my Achilles' heel. I became, if I may say so, an Academy Award-winning performance of perfection. To the world, I was flawless. I excelled at becoming exactly who and what everyone needed me to be. I made myself necessary, wanted, and indispensable. But, as I would later learn, this kind of performance can only last so long.

For 11 months, I honestly believed I had attachment, life, and adulting figured out. My mom was sick, but not always. She was so present, soaking up each moment with us, likely thinking each one may be the last. Our house had such harmony. She took a leave from work to be with us, but she also got very private about her actual health. No one was allowed in the appointments with her. She refused home care nursing to do her port dressing changes. [She had a Hickman Catheter- a port in her upper left chest that exited her skin and divided into 3 different ends. One she had her labs drawn from, one she got her many transfusions into and one, well, I'm not sure what the third one did.] Each week the dressing that covered where the port entered and exited her skin needed to be changed in a very specific and intentional manner, with extreme caution, and she refused help. She would stand at her bedroom mirror, I can still picture it to this day, and change it herself. Each night, however, she had to do heparin and saline pushes into each port (so they didn't clot and close off), and that is where Molly and I got to help. She needed me for those 11 months. She depended on me for those 11 months.

My mom was also very good at positive reinforcement! I got cards and small tokens of appreciation, and my life truly made sense. It also didn't hurt that all of that appreciation was taken, by me, as a reward for being perfect.

Five months after her diagnosis, and just in time, I got my driver's license. Those first 5 months she was, for the most part, just fine. She had many appointments but also a lot of time, strength, and freedom. By the fall of 1998, however, there were days when she would have to spend a day or two at the hospital because of low blood counts or a minor infection.

I would get Molly where she needed to be, I would get where I needed to be, and things would just work out. My grandparents, divorced before I was born, would come and go. My grandma went wherever my mom was, so if my mom was admitted to the hospital for a couple of days, my grandma would stay at the hospital. If my mom was home, my grandma would swing by at times but then go to her house at night. My grandpa took over the 'boy jobs'- making sure the oil was changed in the car, the driveway was shoveled, and those types of things. When I crashed my car into a light pole that winter, I called my grandpa. As an aside, if you are going to crash your car into a light pole just months after turning 16 and getting your license, that was the time to do it. Even the neighbor whose mailbox I took out didn't even seem to mind!

One of the things my mom did those first couple of months was 'getting her things in order'- essentially, dying person speak for figuring out insurance, her will, her kids, and things like that for when, if she did, in fact, die. She immediately got me added to the check book so I could help pay the bills. I learned quickly and took them over almost right after her diagnosis so that if she happened to get admitted to the hospital when the bills were due, nothing was late. I also took over Molly's and my schedules. When mom was home, she would drive us etc., but I knew where we always needed to be and when. We had a perfect flow, and, for the most part, nothing really got disrupted if she got sick, which is exactly what she wanted.

This flow included Molly and I both at school no matter what. I did swimming, basketball and track, I danced and taught dance, and Molly danced—we never missed a thing. I think most people thought she was doing better than she was, me included. I do often wonder when she realized she wasn't going to live, and if she ever thought about changing anything, or telling anyone. I wonder how lonely that must have been. I wonder how much strength that must have taken. I wonder if she thought she was making it all easier on all of us which, in fact, she was, at the time at least. I think now, looking back, I wish I would have known more, especially the terminal nature. There are so many questions I thought I had a lifetime to ask.

She turned 40 on July 12, 1998, while in the hospital. Luckily, she laughed about it. And, in true mom fashion, it made me feel special for it. You see, totally randomly (as in very last minute), I threw her a surprise birthday party for her 35th birthday (I was 10). I have no idea why I decided to do that, but I did. I wasn't even at the party except for the initial 'surprise' bit as I had dance, but the whole party and surprise were fantastic! Her work besties were in on it and managed to keep her late at work so her other colleagues and family and friends could get to our house before she did. We had an ice cream cake from Dairy Queen with 3 blue birds on it, one for her, Molly and I and a matching 'create your own card' from Target that Molly and I had made her. After that, she would tease me for throwing a 35th birthday party rather than waiting for her 40th, but when her 40th came around, she and I had quite the bonding moment because the 35th birthday party suddenly made so much sense. Maybe I was somehow in tune after all.

Somewhere around December 1998, my mom got very sick, honestly, the worst she had been. She was in the hospital for several days, and they thought that maybe it 'was time' for her to [yay] have leukemia so she would be able to start chemo. They needed her to have 20% blasts on her bone marrow biopsy to be actual leukemia. (Side note: I have no idea what the standards are now, so do not take this as medical literature if you or someone you know has MDS. Follow your doctor's guidance.) When she was diagnosed, she was at 10%. It is odd that we hoped and prayed for leukemia, but at that time, regardless of all the time I wished nothing but to be away from her so I could go to my dad's, I wanted nothing more than to help her live.

While they were getting things lined up for her biopsy, they also had her sisters and me have biopsies done to see if we could be bone marrow donors for her after her chemo. It was devastating to me, however, that after I went through that awful procedure, I was about as far away from being a match as possible while still being her biological daughter. (Kids shouldn't be 'perfect' matches for their parents as we get half of our genetics from each parent, I was just the first back up plan to her sisters.) Unfortunately, it didn't matter, as her blasts were only up to 12%. The sense of despair and hopelessness was hard to ignore. Faith and hope kept getting harder.

After that, things got worse. She was so depressed, and it was grueling. She had blood tests sometimes more than once weekly and transfusions just as often. It eventually got to the point that she wasn't strong enough to do anything, let alone drive herself anywhere. She told me once, "Heather, it is a very sad and depressing day when you are 40 and need your dad to wipe your butt on a commode in the living room." My grandparents were with my mom during the day, and then I was with her during the night. We'd brush her teeth with the sponges on a stick you get in the hospital because a toothbrush would practically cause her to bleed to death. I ran to Target late at night for Maxi Pads as she (and in turn, I, by the weird female sympathetic we-all-must-have-our-periods-together thing) had her period daily for nearly 2 months. We lived in a twisted harmonized hell of both chaos and unity with a common enemy and a shared stubborn independence masquerading as "it's not that bad" coupled with an "I can do it myself" attitude. The world believed it all and, in turn, I think we believed it too, ignoring the obvious elephant in the proverbial room of our bubble.

Then, somewhere between Feb-March 1999, there was an amazing ray of sunlight that poked through the darkest of my mom's compartmentalized depression and defeated the biggest storm cloud. But, before I can explain, I'll give a quick background. My mom was married to my dad until I was 3, then was married to Molly's dad for maybe a year right around 1989. Following their divorce, she had two men she dated on and off. She'd date Mel for a while, then would date no one, then Paul, then no one, and so it went. Paul was a farmer who lived on his parents' farm. He was more 'rough around the edges' and more 'fun.' They rented a limo for a Halloween Party once and were just freer and wilder together. Mel, on the other hand, was 10+ years her senior. He was a 9-5, wear a suit and tie to work, polished kind of guy. They went on a cruise once, and after, my mom said he slept in red sweatpants and a red sweatshirt- in other words, he was not wild or crazy. She adored them both in very different ways. I loved them both for different reasons as well, but over time, it was very clear to most that she and Mel were truly meant to be together.

So, back to 1999… one evening, the phone rang. We had one phone in our house- luckily, it was a cordless for my teenage self. I, however, was forbidden from being on the phone past 10 pm, but apparently, that rule did not apply to my mom. Her room and mine were next to each other and shared a wall, so I got to hear the muffled giggles and conversation that lasted well until the early morning hours. The next morning, when she finally reappeared, she had the happiest glow. She was in L-O-V-E!

I looked at her and said: "How's Mel, mom?"

Mom: "What are you talking about?"

Me: "Mom, I could hear you on the phone all night."

Mom: "How do you know it was Mel?"

Me: "I could just tell."

Mom: "Oh, he's great. He's in Colorado visiting his kids (from a previous marriage), but when he gets back, Heather, we're going to get married!" (To set the visual, picture the smitten first-time-in-love teenage girl in all of the movies, practically pirouetting while imaginary heart-shaped bubbles surround her head, and don't forget the completely unnecessary two-octave higher pitch.)

Me: "It's about time."

Mom: "What?"

Me: "It's about time you and Mel got married."

Mom: "So you are ok with it?"

Me: "Yes, mom, please marry Mel when he gets home."

She continued to float for several hours, the healthiest I had seen her since, ironically, the [red sweats] cruise she and Mel went on just before her collapse in May 1998.

Later that day, enter the twisted joke from the universe and another instance where the "why" of my life just doesn't go away, the phone rang. Mel's ex-wife (my mom and she were always friends) called and informed my mom that that morning (after my mom and Mel's 'engagement phone call'), Mel and his son went hiking in the mountains, and Mel had a heart attack and died. WTF!

I wish, at this point, I could offer some Earth-shattering revelation that would make this story ok. I wish I could tell you we all lived happily ever after, although if that was the case, I'd likely not be writing this book- which I'd be good with if the "I wish" was the reality. I wish I could tell you our family bound together to get through the last few months of my mom's life, but unfortunately, I can't.

This is when you now picture that girl in the movie, falling into some dark alleyway, the blackness and lack of light of the movie screen making it almost impossible to see the waterfall of tears streaming down a now pale and gaunt face, where you, the audience, nearly start crying too because we all can, in some way, imagine by pure human connection the raw devastation. I lived that moment with her, the worst reality TV moment before reality TV even existed. Needless to say, the bubble of "I've got this" shattered into a million pieces. She declined from that day and fast.

The bleeding that required the many trips to the drug store for Maxi Pads got to be too much that they couldn't give her blood and platelets fast enough to balance the losses, thus the first big decision. Luckily, I didn't have to make this one. She had to undergo a laparoscopic-assisted hysterectomy, which, by 1999 levels of standard of care was pretty cutting edge. This was her best option in terms of avoiding infection, the ultimate fear factor due to her non-present WBC. The medical team did set my mom up for the best possible outcome. This I fully believe; she was one of theirs after all.

The surgery was a success for a few days. Then the feared inevitable infection happened, of course, in probably one of the worst possible ways- an intra-abdominal abscess. An abscess is a walled-off type of infection—think zit—that had to be surgically removed/drained because if it ruptured (popped), that could, in essence, result in near-immediate death from septic shock. So, back to the operating room she went. Regardless of these 'hail Mary' efforts, she did get septic (the infection was in her bloodstream). And not to be overly redundant, but we were still in 1999, and Vancomycin® (the basically 'catch all end all be all' antibiotic when I was in training 20 years later) didn't yet exist. She was succumbing to Myelodysplasia in the way that so many did/do/will- infection. She was in the ICU surrounded by her friends and colleagues every day and night and received a Queen's treatment as my mom was 'that nurse,' the one that EVERYONE loved. They made an exception to the kid rule and let Molly in to see her (she was only 9), which was a very good thing as Molly was the ONLY person my mom recognized the last week or so of her life. (I will not begin to over-think that.)

Those last couple of weeks were impossible, but we survived. My grandma kept around-the-clock vigil at the hospital, sleeping in the ICU family room. My grandpa kept 'boy busy.' I, well, did everything I could to keep life completely normal, as per my mom's demand prior to her hysterectomy. You see, we had had a very direct mother-to-16-year-old daughter conversation before that first surgery (again, I think she was much more aware of her reality than anyone else was). You know the conversation where the mom basically gives a to-do list, and do and do not list, and a how-to-live life list, for the rest of your life list, a simple list of 'adulting ("that I haven't already taught you or made you do") 101' list, a facts of life list, a welcome to womanhood list, a how to be a good mom list ("just do what I did Heather and you'll be fine"), a how to be a strong independent woman list ("you can do it all, you don't NEED a man. Never NEED one, but if you find one and they can help you, you can let him but don't NEED him. You need to be able to do it all yourself"), a just-in-case-I-die list. In true 16-year-old girl fashion, I told her I already knew it all and not to worry, I would handle it. Ahhh, I can handle it, this would become my double-edged sword of life.

I was also told during that meeting what was going to happen to Molly and me if the worst-case scenario happened. Now I, of course, knew that I was free to make some choices in this department (the whole counting the days until I turned 12 thing), and the only thing I cared about, now at age 16, was that I was NOT going to go live with my dad- amazing how the tides had turned. I was worried about Molly, as her dad, well, her dad was not a great choice. My mom had already gotten all the paperwork signed and completed stating that Molly and I would be going to go live with our Aunt Susan, my mom's younger sister. BEST NEWS EVER! (Ok, please put this into context... This was the best-case scenario for the worst-case scenario, I was not at all hoping to leave my mom.) Susan was the 'cool aunt'!

I did what I was told after that talk. Molly and I kept doing everything exactly as we had been doing. Honestly, I'm not even sure the schools knew just how bad things were since EVERYTHING was done and signed and on time, meaning early per grandpa's standards.

And then came April 9, 1999. It may actually be one of the most burned into my brain days of my life. I, at age 16, was legally my mom's next of kin. I'm pretty sure in all of her planning and preparing she could have changed this to save me what I am about to tell you, but she didn't. Do I understand why she didn't? Yes, I understand it now, but on that day, I wished I was anywhere but where I was. The hospital realized that asking a 16-year-old to make a life-or-death decision for their mother was a bit unprecedented, so they, bless their Catholic-based mission and values, arranged a family meeting to reach a family decision to 'help me.'

How does the Robert Burns poem "To a Mouse" go?

But mouse-friend, you are not alone
In proving foresight may be vain:
The best-laid schemes of Mice and Men
Go oft awry,
And leave us only grief and pain,
For promised joy!

THE DECISION: A Real-Life Drama Featuring Real People (names changed)

The family discussion room players (thinking back, it's almost like a variation of the game *Clue* or a situation in which we were living out a murder mystery plot… though the hospital's intent was good): my grandma and step-grandpa, my grandpa, my Aunt Susan (the younger, cool aunt), my Aunt Candy (the older, bipolar sister, my Godmother), my cousin Emma (Candy's daughter, nine months older than I am and born via a one-night stand, so she was raised in a very interesting home), and me. Molly was off with a social worker since she was only nine and not allowed in the room.

The scene: We all sat down with a case manager or social worker—or whomever this angelic human was. Emma and I took two couches on two walls that met in a corner, where we laid our heads. (These memories are clear as day.) On one side of the room sat my grandma, step-grandpa, and Susan in uncomfortable folding chairs. On the other side were my grandpa and Candy, also in uncomfortable folding chairs. (Candy flip-flopped which parent she was actively speaking to, likely based on who was giving her something or who she needed at that time. That day, it was grandpa. My mom would have been seated in the middle—the peacekeeping Switzerland of the family.) The social worker was seated a bit askew to see everyone in the room. Unfortunately, this placed her slightly closer to the grandma corner, which, to most, would have meant nothing given the purpose of the meeting. But for my family, this somehow just upped the tension of the battle. (No, I am not being dramatic; every edge counted and was noticed.)

Opening act: I'm pretty sure this social worker introduced herself and said something like, "The purpose of this family meeting is to have a discussion to assist Heather in making this decision concerning Kim."

Act II: All hell broke loose. There were a lot of loud voices and accusations—none actually related to my mom or the situation. Instead, they focused on decades-old past hurts and unresolved issues which, somehow, the adult family members in the room thought mattered at that moment.

Act III: Emma, the social worker, and I quietly slipped out of the room unnoticed. Emma and I went for a walk, discussing the absurdity of thinking this family conversation would actually work. She asked if I had any thoughts. I lied and said no. (Of *all* the things my mom put on my "life list," what to do in this situation was *not* one of them. Please, everyone, fill out an Advanced Directive.)

Act IV: After some time passed, Emma and I returned to the room, and it was as if we had never left. Everyone continued to fight and point fingers, no one even noticed we'd left or returned.

Act V: We left again and found the social worker. We told her she might want to try again.

Act VI: The three of us rejoined the battle—unarmed and unvoiced. I sat there and admired her feeble attempts at restoring order before I quietly slipped away, unnoticed and alone.

Act VII: I walked down the long, quiet hall to the ICU and found my mom's doctor. I asked him again what her chances were. He again told me that there were only two options left: pray for a miracle and hope the meds—which hadn't worked in a week—magically started to, or keep her comfortable and let her go peacefully.

Act VIII: I walked into her ICU room after making my decision and sat there in silence, holding her tiny, cold, frail hand. Minutes, hours, or maybe days passed—it just was.

Act IX: I got up and walked back to the "family meeting." When I opened the door to silence, I was stunned.

This silence was broken by, "Heather, where have you been? Don't you know we are all here for you, and you just disappeared? Don't you know how important this is?"

I was honestly speechless. I didn't have the deserved comeback argument. Instead, I simply said, "The decision has already been made. Go say goodbye to Mom."

THE END

Chapter 5: Foundation People

I, in my 40th year, coined a phrase that, I believe, should be added to all psychology textbooks and should be a studied and measurable concept on its own: Foundation People. Foundation People do not have to be biologically connected to a person; however, they are the people who are, typically and ideally, there from the beginning. The ones that the idea of "nurture" (vs. nature or, in many cases, both) define.

The ones that we call "home" irrespective of physical location. The ones who are love and demonstrate love and what it means, and, in many/most cases, unconditional love. They are the ones that, no matter how bad a situation is, are there to support us. They are the ones we call first on the happiest days as well as the saddest and hardest days. They are the ones that, no matter how badly we mess up or how 'dumb' we act, are there (albeit not always pleased) to support us (one's metaphorical, or literal, 'one phone call' from jail). They are the ones you can be your true, weird, awkward, silly, sad, happy, emotional, frantic, anxious, genuine self with because they are safe, and they are 'your people,' and they 'get' you. Or, in reality, it can be a single person.

Some of this, I believe, develops the second we are born, that maternal attachment, which I was lacking, by no one's choice. In the cases of adoption or surrogacy or whatever the case may be that the birthing person does not parent the infant, this attachment can just as strongly come from that first loving chosen hold. That connection of two beings.

Yes, this would also imply that it can (and should) happen with the, for simplicity's sake, male or other partner/parenting person; however, I would argue that there is a 'primary' bond that the infant innately just finds in its person, the innate knowing who is the safest. (And yes, this typically is the mother). I believe that much of this conceptualized feeling, however, deepens in its development in the first days and years of our lives, while the brain is the most vulnerable, pliable, impressionable, and most able to learn.

On a tangent, I would also argue that infants are generally empaths, feeling all the emotions and seeming shifts of the atmosphere around them, further solidifying in their brains what safety feels like and, especially with trauma, what discord and unsafe feel like. The latter raises the stress hormone cortisol in the infant, giving the infant a baseline of fight/flight. Empaths, by definition, have an attunement to those around them and are seeking attachment. The problem arises, however, when the attachment that is formed is not a healthy attachment, a phenomenon, I believe, happens due to the completely not developed frontal lobe (develops in the mid-20s; this is the 'adulting' part of the brain that is imperative to higher level thought and risk/benefit processing).

An empath without a frontal lobe (formally known as the PFC, prefrontal cortex) is vulnerable to many external influences and differentiating safe from not safe is nearly impossible. Further, the development of the PFC can be delayed in the presence of childhood traumas as well, perpetuating a lifestyle of unhealthy and maladaptive attachment seeking. Thus, an infant surrounded by unconditional love and foundation, people who define 'safe,' is typically more comfortable in its environment and within itself. An infant (or even child) who is lacking in foundation people, or the foundation people subsequently abandon the child, can further evolve into even greater attachment difficulties well into adulthood.

Foundation people, within my definition, can be a couple of people, a singular person, or it can be many, much of which likely depends on cultures and norms. A lot of what makes a person a pivotal foundation person is their ability to attach to you and, thus, by pure definitional order of operations, attune. Lucky for you, this will also be a recurring theme in my story. First described in the psychology world by Lloyd Arthur Meeker in 1929, the concept of attunement relates to an ability to feel or sense or 'just know' what another is feeling or thinking. The best example is seen between parents (primarily mothers, or as described above) and their children. (Of note, not all parents have this, as you will see.)

It's the "I just know" feeling or sensation when two people are totally in sync. Scientifically, research is ongoing, but it is felt that attunement works in the brain's mirror neurons, which is evolutionarily important to facilitate bonding between people. Biblically, God created us for community: "And he [John the Baptist] will turn the hearts of the parents to their children and the disobedient to the wisdom of the righteous- to make ready a people prepared for the Lord." (Luke 1:17).

Regardless of which science of philosophy or belief you have, it is known that connection to others is the best predictor of a positive future. More simply stated, attunement, and the following attachment, is super important for safety and mental and emotional (and physical etc.) wellbeing (even if you don't believe in a God or higher power.)

Our 'foundation people' give us that ever important safe connection and attachment to other people, our community. They also model for us what that even looks like. How we should behave toward one another, how we give and receive love, what connection looks like, what acceptance looks and feels like, what trust looks like, what safety looks and feels like and so on. I think that self-worth and value can also be tied to this concept. When one is part of a community of safety, acceptance, and love, one can be themselves without question of judgement or rejection.

One's sense of self and self-confidence can grow in a fostering 'safe' environment that carries with them forward into adulthood. Also, one's PFC also starts its development with modeled healthy behaviors, spoken and unspoken, naturally creating an innate, cliché time, *moral compass* as well as an ability to identify and avoid others who are threatening and unsafe. (This may be in the form of manipulators, narcissists, etc.) No, I am not at all pretending that this is a black-white concept, but rather, what I am trying to depict is an idea that those who are lacking in the very foundation people our species has relied on for generations will have a much more challenging time attaching to safe and healthy others.

I, unfortunately, selectively gave my dad a much larger chunk of my attachment than he had the capacity for. Why this happened is, of course, complex and even beyond what, really, anyone can explain. Much, I believe, has to do with the first few hours of my life and my non-attachment with my mom. The lack of that attachment and eventual realized abandonment that resulted due to my mom and my shared traumatic experience and disconnect pushed me to, in a way, default to the only other human who was a 'constant.'

Ironically, I will come to learn this 'constant' was really not constant, but again, it was the best there was to a newborn brain. Following my birth and my mom's subsequent personality changes due to the trauma, my dad wasn't around as much as photographs would lead one to believe. I also was, surprise surprise, a colicky baby. (We could really rabbit hole this entire phenomenon, but I'll save you that!)

What I will say is that I do think the colic developed due to the lack of attachment I had, which, if you think about it, must have been pretty scary for a newborn. The time following the colic, up until he left when I was 3, seems to have been a trial, a tug-of-war of wills and tolerance for trauma, healing, and, perhaps, attachment to me. Innately, my mom couldn't, but she tried, to a fault, until, as is typical, it was nearly too late. My dad, again, just didn't have the capacity to, at no fault of his own. (I am by no means excusing him or his seeming lack of trying. He still failed me and what I needed at that time.)

My brain, however, didn't clearly understand this lack of capacity, so took it upon itself to do everything to force this attuned attachment, which led to many years (decades) of shaky ground when it came to my male choices in life, for he was who I modeled that kind of *love* on.

I would do, as I was formed at that young age to do, any and everything to force an attuned attachment with my significant others, often at my own expense. I, for some reason, have a miracle of an ability to attune to others, so I thought I could force others to attune to me, a feat that, I know now, is absolutely impossible. We cannot control what another thinks, feels, does and so on, another AA concept. Others can, on their own, work on and develop this, but they must be able and willing to, and they need to recognize the barriers they possess that prevent this from developing. These barriers, unfortunately, are often so ingrained that to be able to evolve, one must humble oneself to their deficits, an act usually prevented by ego.

My mom, however, did do everything she could to attune and attach. She was very successful at the attunement, , but her attachment to me was guarded by my trauma and ingrained fear of losing this attachment. Ironically, though, she was, to so many in her family, a foundation on her own. The last 11 months of her life, she was, finally, my foundation as well. I fully committed to her and absorbed all that I could, and I willed her to live, for I, selfishly, had finally learned to appreciate her. I finally found my foundation. I finally let myself be safe, regardless of the risks.

I felt at home and safe for 11 months of my life.

One person, although not impossible, is often not one's only 'foundation person.' Again, foundation people are different than a family of origin because they just 'are' whereas foundation people are beyond just being. They are the safety and security. So, you may ask, if she was the foundation for so many, why did I not have that group of others as well, who were 'those people', and, even more importantly, what happened to them? And then there is the entire paternal side of my 'family'- who and what are/were they?

To give depth to the players in that family meeting, my 'maternal foundation people,' a digression I have debated even adding to this book, is, in actuality, important because it does impact my years of shaky attachment and abandonment issues. I also cannot put all the discord on my dad, and, to get the full depth of my trauma, my entire maternal 'foundation' is important to understand. (We'll get to my paternal players shortly.)

My grandma: She made her appearance at the beginning of this story. She 'got me' and I was, at least I felt like I was at the time, completely safe with her, probably more with her than anyone else up until my mom got sick. She and my mom had a wonderful relationship as far as I knew, and my grandma took amazing care of my mom that last year. Grandma taught me that women can do anything, as she was the first divisional 'boss' at a large international corporation, but yet she also stressed the importance of femininity. Unfortunately, that did add to my body dysmorphia and subsequent eating disorder.

Still, I do feel that she had the intention of trying to show that women can be strong but also feminine, that they can do it all but don't have to, and that they can and should command a room but also could soothe and be gentle. She, to a fault, however, is also the definition of a martyr. She didn't do much without expectation of something in return. She proved so much to the world but wanted to make sure that it was acknowledged and celebrated, and when she was slighted, it was always catastrophic. My mom had many of these traits, the strength and the gentleness, but mom was the opposite of a martyr and shied away from attention. This difference made Mom uncomfortable at times, but she would have never made it known to my grandma.

My step-grandpa: I loved my step-grandpa. He was Grandpa my whole life as he and my grandma were married several years before I was born. Did we have that special bond? No, but that was just fine. He loved our family and was fiercely devoted to my grandma, if not submissive. (Ironically, when he died, 13 years after my mom, I was not even told about it. Family had completely lost its meaning that even his death was withheld.)

My grandpa: Oh, this man! My grandpa became my person after my mom died, not necessarily in the emotional sense, but in every other sense, as he was my stable and, for the most part, my safety. To this day, my grandpa will always be the closest to *my person*. Non-existent, emotional heart-to-hearts aside, he understood me, he knew how to handle me, he knew when I needed my independence (thus when to get out of my way) and when I needed him, and he was always there.

He was fiercely protective and even more proud of me, and he NEVER left me questioning anything. He is my benchmark for my ever-needed words of appreciation.

Grandpa woke up SO EARLY in the mornings, and when I would stay over, we'd go for his morning walk, which, for my child's legs, was nearly a jog. He made fresh squeezed orange juice and rolled-in-canister homemade orange ice cream. We played the game "Sorry" more times than I can count, and his favorite book to read to me was "Mr. Brown Can Moo Can You?" by Dr. Seuss (and I can still picture exactly how he would make his face funny to look like Mr. Brown on the cover of the book.)

I would get to ride in the milk truck with him to deliver milk for Polka Dot Dairy, and I'd get to help unload the pallets. He'd take me out of school for a couple of days each March to go to the State High School Basketball Tournament (back when North Minneapolis was the team to beat). His favorite food was broiled walleye, which he caught himself. I am not sure if I was his 'do-over' for his lack of being this for my mom and her two sisters, but regardless, he filled so many roles in my life.

My grandpa had an alcohol use disorder, in recovery since before I was born. My grandma supported him throughout that journey, standing by his side as he went to AA and struggled, and she said she would never leave while he was actively working on his recovery. He had one day of return to use around 1980 and got his 'mean drunk.' It was then that grandma did leave, and I don't blame her, I would have left too. He never drank again. I never knew that version of my person.

The most I knew were the stories I would ask to hear and the two cans of beer on the lower right back shelf of his fridge with nearly an inch of dust on them. I asked him once why he had them, and he said it was a reminder of all he had to be grateful for and all that he could lose if he ever drank again. Again, I never knew that grandpa, but my grandma and both of my aunts in that room that April day did. Susan hadn't spoken to my grandpa in over 20 years when we were all put together for the family conference. Candy, on the other hand, on-off talked to him my entire life, motives always questionable. My mom, his very openly favorite, never wavered in her love for her dad. She, like me, forgave people, gave them second chances, and didn't judge them for their disease. My grandpa was my person.

My Aunt Candy: She is my Godmother, my mom's older sister by about a year and a half. Candy was very hot or cold. She was a single mom Emma's whole life and never got married until I was about 20 (her husband is one of the world's gems of a human.) Candy, as you have likely realized, likes to be the most important person everywhere she goes, and if she isn't, she will not talk to you for a while.

She, I have reason to believe, resented Emma and acted like the world owed her for this inconvenience of a daughter. Emma, for nearly her whole childhood, was told a lie about who her dad was and was, essentially, made to believe he left because of her. My mom told me the truth, and I, unintentionally one Christmas, told Emma (I thought she knew?!).

Candy was almost always talking with my mom, sans the Molly Godmother thing, but she seemed to alternate between which of her parents she was speaking to at any given moment. (I don't think she ever talked to Susan though.) When Candy was on speaking terms with my mom, we got along just great. She was my Godmother, after all. After that day in April of 1999, she didn't speak to me again for many years, and maybe only a handful of times since. So much for my caring Godmother.

My Aunt Susan: She was the 'cool aunt' (the younger sister by about a year and a half). Again, she hadn't spoken to my grandpa in around 20 years by April 1999. Susan was, for the most part, always in communication with my grandma. She, like my grandma, is a star martyr who, it seems, felt like everyone owed her something due to my grandpa and the final incident (which I, in part, can understand from their perspectives- just not at the 20-year mark and to the extent that they made 'the decision' [concerning my mom] about themselves and their issues).

Susan, as happens with many who had tumultuous childhoods with their dads (myself, case in point), was in a series of "serious" relationships throughout my childhood with horribly abusive and awful men (luckily, I, although dating and marrying my 'daddy issues,' never experienced the physical abuse). As the 'cool aunt,' I always adored Susan. I looked up to Susan so much and, much like my stepmom Mary (for that time), I wanted to be Susan.

My Cousin Emma: She's mostly been described already, but besides my being jealous of her my whole childhood and teenage years, we got along great. She was so thin and beautiful and mature and had so many freedoms. I don't think I've seen her since my mom's funeral, however.

She is in the grandma/Susan corner, but I think that's because she is smart enough to play it to her advantage. Her childhood was not ideal, see above, so I am sad for however that has played out for her.

My mom, you see, was the glue that held this very broken foundation together. It was a role that, as the middle child who was sick all the time as a kid, she knew very well. I learned this 'skill' for peacekeeping and balancing at a very young age. She was, without a doubt, the worst person to get sick, for even she recognized that if something happened to her, the rest would crumble.

The dynamic of that 'family meeting' with these players was never going to get anywhere, especially since, obviously, my mom wasn't there to keep the peace. Seeing that they all loved my mom so much, one would think that they could come together for her sake, literally, but it is so interesting how they all had such differing ideas on "what would Kim want/do?" It's equally interesting how each of them felt that her dying would be harder on them than on anyone else in the room, including me, her daughter.

Chapter 6: "You Killed Your Mom"

April 15, 1999, was a Thursday, which meant a very busy night as "mom/sister Heather." Molly had dance, I assistant-taught her class and then taught three additional hours after hers. Kendra had become the regular sitter on Thursday nights for me. She arrived when Molly's class was over, got her to bed, and stayed until I got home. Man, I had the whole single-parenting thing down at 16 years, 6 months, and 3 days old!

That night, though, was different. When I got home around 9:30 p.m., I just felt off—panic-like, even. Kendra looked me in the face and just knew she was spending the night. (She had the best mom; this wasn't an infrequent result of these nights, but this Thursday was different, even to her.) During the three-mile drive home from the studio, this feeling of anxiety, dread, and overwhelming something just built and built, and I had no idea why. When Kendra saw my face, she said, "Just go. I've got Molly."

At that moment, I didn't even know what she meant because I didn't know what I was feeling or needed, let alone where I was going. But I got in my car and started driving, eventually ending up at St. John's Hospital. Six days after "the meeting," not much had changed, except Mom just had fewer tubes and cords. She never really woke up, and if she did, it was just mumbling nonsense.

I honestly had no idea why I went there as I was there so often already, but it's as if my car just took me. My grandma kept vigil around the clock, but Molly and I kept our routine because I fully believed that's exactly what my mom would have wanted. Even so, we were there often. I walked into the ICU family area, which had several small cubicle-sized rooms, large enough to fit a very uncomfortable wooden loveseat-sized couch with medical-grade cushions and a very small end table with a lamp. Each room had its own door and housed a family member of someone who was, inevitably, dying.

When I woke my grandma, I thought she might have a heart attack on the spot. She was confused and a bit irritated that I was there at nearly 10:30 at night. I told her everything was fine, but something made me drive there to see Mom, and I wouldn't be there long. And that was that.

I walked into the ICU well beyond visiting hours, but when the dying patient works at that hospital, no one cares when her 16-year-old shows up late at night. I walked into the peaceful calm of a comfort-care-only ICU room. (Yes, she remained in the ICU because of the privacy, room size, and who was caring for her. She wasn't strong enough to leave the hospital on hospice, and the only other option would have been the medical-surgical unit—her unit—and her co-workers and best friends just couldn't be her nurses at that time. Ethically, and emotionally, they needed to be her support system and not care team. She received the greatest care anyone could ask for!)

Walking into that room had a bizarre significance to it. I had this sense that every moment had to be a certain way. I had to sit in a certain place; things had to be "just right." I didn't know what any of it meant or why, but somehow, I just inherently knew and acted.

I walked first to the closest side of her bed, her left, and sat, but it didn't feel right. So, I picked up the clunky hospital-grade recliner and maneuvered it to the other side of the bed, on her right side, next to the window, and I sat down. For a while, I had no idea why I was even there, so I didn't have a clue what to do. Mom hadn't been lucid for more than a week, so I couldn't even have a conversation with her. Regardless, after a while, I started to plead with God.

My inability to cry or feel any emotion just 11 months prior was washed away in this moment—this therapeutic 90 minutes I will never forget. I held my mom's frail hand. (To be clear, her hands always seemed frail. She was tiny, and her hands were always ice-cold and scrawny, so it wasn't actually all that different, even six days into comfort care.)

I looked at that familiar face that Molly so gracefully carries now. I questioned my years of angst, anger, and near hatred. I thought about everything that made her my mom—the cards, the "just because" moments, the special homemade and personally decorated surprise birthday cakes and morning streamers, the multitude of dance recitals and competitions, seeing her face at every game, meet, or event; her wind suits, her pale pink lipstick and blush with just a touch of mascara; her piña coladas, her staying home from work to surprise me with my bedroom painted and transformed in one day; the birthday parties, the perfect gifts, the many times she called me "pumpkin pie," the way she got so frustrated when I only wanted to share my day with her when she'd just gotten into the bathtub.

Her crocheting. Her way of eating M&M's (just the originals, in color pairs). If a bag ever ended with all colors gone and eaten in pairs—this happened only twice, as far as I can remember—we'd have a great celebration. If she got to the end of a bag and had singles left, they were put into the next bag.

The way she just got me—she didn't push me, didn't fight me, yet supported me and cheered for me always. She never left, but she had to pick up the pieces and take the brunt of my emotions. She was my safe place, my home.

Most of these things I thought about; some I said out loud. I apologized. I begged for the miracle I knew wouldn't happen. I begged Mel to be waiting for her with open arms. And I cried.

At around 11:45 p.m. on April 15, 1999, I got direct and bossy with God. I gave Him two choices (yes, I know that's not how it works): He either gave her a miracle, or He had to take her the next day, April 16. That was it. I didn't think about the "after." I didn't think about the "what ifs" or "what's to come." In that declaration, I found peace—because "I had a plan."

Just another example of me being me. Great in chaos. I need a plan, and I can fully handle anything.

Yes, I hoped that at 12:01 a.m., something would happen either way, but I didn't truly believe it would—and it didn't. So, I stood up, kissed her on the cheek, gave her the best hug one can give in an ICU bed with a very sedated, dying person, and drove back home. Somehow, I was no longer anxious, on edge, or full of tension. I didn't feel "off" anymore.

When I got home shortly before 1 a.m., I went right to sleep.

The next morning, Friday, April 16, 1999, was like most others. I got Molly up and brought her to school. Kendra and I had the day off because, of all things, the State Speech Tournament was being held at our high school, so we didn't have school. I have no idea what we did that day, but I know we got to my house around 2:25p.m., so we'd be there when Molly got off the bus.

We had just walked in, and at approximately 2:30 p.m., my grandma called.

My mom died at 40 years, 9 months, and 4 days old. I was just 16 years, 6 months, and 4 days old. Molly was just 9 years, 2 months, and 26 days old.

How did I feel in that exact moment? Honestly, I didn't *feel* anything because "controlling and handling chaos Heather" took over.

1. What time is it?
2. When does Molly get off the bus? (In the next 30 minutes.)
3. Who do I need to call?
4. Don't let them move her until we get there.
5. When will the funeral be?

6... 7... 8...

This is me. I "handle" in chaos. My trauma brain acts, and in this type of chaos, it fights by trying to control it and make it as least chaotic as possible for everyone else. It doesn't feel the moment or what the moment means, it just acts. I had no emotion in those moments.

When Molly got off the bus, I told her the news. She was mad that I hadn't picked her up from school. I told her I had just found out; she didn't care. At that moment, she was mad at me for not picking her up (she needed to be mad at someone), and that was okay—that was the least of our problems. Neither of us cried yet. We just got in the car and drove to the hospital.

When we walked into the ICU room, it honestly looked exactly like it had not even 24 hours prior—at midnight—when I left it the last time. We both started crying. My grandma held Molly. I held my mom's hand, her left one this time, and thanked God for making His choice. Although it wasn't ideal, it was a choice, and I had an odd sense of peace since I "just knew" that was going to be the day.

In a way, I did all my grieving typically reserved for that very "news" moment—the night before, alone, with my mom, the one person who made me feel at home and safe. That may be the only moment in my life, that midnight, that I have ever been that vulnerable and emotional. That was *the moment,* the one moment, in my life where I felt 100% safe. Standing there, in that actual moment on the day she died, it was as if I was watching a rerun that had already lost its emotional appeal. I was already numb, already guarded, and already planning a future without a home or safety. My life changed more in that moment than I even realized, or maybe it changed at midnight, either way, April 16, 1999, everything changed

I suppose a part of me is glad I didn't fully grasp that moment and what it all meant because some of the worst trauma to come was just days away. In that moment, I hadn't lost everything yet, I just didn't know it. Looking back, I wish that moment had been the worst, but it was just the beginning of my *new* life's first big fall.

I would love to tell you all the details of that week, but my brain has clearly tucked most of it away somewhere safe. This brain phenomenon, this protective mechanism, is, in a way, a double-edged sword. On one hand, this suppression protects us. For much of my life, I didn't even realize I didn't remember it, and it, therefore, could not negatively impact me, at least on the conscious level. However, on the other hand, with the suppression of traumatic events, there's always the real risk of them resurfacing due to triggers or because, even though they aren't in conscious thought, they can still impact so much else.

How, you may ask, does that happen? Suppressing traumatic events is like, to use an analogy from Tom Gonzalez—an expert in Adverse Childhood Experiences (ACEs) and a guest on the podcast I co-host (*Addiction2Recovery*)—burying barrels of toxic waste in your backyard. The barrels will leak over time at unpredictable rates and for unpredictable reasons, typically at the worst times.

This slow leak of toxic chemicals—our traumatic experiences, in this analogy—starts to spread throughout the yard, coming to the surface in various places, potentially killing off things (especially the most sensitive plants or flowers) and creating all sorts of other possible illnesses, diseases, or troubles.

When we have no idea what's going on because we don't remember burying them—thank you, brain protective mechanisms—it can take a very long time to eliminate them. We typically start by patching the grass, replanting flowers, or applying various other Band-Aids since, again, we don't realize what's causing all the turmoil.

Our traumatic events behave in the same way. Maybe we do remember burying some of these toxic things, choosing to forget them or to "just move on" by sheer force of will. Then, when the reemerging or seeping damage happens—often so slowly at first that we don't even realize what's occurring—all of the intentionally buried toxic events come back and impact us even more than they initially did.

This now exaggerated effect results because we didn't realize or remember burying the initial toxic events in the first place. When the toxic chemicals slowly seep to the surface, they often manifest as symptoms of anxiety, mood instability, depression, heightened stress, overreactions, sleep disturbances, etc., which we then—thank you, again, midbrain—try to suppress with coping mechanisms.

These coping mechanisms are, more often than not, maladaptive. Because we chose, or didn't choose, to bury our trauma, we didn't develop, or learn, healthy coping mechanisms in the first place. Compounding that, we likely didn't have these healthy coping mechanisms modeled for us, as the very people we were supposed to be learning from were often the cause of—or at least a player in—the initial trauma.

The maladaptive coping mechanisms, viewed through society's judgmental lens of "choice," look like addiction, eating disorders (my personal favorite), or behavioral troubles. These, when viewed through the trauma lens, are byproducts and additional symptoms of the toxic chemicals that, until properly addressed, we will [always] struggle to fully recover from.

There are, however, a couple of details from those days that will never leave me and are as clear as if they just happened.

First came the innocuous, non-traumatic question of, "What are we going to bury Kim in?" Molly and I made that choice very easily—her white nursing uniform with her Looney Tunes scrub jacket. (Not my grandma's first choice.)

Next, who would be the pallbearers? That was obvious—the nurses she worked with. They all had to wear their white nursing uniforms and a colorful scrub jackets, too. (Not their first choice.)

Then came the visitation, which had a few minor hiccups. She had an open casket, and I am very grateful we chose that for many reasons, none overly pertinent to the story; however, her simple light-pink lipstick, blush, and a touch of mascara were not at all what I saw. I responded to that shock by washing my no-longer-living mom's face. I reapplied her light-pink lipstick and blush and added just a touch of mascara.

After years of her attempting to apply my dance makeup, it was my turn. I will cherish that moment always. And yet, looking back, I have no idea how I managed to do that.

For the actual visitation, the funeral home had a basement where all my friends hung out. There was a TV, snacks, and games—it was like a party, exactly what I needed during the small breaks I got. Unfortunately, the only person I distinctly remember talking to or seeing was my dad. Again, I ask myself: why, of all the people I saw and talked to that day, did my brain choose to remember just him? I hadn't seen him since he disappeared from my life when I was 11 years old, five years prior. Maybe that's why it's him, I remember. My hero, my first "He," my goal for so long. It wasn't until the last year of my mom's life that I finally saw the truth of what I had always had but chose not to see.

Was his being there a new trauma, or was it my traumatized brain being triggered by his presence? Did it bring buried memories to the surface, blending the long-term with this new situation and giving his appearance greater significance than all the other active moments happening in rapid succession? Or maybe it was the way it happened. He strolled in wearing black jeans, black leather chaps (he rode in on his motorcycle, of course), a black shirt, and a black jacket—at least he had the color right. Next to him was my stepmom, whom I was meeting for the very first time, at my mom's funeral.

My actual memory of that moment is brief—just a few seconds—though the reality was undoubtedly more involved. My memory begins and ends with them walking through the door and me, at that same exact moment, rounding the corner and nearly bumping into them. I froze. End memory.

The next vivid memory is the funeral service itself. For some reason, I thought I should sing "Amazing Grace" at my mom's funeral. I have absolutely no idea why or where that idea came from. Luckily, Kendra has an amazing voice and rescued me. She couldn't, however, rescue me from the eulogy—my first of four that I've now given to date. I wish I remembered the eulogy or had a copy of it somewhere. I couldn't even begin to guess what I said. I know I ended it with "Amazing Grace," and I know I failed miserably at that because I was crying. I can only assume that whatever I said wasn't easy to deliver.

Between the butchered singing and going home with Molly afterward, there's one more moment I remember—one that stopped the sad tears and brought happy ones. It was just after the burial. As everyone began turning to their vehicles to leave, I lingered by the now-occupied hole in the ground. When I finally turned away, I froze again. There stood 20-30 of my classmates, huddled together, just looking at me. The shock of seeing them there, offering their support, was overwhelming. It was such a moment of love. Apparently, our AP History teacher had canceled class for the day, freeing up their schedules. Beyond that initial moment of shock, the rest of the memory is gray.

I don't remember who, if anyone, came back home with Molly and me after everything else that happened that day. What I do remember is how quickly everyone's attitude toward me seemed to grow cold. Sometime that week, when I confronted my grandma about her absence, she looked me straight in the eyes and said: "You have no idea how hard this is for me. You lost your mom, yes, but I lost my daughter, and that is so much harder. You cannot tell me it is harder for you because YOU KILLED YOUR MOM."

That statement changed everything—my life, my foundation, my future, and my understanding of love, family, safety, and security. All of it was gone. The floating and treading water that became my status quo for decades was all I had left. Any abandonment I'd felt before—including from my dad—was dwarfed by that moment. Whatever trust I had built, especially in the last year of my mom's life, was obliterated. My grandma, the one who had always "gotten" me growing up, had destroyed the last of what I thought I had.

My response was nothing. It's one of those moments in life when someone says something so unexpected that you can't possibly have a good response. Later, all the things you wish you'd said come to mind, but by then, it's too late and never worth it. So, I did what I'd learned to do—from both my mom, who was independent and capable, and from the prior year—I handled it. My mom's "if I die" speech was very much on my mind.

The plan, as it had been laid out, was that Molly and I would go live with Susan as soon as it made sense. Logistics being what they were, this would likely happen at the end of the school year, less than two months away. So, immediately following the funeral, we carried on much as we had before. I continued to pay the bills and take care of Molly and myself. No one seemed to be bothered by this setup. I think most people assumed a grandparent was living with us full-time. I might have assumed the same in their position. But that wasn't the case. (My grandma was clearly in no condition to do so, and my grandpa—though still around to handle things like mowing the lawn and maintaining the house—didn't take on the "kid stuff" or stay with us.) The situation was manageable, and things were okay. Molly and I were "fine".

But then, of course, things got worse. I don't remember exactly when (sometime between April and May 1999), but the moment itself is as clear as day. Susan and I were sitting in the kitchen, discussing what was to come. I was seated with my back to the window near the counter while Susan sat across from me, near the door. Molly suddenly burst in, excitedly flinging the door open and hitting Susan with it on her way to give her a hug. "Is it time to come to your house now?" Molly asked. I jokingly said, "Well, thanks a lot." Susan replied, "That's what your sister and I are about to talk about. Why don't you go back outside to play?" Innocent of what was about to happen, Molly ran back outside.

Susan turned to me and, without preamble, said, "Heather, I can't take you guys."

"What do you mean? That's what Mom said the plan was," I replied.

"I know that was her plan," Susan said.

Now, growing anxious, I asked, "So what's the problem? Why can't you take us?"

Then, it happened again.

"Heather, I can't take you and Molly. I didn't think she would actually die, so I told her I would take you both to make her feel better."

That statement from my "cool" aunt, my "favorite" aunt—the one who had promised her dying sister she would protect her daughters—was a rejection and abandonment I couldn't process. (I'm done counting at this point.)

At some point after delivering that news, she left. I haven't seen her since. (We were supposed to have lunch in the summer of 2006. She stood me up.)

When the school year ended, Molly left. I stayed in my house until I had no choice but to leave. Apparently, at some point, I packed and cleaned my childhood home with my grandpa's help. I remember none of it, which is probably a blessing—I can't imagine how much it must have hurt. What I do remember is sleeping on a sleeping bag in the living room and conversations about where I might go next: live with my dad (which was never going to happen) or with my grandpa (a 16-year-old and a 72-year-old was equally unlikely). Eventually, my cousin convinced my aunt and uncle (my dad's brother and his wife—whom I hadn't seen in over five years) to let me live with them in the next town over so I could graduate from my high school. For reasons I don't understand, they agreed. Apparently, I moved in, but I'm glad I don't remember the details.

That summer of 1999, however, Alex happened. It was another event that shattered my life, trust, safety, and whatever concept I had of stability or unconditional love.

Far more important, though, was the very thing my mom feared and fought to prevent. Molly had to go live with her dad. I won't tell Molly's story—it's hers to share. But I will say this: Anyone who thinks I overcame a lot in the years after our mom's death has no clue what Molly endured from fourth grade until college, for what she endured was far more. My sister is resilient, a survivor. She is my mom—in looks, compassion, integrity, and all the ways that matter. Molly is a social worker in Child Protection with a passion for grief therapy. But Molly's story is Molly's story.

Chapter 7: Walls

Walls can be seen as a concept and/or a "lifestyle" (albeit a mostly maladaptive one) when you consider how they play a role in one's actual life. Let's, for a moment, use walls as a visual—something easy for most to understand. Walls can have holes in the form of windows and doors, easily opened to let things/people/etc. in and just as easily shut when needed. Walls can also be implied, such as the division between one's yard and a neighbor's yard, or they can be full barriers of brick and stone, hardened over centuries to protect what is inside from attack. Thinking through just those three examples, it's easy to see how walls play a part in everyone's life. However, most do not actively—or nearly constantly—think about, construct, deconstruct, and strategically plan their walls. For me, however, that is exactly what I have done. Honestly, though, I was—especially in the past—very poor at choosing which types of walls to place where.

I am not quite sure when my walls started to be built, but does anyone really know? Can anyone truly pinpoint the moment in their lives when they just knew something had to happen to protect themselves—like, "Hey, self, it's time to protect and suit up for battle"? Of course not. That's the whole midbrain protection thing. It just happens over time, like your kids getting older, like the grass growing, or like water boiling—it just happens. It's only after the fact that one can see it has happened.

Needless to say, I have walls—plural—as in a fortress of walls. There are layers of walls. I honestly have no idea how many layers there are or how thick these walls might be. Fortunately—or unfortunately—I was too busy surviving to pay attention. At this point, it would likely be re-traumatizing to even try pulling them apart or figuring out where one begins and another ends. Like wet tissue paper, many of them just became one, blending into a brown, indistinguishable mess. For most of my life, it became easier to simply put up a solid stone wall than to leave myself vulnerable.

There are a few key situations I can pinpoint, in hindsight, where another wall was built. As in the exact moment a wall was erected, the reasons why and now are as vivid as if they were happening right now. These walls usually went up so quickly because they replaced a wide, trusting, and vulnerable expanse of myself that I had given to someone else—only to have them follow in the footsteps of many who came before, washing their hands of my needs, feelings, wants, desires, and worth. Unfortunately, I wish I could say that the moment such a dismissal happened, a wall was erected because of my own self-worth, a boundary if you will. But the reality is that I would try—over and over—to change myself to fit whatever their capacity was, often diminishing myself in the process. As if behind the wall I was changing into a better costume to fit the part I was *supposed* to play in their production.

A quick tangent on this idea. I see self-worth and ego/narcissism on a spectrum, paralleling the responsive sides of martyrdom and selfishness. I believe that to be in a healthy place on this spectrum (and I believe everyone fits on it, fluidly shifting if nurtured to a "healthy" place or swinging fully to the extremes if not), many factors are involved. One key factor ties back to the idea of foundational people. If you grow up in a stable situation with a strong foundation, then confidence, empowerment, worth, and value are naturally modeled—and, more importantly, fostered within you. You live with minimal trauma (or if trauma exists, you have your village's support and guidance to navigate it) and naturally develop a [healthy] sense of self.

This self-awareness is displayed in actions toward others: compassion, empathy, and support. Yet, you also possess the confidence and self-worth to voice your needs, wants, and desires, advocating for yourself when necessary. Not everyone possesses this "picture-perfect" ability, even when near the middle of the spectrum—personality differences play a role—but they likely still inherently believe in themselves and their basic worth.

For people like me, who have experienced traumas and abandonments, that innate self-knowing often doesn't exist. I constantly question whether I'm being too greedy, picky, selfish, needy, or demanding, living in a persistent state of imposter syndrome—never feeling good enough, regardless of the situation. This mindset sometimes leads to doing too much for others in the hope it will be reciprocated. It's like a non-verbal modeling of my own needs and wants, wishing others could pick up on it or read my mind. Asking for it outright feels impossible (and what if I ask and get rejected? That's even worse!).

I tend to sit on one end of the spectrum for too long—nearing martyrdom—molding myself to others' needs, wants, demands, ideas, and desires while neglecting my own. I convince myself I'll be fine in that space, ignoring "me." I believe that if I mold myself perfectly to fit another's world, I'll finally be worth it. Unfortunately, the molding and waiting and hoping and ignoring of me only works for so long before frustration, irritation, resentment, and pain build to a breaking point where I just cannot not be me anymore.

At that point, the pendulum swings the other way, and I stop caring about what the other person feels or thinks. I rationalize it with they haven't cared about my feelings, thoughts, or needs for so long. And there lies the breaking point. I fully understand it's unrealistic to expect someone whom I've never held to a standard to suddenly care, feel, or prioritize me. They've had it easy for so long—why would they change? Their defense mechanisms then kick in, and everything implodes. And just like that, a new wall is built.

Can a relationship come back from that point? Honestly, I'm not so sure. It would require a genuine commitment from the other person and my willingness to rebuild the trust in promises and standards of worth that were never met before. Given my history, I doubt I could fully trust again, and I doubt anyone would even know where to start without inadvertently accusing me of being insatiable: "Nothing is ever good enough for you. Nothing will ever make you happy." Both so easily thrown in my face.

To end this tangent: lacking innate comfort on that spectrum—where, from the beginning of a relationship, standards, and expectations of worth and needs are established—can be a significant challenge. It's deeply uncomfortable. I'm terrible at voicing my worth, needs, and boundaries from the start, which is crucial for a healthy relationship. Without it, I'm not sure the foundation will ever be strong enough to trust fully. Although this leans heavily toward romantic relationships, it applies in other situations as well, with nuanced variations.

Back to the walls. I am fully, painfully aware of the weak spots in mine. These weak spots weren't intentional. I like to think some greater force put them there so I could inherit the compassion and empathy from my mom. These—perhaps it's unfair to call them "weak" spots—make me human. They've also made me a good doctor and mother.

I'm not naive enough to allow the weak spots to align (think of the holes in slices of Swiss cheese), as that would make me far too vulnerable. These weak spots are very specific, describable, and—much to my dismay—obvious to the very people the walls were built to protect me from. I know them well. Not only are they anyone's chance of reaching the real me, but they are also the exact points where I've been manipulated and taken advantage of—repeatedly.

This manipulation brings me the deepest shame. Each time someone exploits one of these weak spots, it not only builds another wall but also compounds my internal shame, as though I must own their manipulation.

There are two kinds of shame involved. The first is the shame I feel from the manipulator's actions. I invariably own their behavior, blaming myself because manipulators excel at making themselves appear flawless. When they fall from their pedestal, it's presented as my fault—and I believe them every time.

The second shame stems from my inability to prevent it. Why don't I see it coming? Why do I hope for something different? Shame on me for being fooled again. Although I am acutely aware of these weak spots—and even though they are always the same—I still fall victim every single time.

In therapy, I'm told this is my "pattern." I struggle to close these weak spots completely because they are part of what makes me who I am. They form my attunement, compassion, and other good qualities. Striking a balance, much like navigating the aforementioned spectrum, is my challenge.

In my world of walls, I am fully aware of one more concrete fact: unless you came out of my body or are, in all likelihood, dead, the only solid truth is this—I am my own foundation, I am my own strength, and I know how to hold up the fortress of these brick walls.

Yes, this seems extremely melodramatic, very self-serving, and perhaps even self-sacrificing. But, as you will see, it does have some basis in truth. With each wall I've built and each manipulated weak spot, my self-foundation has had no choice but to become stronger and thicker. In a way, that self-created foundation is the cumulative platform for my walls. It's also, as I like to think about it, what keeps my head just above water when I'm frantically treading to survive.

Where you may ask, is my true foundation—the foundation of home, family, and safety? Great question. And if I ever learn what happened to mine—or why the complete disappearance from literally everyone occurred—I'll let you know. Some of this, however, will reveal itself in fragments throughout this story.

Foundation tangent: The absence of the "was supposed to be there since birth" foundation is the most painful and my biggest Achilles heel when it comes to letting real people (i.e., not manipulators) through my walls. This absence is felt daily in some shape or form. Take, for instance, my divorce. (Let's speak of my divorce for now from a very high level.) My in-laws were my family, and combined with the isolation they pushed upon me for my "not refined enough" dad [his presence in my life following my mom's death waxed and waned, as you'll see], they were all I had. My best friend was my sister-in-law. I was my father-in-law's confidant (which he seems to have forgotten quite quickly). I played the perfect exterior role.

Then came the divorce, and they—though I can't fault them for choosing their blood—not only erased me from existence but also contributed to the slander and defamation of my character. Leading the charge? You guessed it: my father-in-law. Amazing how that works out. It's one thing to step away; it's another to destroy someone based on assumptions, misinterpretations, and one-sided declarations, so much for ever belonging. Was it ever really real?

Without a foundation of my own, where do I get to be sad, vulnerable, heard, and accepted—no matter what? Where am I supported—no matter what? Who has my back—no matter what? For many, the answer is their chosen family, their friends. Well, I already mentioned my sister-in-law was my best friend—she fled so fast and even found my ex-husband his new girlfriend (she planted her ally, I believe, since well...). I can't completely fault her silence, being married into the family herself, but still. My "next best friend" threw me under the bus with my ex [in the most hypocritical of ways] and tried to destroy my career (cliffhanger—more to come). So there's that.

Seeing as we lived in his small, rural hometown, I stood no chance. Nearly all of my closest friends heard and believed what they wanted to or what they were fed as gospel. I was blacklisted. That's a bit of an exaggeration—I do have a couple of girlfriends who stood by me through the worst four years of my life. But, as much as I love them, they joined my life in my mid-thirties. Time doesn't define a bond, no, but I still lack that foundation—someone who "just gets me" and has my back no matter what. To fully trust anyone after what my closest friends did is impossible.

The foundation I was left with? Myself. Because it had to be.

Back to walls... Where someone lands in my world, in relation to my walls, depends on many factors. First, how well they manipulate their way through. (Yes, see above.) Second—well, maybe for the vast majority of my life, it really was just the first one. There's a reason for that. Not a good reason, but a reason: self-preservation.

Very few people have genuinely broken down any of my walls (I'll spend time on who these people are in their own chapters). Only one non-child-of-mine ever started to shatter them all. But even that building foundation is terrifying and hard to trust, how can I really ever be sure it's genuine and not further manipulation.

Also, as walls are taken down and with each move closer to the real me, the urge (anxiety) to rebuild gets stronger. Even the slightest over-thinking or stress wants me to run for the hills, or mortar.

The first question one might ask at this point is: why the need for such a fortress of self-preservation? The second: what's inside the walls?

The first question is the easiest: trauma, abandonment, resilience, self-sufficiency, and the honest ability to handle everything, it seems, on my own. When you can do it all, why on earth would you break down walls just to let someone else try to manage what you can already handle yourself? Living in a cave of walls is completely fine if you can truly handle it all. (More will become clear as the story unfolds.)

Although this concept of singular self-reliance goes against everything it means to be human—the need for community, survival is even more primal. One caveat: I do NOT want to live this way, it's truly not a higher level of thinking choice.

The second question: what's on the inside of the walls? The true inside. Inside the outer strength, the proven abilities, the resilience, and the unrecognized (because if it were recognized, I'd have an Oscar by now) facade is an abandoned newborn. A terrified child. A lonely, lost girl who has only ever been searching for one thing: unconditional. Unconditional love. Acceptance. Safety. Home. Worth.

My inner child—her age, I haven't perfectly pinpointed. My therapist and I likely disagree. At the oldest, she's 11. But honestly, through countless hours of therapy, I surmise she's likely between 3-5 years old. (My therapist, however, would say, at most, she's hours old.)

Regardless of her age, she's a badass. This girl, protected inside my walls, saved my life. Without her, I wouldn't be here today.

My inner child-he's my hero.

I'm supposed to, in my trauma healing, acknowledge her fears, sadness, and vulnerabilities, console her, and "set her free" to be the child she should have always been. But this is an impossible ask. How can I honor her badassery while also telling her it's okay to be scared and vulnerable?

This dichotomy is unnerving.

She became strong and self-capable because she had to—because those foundational people weren't there to support or protect her. So, if I "free" her, who plays that foundation role in her healing? Do I create false narratives about the people who should have been there? Or do I give her the foundation I know now and play that role myself?

That doesn't make much sense either. How can I heal by freeing her while also giving her a solid, healed foundation to stand on?

If I just free her without expectation, then where do I stand?

As usual, I'm likely overcomplicating it. This is all supposed to be theoretical because the past can't be changed.

What I can do is honor her. Thank her. Forgive her.

Without her grit—and sometimes even her destructive drive—I wouldn't be here now.

But forgiveness, not just praise and gratitude, is essential. What happened to that girl wasn't her fault, but some of her reactions and choices weren't ideal.

On one hand, everything was survival-driven. The circumstances were an explanation, even an excuse at times. But not all those actions and behaviors were good ones—and as I got older, they got "less good."

I want to take another small tangent here to explain the importance of the concept of "less good" because it is crucial when discussing, and choosing to heal, the inner child. Firstly, if a child, adolescent, or even adult always chooses to do, say, and be the right thing, and yet the world and foundational people continue to disregard, ignore, and reject them, doesn't the very idea of the right thing come into question? If you don't receive appreciation or positive affirmation for doing well, why would you keep doing it? Especially when it seems that others around you can continue to do the "not right thing," "get away with it," and still receive love and attention. And when there are no foundational people—no "safe" people—who are always supposed to be there to support, love, and reassure, then what happens? Well, the concept of the right thing starts to grey. It begins to blur.

If those "less-than-perfect" responses aren't redirected or balanced with love, it becomes a slippery slope. The responses become more selfish and self-serving, often subconsciously so. They become justifiable because why not? When no one was ever there to positively affirm the "right" and help guide you down that path, the very concept of doing the right thing gets questioned. There wasn't a stable foundation where this standard was defined, and therefore, the outside world sets the standard—or worse, we look to the wrong people to help set it. (In my life, there's a specific type of person who loves to set that external standard for the traumatized.) These wrong people often use manipulation to mold you (me) into someone that suits them best, setting a standard for their own benefit.

During trauma healing, however, this dynamic is uncovered, leading to even more painful therapy and feelings of foolishness. So, what does this mean for me and my inner child? Well, I made some very bad choices as a subconscious cry for help. I say subconscious because, on the surface, I knew some of my choices were wrong—or retrospectively, I can see where things started to spiral or how my actions led others to think or feel a certain way about me. But deep down, I just needed to be loved. My inner child had her blinders on, focusing solely on the human need for love and connection. I was so broken and alone. No matter how good I was, I still felt lost to everyone else, burdened by so many unacknowledged expectations. My worth disappeared into this foundationless slope, and I was dying inside for connection.

Now, back to the relationship between this inner child and the walls. Each time a new wall is built, the inner girl becomes more terrified and retraumatized (hence the new wall of "protection"). Each time someone gets through a wall, and closer to the core, that little girl reacts. (I love how simple I just made that sound!) "Reacts" is anything but simple. Also extremely important to note, before I describe what "reacts" means, is the very difficult-to-explain idea that "reacts" is not intentional, personal, wanted, relied on, or any other description implying I have control over it. "Reacts" lives in the reptilian brain, where we have no control, especially in the world of trauma.

Maybe that makes it sound like I have dissociative identity disorder (and I am not shaming those with that diagnosis—it is itself a form of severe PTSD with a more obvious outward protective mechanism) or that I am truly a completely separate person. I don't, and I'm not. The reptilian, I-have-no-control-over-this "reacts" is mentioned simply to highlight the innate nature of the fight/flight/freeze response, where higher-level thinking doesn't exist. This is not an excuse either—darn it, I'm working on it! I'm owning my not-so-pleasant primordial reactions. But, again, decades (or, per therapy, literally a lifetime) of "this" doesn't change overnight. It's made more complicated by the fact that I don't have the foundation of not only support but also modeled and learned "how-to." Essentially, if you want to traverse, with good intent, toward "me," you better have a lot of patience. Just kidding—it's not on anyone but me to do the work, to have faith and trust in people. (But I ask again, where do we learn these concepts? And if we didn't learn them from our foundation, then when and from whom?)

Yes, this is a full conundrum. I want connection and love but seem to act in complete contradiction to that.

What does "react," however, even look like? The two easiest descriptors would be self-sabotage and pushing people away (i.e., self-isolation). Ironically, these two behaviors serve the exact opposite purpose of what my inner self wants and needs. All I want is that feeling of unconditional acceptance and love. Yet, as anyone gets closer to giving me that, I somehow innately react in the opposite, paradoxical manner. And if that person manages to survive this reaction and reaches a new, closer layer of blissful stability, they end up encountering another wall to circumnavigate. Of course, this results in my inner self reacting again—this time, even more strongly because that brave soul is even closer to the core.

In essence, surviving me and my reacting inner child can be challenging. It continues until either they outlast me (confidently stay, fight, love hard, and not take my reactions too personally because they understand them) or, preferably, until my trauma healing finds balance.

One major stumbling block: this reacting inner child would be so much easier to understand, accept, console, and be patient with if I were actually a child—because childlike reactions make sense coming from an actual child. Reactions coming from someone who, from the outside, appears to be a well-put-together doctor are extremely difficult to reconcile. Understandably, they can seem and feel as if I'm intentionally creating conflict or falling out of love and trust, building more walls. The reality, however, is that I need the same understanding, acceptance, consoling, patience, love, and—most importantly—grace that would be given to that small child. Lots of grace. This reassurance concept seems to evade manipulators (you'd think that would be an obvious red flag), but alas, I hold onto hope for far too long.

I am fully aware that this sounds very paranoid and excessively extreme. This is no longer a 'healthy' situation of playing things safe and building trust as per what might be considered 'normal' behavior. There is little normal in this. Yet these walls—and my reactions to them—weren't built in an environment of health or safety. Every situation that helped create the walls and the holes created such trauma that my inner self had no choice but to always be on high alert, always suspicious, and always ready to react.

There have been people in my past who got very close to the innermost area—people I trusted, people I gave my heart to, people who nearly reached the center—even before there were as many walls. They, frankly, are some the very people who built and forced the subsequent construction of the thickest, strongest walls. They are the very people who masterfully manipulated each weak spot, leaving me now less comfortable trusting my 'higher-level thinking' recognition of sincerity, genuineness, or true love. I fully and completely trusted them. But, as I see now, I was being groomed by some, used by others, and was simply a figurehead of sorts for even more. I learned that it is far easier to just not let people that far in. These master manipulators destroyed me despite not even being all the way in—so why on earth would I ever let anyone all the way in?

My inner self cannot trust until some brave soul proves truly sincere, genuinely driven by love, honor, and respect, and capable of surviving the 'reaction.' God bless the heart that tries. (To be fully transparent—there was one, maybe two, others who 'should have' been 'my person.' But in true trauma-response fashion, I sabotaged so quickly. More to come, but at the time they were in my life, I definitely wasn't at a place of believing I deserved it. I had not yet started the intense trauma therapy I needed to begin understanding and healing.)

In a way, it does indeed sound like a crazy 'test' for anyone. And maybe, to the bones, it could be considered that. But that would, again, imply intent on my part, and there is no intent. I want that connection more than anything. I do not like the inner-me 'reaction' because I very clearly see the hurt and confusion I cause. I can literally see and feel others' walls being put up to protect themselves from me—and man, does that hurt. Oh, the irony. It puts me right back in that place of feeling not quite good enough, not quite worth it enough. I'm too much work. And I get it.

After the reaction, my inner self sits raw, devastated, silently screaming for help, for understanding, for someone to fight it, fight me, and say I'm worth it. All the while, following the 'big reaction,' I feel the chest tightness of the breath being taken away and the slow, upward creep of another wall getting ready to be built. Silently, with tear-filled eyes, I hope and beg to be worth it just one time—to not have to build another wall. To know I'm safe, loved, and accepted as me.

But maybe that's part of the problem. I needed to find worth on my own first and not rely on any one (non-offspring) person to climb all the walls without manipulating the weak spots.

I understand my worth now, but it has taken a long time, and the process doesn't end. I am, and will always be, a work in progress—constantly growing, learning, and healing. And I am okay with that because my trauma deserves that respect, understanding, appreciation, forgiveness, self-love, and self-grace.

Chapter 8: The Drowning Lifeguard

On February 6, 2020, I became aware of a very disturbing news story. This story struck me cold, for "my Alex" was the star. What followed initiated a nearly four-year-long midlife crisis of sorts. It changed my life in many ways, causing me to question everything even more. All my traumas were torn open, revealing truths until only I was left. After seeing the story, I called the police department listed—purposely after they had closed. (I really hate talking on the phone, and I didn't know if I was even doing the right thing by calling. I needed overnight to process what I had seen, but I knew if I didn't call that day, I might never call.)

The following pages, I warn you, are not easy and may be triggering to some. This is the summary of my story with "my Alex" and how this one "man" impacted every relationship I have ever had since. This one "man" became my next *He*—the worst to this point, but, unfortunately, not the worst of all.

In the summer of 1999 (I was 16), just a month and a half or so after my mom died, I stopped playing mom for my sister and was just me—alone in my house. I was not going to leave. I was living in my house with a sleeping bag. At some point, yes, the house was cleaned and sold, and I had to move, but, as I've already stated, those memories are non-existent compared to Alex. (Intertwining traumas—did one completely overshadow the other, or do they both exist deep inside, one just buried deeper? And if so, why? Trauma and our brain's response is such a fascinating thing.)

That was my first summer as a lifeguard. I was a swimmer; I loved the water, and it was the outdoor pool I grew up visiting nearly every day of every summer when I was younger. I was assigned the afternoon/evening guard shift, and Alex was my direct supervisor—my "boss." It was him, me, and four other girls who worked our shift. I knew two of the girls when I started, as we went to high school together. Alex and the other two girls were older, but I went to school with several of their younger siblings.

Looking back now, I can see that Alex was my very typical *He.* He was nice, complimentary, and kind. He was charming, funny, and flirty. He was tall, dark hair, handsome, solid—not scrawny. The "hold you in his arms and protect you" kind. He was the type of guy who made girls giddy and awkward, and I was no different. I was, however, very different in a few other respects.

At the time we met, I felt beyond alone in the world. I had just lost my mom and my sister, and soon, my house would be gone too. All my maternal foundation people had disappeared except for my grandpa. I had to move to a town I didn't want to, to live with my dad's brother, my aunt, and cousins, whom I hadn't seen in five years. Although I had Brandon for a boyfriend, it was a mere title. Unless I was fawning over him or conforming to his ideas and thoughts, I was on my own. That summer, I was basically a neon sign begging for attention and love.

Alex and I progressed to friends, not just boss and employee, and soon started to hang out more—with a flirtatious undertone. Alex treated me like I mattered. I confided in him about my struggles since my mom died. I told him about my dad and how I really didn't seem to be wanted anywhere, but how my aunt and uncle were kindly letting me live with them for two years. I told him about Brandon. I told Alex everything.

Alex listened, and he held me. He gave the best hugs, and I could get lost in his arms because he was so big, so strong, so protective. He knew what to say and he made me feel special. He also told me about his life. He shared stories about his daughter, whom he had in high school, and the struggles that came with that. We would take her to get ice cream—she was the sweetest little thing. He told me about joining the Army and his hopes and dreams for the future.

At work, I started to be treated differently, more special. Everyone noticed, but what could they do? He was in charge. I was entranced.

Then, one day, everything changed. I had just moved into my aunt and uncle's, the town over, so my drive was now much longer. After I had already driven to the pool that day it started raining and the pool was closed until the rain stopped. Since I no longer lived close, Alex invited me to his house to hang out. The excitement I felt!

When I got to his house, he took me to his room in the basement. He started to playfully tease me because, just the day before, we had gotten new wind pants and lifeguard sweatshirts, and I was already wearing mine. We started by sitting on his bed, and he turned on *Full Metal Jacket*—a movie he always turned on, even in the guard room—so I had already seen it at least half a dozen times. So many details of that room, that day, that just won't leave me.

He then pulled me into him—the cozy, sweatshirts-on-a-cold-day-watching-a-movie kind of snuggle. Seriously, 16-year-old me felt like she had died and gone to heaven in the arms of my 21-year-old boss! And then came the compliments and charm.

Apparently, navy wind pants and a gray sweatshirt over a one-piece red lifeguard swimsuit, with my hair tied up in a scrunchie, made me the most beautiful girl in the world. When he realized I was wearing my swimsuit, he questioned how on earth I could be comfortable. Smooth—so smooth he was. Oblivious, how oblivious and naïve I was. He reached up to feel my swimsuit and realized I didn't have the straps over my shoulders. (This was common for swimmers like me when not swimming because, honestly, those straps could be so uncomfortable and dig into your shoulders.)

The next thing I knew, my swimsuit was pulled down from under my sweatshirt. Then my pants and swimsuit were off. (So classy—yes, even at this point, I was still wearing my sweatshirt.)

I lost my virginity that day to *Full Metal Jacket* playing in the background. Nothing sweet, nothing special, nothing gentle. Nothing with foreplay. Nothing but a two-minute, edge-of-the-bed, rapid release for him, quickly followed by, "We should get to the pool." I wanted to vomit.

Shock. Disappointment. Anti-climactic. *That's what sex is all about? Did that just happen?* The drive back to the pool was a blur. Honestly, it didn't feel right, and it didn't feel good—physically or emotionally. Did I think it was "wrong" during that quick drive? Not really, since I didn't say no. But I also didn't say yes. I didn't say no. I didn't say yes. Did I consent? No. Did I fight? No. It all happened so fast, and then it was over. And we left.

The question I've always asked myself: was that assault? Was it wrong? Was what he did wrong? Did I bring it on myself?

Over the next 25 years, I went back and forth, typically keeping the whole situation very vague whenever someone asked about "my first time." Over those 25 years, however, I also loved "my Alex." I'm going out on a limb here and saying that most people probably have a special place in their hearts for their first. Because of that, I found it really difficult to think it was wrong—especially since I never said no.

There were many times over the next 20-plus years when I would come face-to-face with that question.

The first moment of questioning came when we arrived at the pool, just minutes after it happened. Amanda, one of our co-workers—Alex's age—was in the guard room when I got there. She asked me what I had done during the delay (knowing I didn't live in town). When I told her I had gone to Alex's, the look on her face was one I will never forget.

She didn't ask. She didn't have to. I felt shame and embarrassment and escaped, in my typical fashion, to the bathroom—a cement block space, damp, cold, and gray.

And bloody.

Oh, so much blood I found when I went into that stall that day. I sobbed. Nearly vomiting, I was overwhelmed with regret—regret that was quickly interrupted by Amanda's voice asking me if I needed a tampon. She knew.

Her response for the rest of the summer was, I assume, like what a mom's would have been. She never directly asked me about it and never mentioned it again, but she never left me alone with him at the pool. She checked on me all the time, especially if the pool ever had a delay. She was the big sister I needed that summer. She cared.

Alex never invited me over again, never gave me any extra attention, never complimented me, and never was flirty or sweet. He lost his charm, but he was never mean, rude, or aggressive. He moved on to another lifeguard on our shift, one a year younger than I was. Together, they isolated themselves from the rest of us—a painful blessing for me. I was so jealous because, again, he not only stole my virginity that day, but he also stole a part of my heart. I felt rejected by him. Yes, Amanda was protecting me, and I didn't want to be with him or alone with him, but he didn't even show that he cared. What happened meant nothing to him; I meant nothing to him, and that is what broke my heart. I clearly was not good enough for him, whereas he and the other girl dated for nearly two years.

Fast forward several years. I was in college; Alex was in the Army. One day, I got a message on Facebook—many "I miss you," an apology for the time passed, and an update on his loneliness, especially with a deployment. Like the Bermuda Triangle, I was sucked right back in—a victim of his charm and attention—for it all came back tenfold.

Wow, I must have meant something after all! Why on Earth would he have cold-messaged me [of all people] if he didn't care?

We would message often. The messages were innocuous: "How's school? How's work? How's your daughter? Do you have a boyfriend?" He was just about to be deployed to Kuwait and was afraid—understandably so—but he was also feeling alone. He needed "someone," and he decided it should be me. I complied almost instantly. In true Nicholas Sparks fashion, to my hopeless romantic self, I was his "letters home." Almost weekly, I would get handwritten, multi-page letters describing his days and his loneliness, his dreams of me, and how he couldn't wait to have the rom-com reuniting... so smooth. I was completely hooked (and so the grooming continued…I mean, it worked the first time).

When he returned from deployment, it was perfect. Within a week, I went to visit him. There was a welcome-home gathering at a bar and grill. I walked in and saw him, looking terrified at his own party, back to the far wall away from the door. I approached him, and he hugged me as if I was a life preserver. This party was too much for him, having just come back from war, and apparently, I was the only one who noticed him struggling. We talked about how afraid he was and how happy he was to be home.

He had a lot to catch up on over the next few days, but he asked if we could connect in a week or so… because I was different, and I understood him—he needed me. Yup, hook, line, and sinker: I'm "special," and I'm "chosen," etc.

A week later, I went over to his house. We went back to his room so he could share things "I can't share with anyone else." This time, however, I was not naïve. Did I know what "could" happen? Yes. Was that the plan? No. Did I want it to? No. Did he hint at or imply it would? No. Did I up front say it wasn't going to? No.

We talked for a long time. He cried while telling me about his deployment and return home. Crying turned into hugging, which turned into kissing, which turned into the rest. This time, despite my more mature awareness, it went very wrong again. I did consent to the act itself. Honestly, I think it was to take my power back from the first time. For now, in my mind, at least, it made the "ick" and wrong from the first time easier to minimize.

I didn't, however, consent to the anal sex. Nor was I warned it was going to happen, nor was anything done to prepare, nor did I enjoy any of it. It was humiliating, painful, and even more demeaning than the assault at age 16, roughly five years prior. Again, it was over fast; again, it was aggressive; again, there was so much blood; again, I thought, "What just happened?" "Did that just happen?" And, again, we wouldn't speak for years after I left his room.

One would think this would have been a huge "news flash." Move on, Heather. This isn't safe, healthy, or a person who should be in your life. But, as you'd probably expect by now, I didn't take that route.

Much like with my dad, I would do ANYTHING to hold tight to all people regardless of the harms. Harms, you see, are very easy to "forget" and minimize, especially when they are so easily overshadowed by attention, appreciation, and "love." And when the faux pas are so easily explained and blamed away, I am also a very forgiving person. When the explanation of the wrong is matched with attention, fancy words and promises, and grand gestures, I stay.

Did we eventually reconnect? Of course, we did. Whenever his marriage—or mine—got stressful, we would message, email, or send snaps. (We never met or actually saw each other). "Someday" was a common statement. "You were the one that got away" was another. And "when the timing is right in the future, we will be together" became the nail in the coffin. He was "my Alex." (One of my upcoming "Hes," upon hearing about Alex for the first time, was the only person who questioned the 'okay-ness' of the whole situation. Ironic, as you'll see.)

Fast forward to 2019—20 years since the pool and 15 or so since the last time we saw each other. It had been roughly three years since we'd had any contact even electronically. He reached out in early 2019, telling me he was the school resource officer at our old high school. He said they had an annual conference and wondered if I would be a presenter, discussing addiction, substance use, and substance use disorder. (At that point in my career, this was a common and frequent ask from many people.) I looped the rest of my team into the conversation, and we attempted to work out the details—none of which ever came to fruition. [Another big red flag I missed.]

I was going to be in his area in late summer, so Alex and I decided to meet to discuss more, just the two of us. We planned to meet at a restaurant—a restaurant that had a special place in my heart because of my grandpa—to discuss the conference over lunch. However, when I arrived, Alex informed me the restaurant had closed years before—enter red flag number two. He suggested we go to the bottoms, a slightly isolated, wooded area along the Mississippi. It wasn't an uncommon hangout spot for locals, but it was definitely red flag number three. He also insisted on driving—red flag number four.

The initial part of the drive was pleasant enough until he drove past the parking lot, leading us down a narrow, muddy road, past shanty dwellings, and ending at a spot where the next closest person was at least half a mile away—red flag number five. (Did I mention I'd left my cell phone in my car, back at the "restaurant," five miles away?!) We got out of the truck anyway and walked toward the river. I found a fallen tree to sit on so we could talk. At this point, I was entirely focused on discussing the conference, naively oblivious to any other intentions for the meeting.

As I turned around to tell him I found a place to sit, he was right there. He gave me a hug and didn't let go—beyond my comfort level. He was a good 4–5 inches taller than me and outweighed me by around 100 pounds. I wasn't going anywhere.

I asked to sit down to talk about the conference, at which point he laughed and said, "You actually believed there was a conference?"

I replied, "Uh, yeah. Isn't that why we got together?"

He laughed again and said, "No, that was just an excuse so we could meet since we haven't seen each other in so long." He leaned in to kiss me, but I turned my face away.

The laughter stopped. His charming, charismatic "Alex" began to crack for the first time ever. He said, "Are you serious, Heather? All the talk about your bad marriage and my bad marriage—it's finally our time. You know you want this."

Shocked, I said, "You're right—things aren't great—but I can't do this. There's too much going on, and it's not the right time."

He wouldn't let go. All my fight-or-flight instincts kicked in.

More aggressively, I said, "Alex, let me go."

He responded, "No. You know you want this. I took a day off work for this, and we are going to do this."

"Alex, let me go."

"No."

Thinking quickly, I remembered telling him about my breast augmentation (a line I should never have blurred for attention, regardless of why I did). I said, "Hey, remember I told you I got fake boobs? Do you want to touch them?"

Pure joy spread across his face—he thought he'd won. He started to grab both at the same time and when he did, I stepped away. So proud of me! However, I made the classic "girl in a scary movie" move and walked toward the river instead of toward the road back to the truck. For some reason, I thought I could reason with him because I still naively cared about him and was still struggling to make sense of how he was behaving.

He was fully upset now, fully himself, the monster I'd somehow not seen in 25 years. "Heather," he yelled, "Heather!" I was about 10 yards away.

I turned around at the way he said my name. There he was—pants around his ankles, fully erect.

"Alex, what the hell are you doing?" I asked.

"C'mon, you know you want this. That's why we came here today."

"No, I came here to talk about the conference you told me about."

"There is no conference. And now you owe me."

"What do I owe you? Pull your pants up. We are not having sex."

"Then you owe me a blow job," he demanded.

"I don't owe you anything," I said, walking a wide berth back to the truck. "Take me back to my car."

"You bitch. You're such a bitch and a tease. You only want me when you need me. If you don't do this, we are done."

"Take me back to my car, Alex. We have never been a 'we,' and we never will be."

Surprisingly, when I got to the truck and turned back around, his pants were up, and he was stomping toward the vehicle. We got in. Silence. I was running a Ragnar (a 200-mile, 12-person relay) the next day. I wasn't wearing tennis shoes, but I was doing the math, formulating a plan to run back to my car, five miles away if needed. Someone would see me and help a mile or two in, right?! I kept my hand on the door handle the entire ride, planning how to jump out and roll if needed. Luckily, it didn't come to that. When we got back to my car, I barely had time to close the door before he sped away.

For the third time with him, I had the "Did that just happen?" thought. The shock of the dichotomy between my "Stockholm Syndrome love of my life" and the undeniable monster of truth was overwhelming. (Stockholm Syndrome: a coping mechanism in abusive situations. People develop positive feelings toward their abusers over time, forming a psychological connection and even sympathizing with them. Cleveland Clinic definition.)

Where did I go from there, you may ask? I went to the cemetery where my mom and grandpa are buried—my "people." I cried, then denied it happened and boxed it up with a pretty little bow. I met with my friends to get ready for the Ragnar. I was "done" with Alex.

But to be fully honest, if nothing else had happened and years had passed, I can't promise I'd have truly been done. That's the problem with Stockholm Syndrome, trauma bonds, and being an easy victim for manipulators and narcissists.

Five and a half months later, on February 6, 2020, that mugshot would forever etch itself into my memory. When I met with the detective in that soft interrogation room (it felt like a living room, complete with couches and a dog), he asked if I realized how many times I'd called myself stupid during the two hours it took me to tell this story. I didn't. He said I wasn't stupid—I was a victim. But I didn't believe him. I was still in shock, questioning every decision and every "He" who had been part of my life since Alex. I felt embarrassed, sad, mad, humiliated, angry, full of shame… and still so, so alone.

Chapter 9: Lost At Sea: Part 1

When my mom died, I was essentially parentless, family-less, and living alone at age 16. Sometime that summer, my cousin convinced her parents to let me live with them. I did not know this family all that well, as I had not been to a Christmas, holiday, or, well, any gathering since I was 11 years old. They, however, welcomed me with open arms. My uncle finished off part of the basement, giving me a very large bedroom and my own bathroom. I even managed to convince my school to let me open enroll. Things, at this point, were going as well as they could for an orphan—well, until Alex, a couple of weeks later. But for now, we'll focus on what else was happening at the same time.

Because, little did I know, there was quite a bit going on behind the scenes. My mom's two best friends, Michelle and Barb, were doing everything they could to help Molly and me. They knew my mom had arranged for Susan to take us, and they knew the last thing she would have wanted was for Molly and me to be separated. However, they encountered many roadblocks—primarily my grandma. Their plan, once the prearranged and agreed-upon arrangement with Susan (and the lie it was built on) fell apart, was for Molly and me to live with Michelle, her husband, and their two kids. Michelle had even already called my school so I could open enroll. They fought for us.

Grandma, I'm told, was concerned about the money. She was somehow convinced that all Michelle wanted was the Social Security money Molly and I would be receiving from my mom. This is particularly ironic, considering who actually ended up getting it—clearly, she didn't think that through very well. Also ironic is the fact that, although I was old enough to make an end-of-life decision, I was somehow not old enough to even be asked what I wanted in this situation.

(Why didn't I fight to live with Michelle, you may ask? Well, I learned about this behind-the-scenes battle approximately 23 years later. Yes, I didn't know any of this until long after it had happened—and what I would have done if I had known is completely irrelevant at this point.)

Yes, I did some digging and fact-checking, asking all the right questions to make sure this was even a thing, and yes, it all checked out—someone actually WANTED us and was FIGHTING for us.

Not only was I abandoned by my dad countless times by the age of 16, but losing my mom felt like the worst abandonment of all. My therapist will, again, argue that I had a level of [unintentional] maternal abandonment the moment I was born, but that, to me at this point, seems very semantic. Losing her when I did not only felt like she was abandoning me, but it also felt like God was abandoning me. Yes, this is arguably very dramatic-sounding, but at 16, I just didn't get it—especially because of all the work I and we had done that last year to finally get to such a great place as mother and daughter. It felt like such a twisted joke.

And why her? Why did my mom have to die? I played and replayed the song "Only the Good Die Young" over and over—which did help in some weird way—but it didn't change the fact that I was mad. There were many days when I felt like I was being personally punished because of all the years I had been awful to her, but I did get over that because that really made no sense when it came to Molly. The ways our minds need to try rationalizing things...

P.S.: Now, more than 25 years later, I still can't make complete sense of it. Christian leaders will encourage us to step back and not look back at the situation to try to make sense of it specifically but rather to see how it has impacted our entire life and what has resulted because of it. Not a direct "this positive happened because the negative happened first," but more of a way to find peace (and forgiveness—even for God) in the negative, for everything fluidly impacts so many things.

So then, to hear—23 years later—that someone wanted me? It was a lot. It was so hard to hear that and so great to hear that, especially because of all my 'foundation people' who didn't. After the shock of it all, I had a bizarre mixture of anger, sadness, and grief. I heard this news while standing at my son's baseball game, and in one moment, I managed to feel like both the "mom" and the "lost child." I cannot even count how many times since that phone call that I have played out what that situation would have looked like for my life and for Molly's. Honestly, it is nearly impossible to imagine.

Some may say—and have—that I should be grateful that someone wanted me, that I should stop being so dramatic about having 'no one,' that I should just 'get over' all the years of feeling so abandoned, and that I should just move on. Somehow, I am supposed to take this new knowledge more than two decades later and feel comforted that I was wanted—to reframe all the moments and years where I felt anything but that. Clearly, these people have no concept of trauma. How do I 'un-traumatize' myself based on something that didn't actually happen just because someone wanted it to? Trauma changes our brain chemistry so that we, who have trauma, simply have exaggerated and sometimes ill-placed fight-or-flight responses.

The significant trauma I experienced at 16 (not even counting the Alex situation in this), with the knowledge and information I had at 16, changed the way I respond to situations in which I feel threatened, unloved, unwanted, rejected, etc. I shut down and isolate (freeze), and/or I 'run' (flight). It is how I protect myself from having to 'feel' the rejection. (Okay, I still feel it, but my reptilian, traumatized brain cannot tell the difference between this emotional experience and a life-or-death situation—like being chased by a sabretooth tiger. The species is still evolving, after all.) Just because I, decades later, learned that someone did want me doesn't change the experience I actually went through.

Can the new information be used to help heal this trauma? Yes. Is it easy? No. Is it a process to unlearn, at the innate level, things and responses so ingrained deep inside? Yes. Am I working on it? I probably always will be. One moment in time completely changes the trajectory of the dominoes that fall following it, so it is impossible to know how changing something decades prior would change the now.

The other thing that needs to be understood is that trauma responses live in this 'reptilian' brain (midbrain) and not in the frontal lobe (the 'adulting,' logical, processing brain). The frontal lobe develops in the mid-20s (already after my mom died—also an important time frame to note, trauma-wise), and unfortunately, the frontal lobe, in trauma—simplistically stated—gets 'shut off' by the very fight-or-flight responses it's supposed to be calming down with all the new tools learned.

Here's an example: Your 18-month-old puts his hand on the stove, which is not even on. Your parent self sees the hand going toward the stove, and you freak out, run to the stove, take the hand away, and then realize it's not even on. That's your midbrain responding to a threat to your offspring, and it all happens very fast. Your adulting frontal lobe did, in fact, already know the stove wasn't on, but in the moment of threat, the reptilian brain shut all that logical nonsense off to respond to the situation. Okay, not the greatest analogy, but I think you get it.

Getting this new, albeit positive, information is now supposed to interject in the exaggerated and very rapid fight-or-flight response? I think not—at least not until it, too, is learned and becomes just as innate as the feeling of abandonment. A child, for instance, who always had loving parent(s) probably doesn't think twice when their parent drives off to work or has a change in routine. I, however, did not handle this well because of my dad. After my mom died and everyone else disappeared, I trusted no one not to disappear. This translated into any time there was even a hint of adversity, argument, or situation where I did not feel that I was valued, I shut down and prepared myself to be, once again, abandoned.

For most of my life, therefore, I have, innately, felt that the only way I would not be abandoned was to be, do, handle, accommodate, and and and—everything myself. My needs and wants were always secondary because, much like they didn't matter to my very 'foundation people,' why on Earth would they matter to literally anyone else? My needs and wants adapted to what those around me needed and wanted, and by sheer will, I would make sure that their needs and wants were achieved—because then I had value.

As you will see, therefore, learning this new and 'amazing' information and being told, 'See? You were wanted. Now let go of it all,' nurtured in me a sense of "it's my turn." I felt that since I had, in fact, revolved my life around everyone else's wants and needs, I should be able to start expressing my wants and needs, and my 'people' would reciprocate to some extent. I was so wrong.

Chapter 10: Never at Home

In August 2001, just months after high school graduation, I completely moved out of my aunt and uncle's house and into the dorms at Gustavus Adolphus College. Several things happened during the two years of high school that I lived there, which ultimately drove me to move out. The underlying reason, I believe, was that I was struggling with so many things—coping felt impossible so leaving everything felt the safest.

My mom's family was never very fond of my dad's family, with whom I, at that time, now lived. My mom, however, never once said a bad thing about them, but since my dad disappeared so many times, I just didn't see them. My maternal grandma and aunts, after shunning me, essentially told me I was going to amount to nothing and that I would end up just like my dad—whatever that meant. So, there I was, living with my dad's family, essentially very kind strangers who had taken me in, wanting to do everything in my power to spite my mom's family and prove them wrong.

You would think that the very idea of these essential strangers letting me move in would have trumped all the negativity I had heard over the years—but it didn't. I was terrified of being like my dad after that last year with my mom, yet I found myself living with his family, feeling lost and alone. I isolated myself in my room, trying to do and be the exact opposite of what I saw around me and what I had been told my entire life by my grandma in particular. They drank, so I didn't. They smoked, so I didn't. My cousin had parties—I locked my door. Another one of my uncles got out of prison and, for a short time, moved in with us. He and I shared a bathroom. He had drugs—I flushed them down the toilet. He got mad (it was worth a lot of money), I got scared, I actually told my dad, my dad threatened that brother, that uncle moved out… (Yup, this family was way different than living with Mom.) There was more that I won't share.

One of my cousins—thank God for Michelle—and I would hide in my room rather than partaking in the 'fun' upstairs. We played Bubble Bobble on the Nintendo and binged on Schwann's Ice Cream. Michelle started to feel like home for what was, essentially, two very short years.

Looking back, however, I see how real that house was. How real my aunt and uncle were. How accepting my cousins all were. How welcoming it was. Yes, there were issues, clearly, but the people were real. I'm sad I didn't see it then. I'm sad I didn't feel ready to just be and allow myself to feel safe and welcomed. At the time, I felt like an inconvenience, so I thought I had to be 'perfect.' But honestly, I probably would have felt that way anywhere I went, which makes sense, considering everything.

I feel sad for the 16-year-old me who felt that way, who further perpetuated the feelings of being unwanted and abandoned, of needing to be perfect all the time so as not to be left again. Why did the system not force therapy on me, or at least something? Apparently I was old enough to make a life-or-death decision but not important enough to check in with.

Regardless, it wasn't home. I knew I didn't quite 'fit.' I knew it was time to leave. So I left—and I didn't step foot back in that house for 22 years. When I finally did, after having a panic attack in the driveway, Michelle had to come rescue me just to get me in the door. I couldn't even bring myself to go look at 'my room.' But do you know what? The people inside were still welcoming, kind, and real.

I wish I could go back and exist in that time without the trauma lens because I'm guessing it was probably pretty great. But unfortunately, that's not how trauma works—we can't just choose to 'let it go.'

Decades later, I would uncover how much of what happened in those two years—things I was consciously aware of, things I was subconsciously aware of, and things I was completely unaware of—shaped my adult life and career. People always ask me why I ended up in addiction medicine, and my answer is usually vague. I don't have a great answer outside of "it just happened." Sometimes, I jokingly say, "I lived in a drug house in high school," though I can only truly speak to the alcohol and the one-time situation of drugs in the bathroom from an uncle who was only there temporarily (not the homeowner uncle). That exaggeration is unfair based on my actual memories and whatever else was actually going on, I can't say.

What I have since learned, from my dad of all people, upon reconnecting, is that there was more going on with him and his family throughout my entire childhood than I could have possibly known. This is fascinating because I neither saw it nor heard about it. The more I dive into my past, my trauma, and what makes me who I am—how I interact with people, particularly those with the disease of addiction, and how I respond to adversity—the more I see how it all ties back to those times.

Therapy has challenged me to consider not just the concept of modeling, which is more intentional, but also the idea that simply being in certain environments and situations—even without a conscious awareness of anything being awry—can influence how we act, think, and interact with others well into the future. There was a reason my dad disappeared when I was between the ages of three and five—it was intentional and for my safety (though no one was told that). There was a reason I spent most of my time from ages five to eleven with Mary and not my dad. There was a reason he fled to Iowa rather than staying where he had two kids. There was a reason I felt 'off' living with my aunt and uncle despite all evidence to the contrary.

I think people who have experienced trauma are much more in tune, even subconsciously with everything around them—it makes sense for survival. Unfortunately, this attunement can make them more susceptible to subsequent trauma because of their hyper-awareness of things that may never have directly impacted them (as in my situation at my aunt and uncle's house). This subsequent trauma can have far-reaching consequences. It can perpetuate and deepen the historical trauma of underserved and underrepresented communities, and it can also lead to a heightened ability to relate to others in ways that don't, on the surface, make sense.

Although I do not have a substance use disorder and do not have a story of a family member being blacked out, violent, or doing XYZ while drunk or high, I still somehow empathize in a way as if I had. Rather, my experiences consisted of several small things happening around me—like those time periods with my dad—several small things when he was 'around,' and several small things in high school that I subconsciously processed. That processing and imprinting have made me very effective in my work and help explain why and how I do what I do, even if I wasn't fully aware of it at the time.

This is why children who live in unstable environments need extra support. They may 'know' more than they even realize, and they are at risk of carrying those unhealthy patterns into their future, continuing the cycle—even if they were removed from the situation or were exposed to healthier modeled behavior. A child under three, for instance, does not have 'real memories' of drugs being used or violence in the home, yet they are often hyper-vigilant and aware of these things, making them more at risk, even if they were removed from that environment before forming concrete memories.

At the time, my decision to fully move out of my aunt and uncle's house was simply because I didn't feel like I fit in. I appreciated everything they did for me, yet it never felt like home.

I left high school with essentially two people: Brandon (my high school boyfriend) and Miranda (my best friend). Gustavus was not, however, my first choice for college—Notre Dame was. Ever since I was in first grade, I had the goal of going to Notre Dame. I have no idea why any first grader even knows about Notre Dame, let alone has a goal of going there, but I did. So how did I go from Notre

Dame, a large Catholic Ivy League college, to a small Lutheran liberal arts college in southern Minnesota?

It's an easy answer—my grandpa.

When my mom died, my grandpa became my person. Even though my mom was, in his very open declaration, "his favorite," he managed to put that aside, realizing that I—and Molly, to some extent—needed him. Molly didn't lose our maternal foundation despite having to go live with her dad. If anything, she got smothered, but again, that is Molly's story to tell.

For the remainder of high school—my junior and senior years—when I lived with my aunt and uncle, my grandpa was the parent for all things logistical and necessary. I did not go live with him when my mom died because I'm not even sure it was an option. Imagine a 16-year-old girl and her 72-year-old grandfather cohabitating—hmm.

For the good part of, well, the rest of his life—13 more years—he did the things, taught me the things, and made sure all the things were in order. The "things" being: insurance; a credit card (to be used only for gas and paid off each month to build credit); my car and all its maintenance (he finally let me get a red one despite his fears of it being a ticket target); and, if anything went wrong, he was the call. The only thing I had to do to balance out the "things" was to make sure he got a copy of my college transcript every semester—done.

Over time, as he got older and dementia crept in, as happens, I became his person to do all the things. We trusted that capability in each other.

Emotionally, however, was a different story. I cannot even imagine going to him with the emotional turmoil of being a teenager, a college student, or beyond. I knew which guys I dated that he disliked—he was never shy about his very honest, very direct opinions—but aside from him just telling me his thoughts, there were no tears, no emotions, no deep heart-to-hearts. That man, however, loved me more than anything. He was proud of me like no one had ever—or has ever—been.

I always knew where I stood with him, even when it was tense or not the most ideal situation. For instance, I eventually had to talk to him about making the decision about my mom. He, like my grandma, would not have made the decision I did. He was devastated, but unlike my grandma, he trusted that I understood more than I should have, and, more importantly, he knew Molly and I still needed him.

We did eventually talk about it—five years later, right after my medical school interview. It was a much easier conversation than I had expected. I think that was partially because one of the professors who interviewed me happened to be an expert in myelodysplasia, and I, therefore, spent much of my interview essentially interviewing him about the disease. He very much reassured me that I had 100% made the right decision and gave me a list of the reasons why. I simply had to share all of it with Grandpa, and then peace was had by all.

So, choosing to go to Gustavus rather than my dream of Notre Dame was an easier decision given my, at that moment, life situation. My grandpa could easily visit since Gustavus was so much closer.

One major problem with Gustavus, though, was that Brandon had also chosen to go there. An odd statement about one's boyfriend of 2.5 years, but the reality was, Brandon was, again, another He.

I still, to this day, cannot wear jean shorts with a T-shirt because he said the combination didn't look good on me. (Insert Schwann's Ice Cream.) On more than one occasion, my back hit a wall with my feet off the ground. That was the extent of physical violence (no, that amount is not okay either); it was much more emotional and psychological. Everything we did was with his friends and was what he wanted to do. It was not healthy—at all.

Why I "allowed" it to happen that way and why it went on as long as it did is actually quite simple—he knew my mom. We started dating six months before she died (five months after she was diagnosed—not a good time to start any type of relationship… we could analyze this further, but it's a pretty easy one, so I'll let you all do that on your own). And although she didn't like him very much, they still knew each other.

Back then, if there was someone in my life who had met my mom, I had a really hard time letting go of them. Since we started at Gustavus still together, I, unfortunately, did not experience the full freshman experience of going out, meeting a lot of new people, or rushing a sorority—not sure I would've done that anyway, but who knows?

Brandon did, however, have a silver lining, and it's that silver lining that explains why God let that relationship go on as long as it did. I can 100% fully say that I forgive him (Brandon) and those years.

Since I completely moved out of my aunt and uncle's when I moved to Gustavus, I was essentially homeless. Although my dad and I had, by my senior year of high school, superficially reconnected, he was still not even close to being "home." (He also lived more than five hours away.) And truthfully, the reason we reconnected was because I had a sibling born in January of my junior year of high school, and I made the commitment to be there for them.

By Christmas of my freshman year at Gustavus, it was glaringly obvious that I did not have "family" or "home." I spent weekends at Brandon's prior to Christmas, but when it came time to go "home" for Christmas, it all became very real. That Christmas was actually harder than my first two Christmases without my mom because, for those two, at least, I was with people—at my aunt and uncle's and with cousins.

Leaving Gustavus at Christmas to go to Brandon's house was hard. Everyone was all excited to go "home" for the break and see their friends and family, and I realized just how little of that I had. (Yes, I was going to have Christmas with my grandpa and sister, and yes, I was going to see my couple of high school friends, but it was not the same.)

I am more grateful to Brandon's parents than I can explain. They, much like my future in-laws, were the family I always wanted but never had, and they made putting up with a less-than-ideal relationship possible. Going home for Christmas to their house, I was that "troubled teenage girl" in the movies who moves in with her boyfriend's parents.

Feeling so homesick, missing my everything, that Christmas was a struggle. But I got the greatest gift imaginable—Brandon's aunt and uncle, Nancy and Ron, whom I had met a couple of times before, asked if I would want to move in with them after my freshman year of college. (They had one son who was married with kids by that point.)

I have no idea what compelled them to say that to me, what happened that led them to offer that, and I honestly never even asked them. It was a dream I didn't want to accidentally wake up from.

The rest of that school year, however, my anxiety built and built. What if they changed their minds? What if they didn't mean it? Am I supposed to call them to verify this? How does this work? Where's the catch? I really didn't know them well at all—maybe they said it on a whim because they felt sorry for me on Christmas... So much fear!

(More to come on Ron and Nancy!)

In terms of college itself, it was awesome. All my friends played hockey, which is comical because this girl can barely stand on skates. All their boyfriends and I would travel around, watch them play, and act like the obnoxious section of groupies.

I was comfortable with my group in college, and I felt like I actually belonged. I had to work quite a bit on campus—still had to budget for toothpaste—but Gustavus was very kind to me.

Honestly, I think if I could have stayed in college, with my people in college, my magnificent downfall that was about to happen wouldn't have!

Chapter 11: Bonus Parents

They meant it! When I moved out of the dorm in May after my freshman year, I moved in with Ron and Nancy. Within the first week, Miranda and I had completely repainted their upstairs bathroom—MY bathroom. It is unbelievable how fast that became home. It is unbelievable how comfortable, natural, and normal it was. Honestly, more than 20 years later, I still can't believe it. Why would I?

Ron and I had so much fun that summer together. We took dinghy trips down the river, spent a lot of time washing the boat, and were always busy being busy! Ron never sits down and can talk as much as I can! Ron became 'Dad' very fast. I never had a dad growing up who did things like this with me, so at the age of 19, it was a dream!

It was a slower burn with Nancy. She was a nurse, just like my mom, and they had very similar personalities. This was very hard for me at first, as my mom had only died three years prior. Even that first summer, I spent more time with Ron and shared more with him. By the second summer, though, everything changed. Due to unforeseen circumstances with Nancy and her mom, we spent nearly all day, every day, together. Nancy became, for all intents and purposes, my mom from age 19 to 32. The biggest—and seemingly only—difference between my mom and Nancy that I discovered was that Nancy liked to go shopping and to the salon; Mom did not. But the way they cared, the way they talked, the way they comforted, the way they reassured, and the way they just 'were'—was so alike.

Nancy filled that mom role as best as she could while taking on a 19-year-old with my history, trauma, walls, and abandonment issues. I was—and have historically always been—an over-sharer, as opposed to the more common reaction of isolation for someone with my history. It's somewhat strange, considering my past rejections and lost trust. I think the oversharing was my sideways attempt at showing others that I was vulnerable, hoping they would also be vulnerable with me so we could build a deep friendship. Or maybe it was a horribly sad way of wanting people to see how much I needed them. I was hopelessly screaming and desperately searching to belong and to be wanted. Of course, this just scared most people away—but not Nancy. She listened and didn't judge. She didn't give unrequested advice. She did, I fully believe, genuinely care.

Looking back, however, I believe I was subconsciously keeping a wall up to protect myself from the inevitable rejection and abandonment that I somehow just knew had to be coming. She was safe, and deep in my core, I knew that. But trauma-induced fear kept me from allowing myself to just 'be'—the very thing I yearned for the most. It was like the safer a person actually was—which I did somehow inherently recognize, especially after the fact—the more I protected myself. My fight-or-flight response had a paradoxical reaction. Since I lost my real mom, I had an underlying fear that I would lose Nancy too when (not if, as I always expected the worst) she got sick. And, as it turns out, I did.

There were times when I had somewhat of a panic moment with Ron and Nancy. Not full panic attacks, but moments where I questioned if things were too good to be true, and my response would be to push them away. In those times, I would isolate or lean more into another relationship. The thing about it all, however, is that they understood me in a way that even my mom and grandpa didn't. I attribute some of this to the fact that my grandpa was from a completely different generation and that my mom died when I was way too young. That, and the obvious fact that her death and the trauma surrounding it shaped so much of who I was that she clearly couldn't have understood me in that way.

For instance, at the very beginning of my sophomore year of college, Ron called me and told me to break up with Brandon once and for all. This had been a topic of discussion several times, but Brandon always threatened that if I broke up with him, I would lose Ron and Nancy. As manipulative as that was, it was a real threat to me. That day, however, when Ron called me, he said the most magical sentence that I will never forget: "You will never lose us. You are our daughter." After the shock of that statement set in, I very easily walked into Brandon's dorm room and broke up with him. He threatened Ron and Nancy, I said nothing, and I walked out. After four years of dating, it was that easy.

For her part, Nancy even understood when I was triggered or about to be triggered and always knew the right thing to say. Very early on, she realized that she should never directly question any of my choices because that would make me even more adamantly commit to them. When I ended my relationship with Dane (next chapter), which I'm not sure she ever forgave me for, even years later, she took my wedding dress out and paraded it around in front of the next guy I dated. She also very directly called me out on my 'HE' pattern with Carson, recognizing even my reasoning for choosing him. (Unfortunately, I didn't see or understand my pattern until years and years later.)

Even while decorating the reception venue for my wedding to Carson, she questioned me by pointing out how lost I was and how much I was investing without much in return. I didn't see it, and even if I had, it likely wouldn't have mattered back then when I was still so broken. Nothing anyone said or did was going to change me. So she did the next best thing—she loved me through it. They were the greatest parents in that regard. They listened, suggested, and questioned but didn't push. Ultimately, they supported me and my decisions fully, even if they didn't agree with them.

So then when I ultimately, of course, lost Nancy, it was, in most respects, harder than losing my mom. Losing her pushed me further into investing in Carson's family and further into believing that I could and should just accept my role in it. I didn't know what I deserved, so I either overcompensated or undercompensated for my own lack of 'foundation.'

In my hardest moments, when I need 'my people' and they are just gone, I ask the most painful question: Why did He take both of my moms?

Chapter 12: Too Good but Also So True

The saying goes, "too good to be true," but Dane was so good and so true. He is the cliché—"the one that got away." However, he didn't *get away*… I pushed him. Or did I just run? Or did my trauma simply not understand that I was worth him?

We met several months after I ended things with Brandon (and just after the whole Alex-return-from-deployment situation). Was it love at first sight—if that's a thing? Yes. He got along with my friends; he got along with everybody. Ron and Nancy loved him. My grandpa loved him. And I loved him with all my heart. He was safe, he was genuine, he was kind—he was, well, the full package.

Dane played football and was in a fraternity, but unlike the stereotypical *frat guy*, he had absolutely no attitude. He wasn't cocky, and he understood that I didn't necessarily fit in with all the sorority girls that hung out with them—and he was okay with that. Across a room, he would notice if I was getting uncomfortable, and he'd make an excuse to leave or do something to ease any feelings of anxiety I was having. He was so in tune with me that I very rarely even got to the point of feeling anxious. Dane was kind to everyone, he was considerate, he was caring, and he was great at communicating. People liked Dane. I loved Dane. And he loved me too. We trusted each other and were so confident in *us*.

Dane also had the most amazing, loving parents. They welcomed me with open, genuine arms. He had an older brother whom he respected and who was kind to him. He had a younger sister whom he protected and loved with everything. His extended family was true and genuine, and even when things ended, they were still kind.

All throughout college, we never had the same classes, nor did our majors even *sort of* align. He supported my goals and dreams, encouraged me, and truly was a very loving partner, even knowing that medical school could take me—or us—far away. I supported him as well. I didn't miss a football game. I went to the fraternity's weekend-away parties. We both always put each other first—but never in a weird, possessive way. I had friends. He had friends. We all got along just fine. We didn't have to be glued to each other because we had such a true connection, trust, and friendship.

At Gustavus, there's a January term—basically, a full-time class Monday through Friday, all day, for just the month of January. Dane, my best friend Bobee, and I took a class that brought us to New Zealand, Australia, and Hawaii. It was beautiful. It was perfect. Bobee and I decided we *had* to go bungee jumping—something Dane was in no way going to do. He stood there and cheered for us the whole time. Bobee and I decided we needed to go do something just the two of us—he supported that as well. And when Bobee decided to go home for the optional week in Hawaii, he and I did all the things.

My brother was born while I was in college, and Dane and I would go to my dad's house to visit. Dane, single-handedly, was the one who convinced me that family is important and that I should really give my dad another chance. He made sure my family was always included and part of our plans—even when I didn't. He didn't judge them. He didn't question them. He didn't hold the past against them or against me. He saw them as *my family*, no matter what, and that was all that mattered. Even when our schedules conflicted with his family's, he was the one who made sure we honored both.

Then there was March 2005. You see, Dane and I hated the month of March—probably me more than him, but I totally convinced him it was the worst month. March is a cold, *blah* month where nothing exciting ever happens. There are no major holidays. I just really didn't like March. Dane, being Dane, decided he would make March the best month ever. His mom, sister, Dane, and I went to Chicago to visit his older brother. One morning, for no good reason (other than it being gray, raining, cold, and *March*), I was in a crappy mood. Of course, he knew exactly how to handle whatever mood I was in—where to push me, where to give me space, how to just love me.

That was the day we were going to the Sears Tower. The tour started with a video, and during it, Dane managed to get me to relax and just enjoy the day, saying something along the lines of how he *knew* we weren't going to have a view, which just meant we'd *have* to come back again soon. After the video, we got on the elevator to go to the top of the Tower, to the viewing deck. Being March, and the weather being what it was, there was, like he guessed, absolutely no view. He suggested we walk all the way around the space, just to see if there was *any* break in the clouds—anywhere—

to find *some* kind of view. However, about two-thirds of the way around, we stopped. No view yet in sight.

And then—he got down on one knee and proposed.

On top of that, his sister had gone the other direction around the viewing deck and captured pictures of the whole thing. I was arguably the happiest person in the universe! March became my favorite month. Chicago became one of my favorite places. And Dane—once again—had planned *exactly* the right thing.

We started planning our wedding for that December. I was graduating in May and starting medical school in the fall. Dane was a year behind me in school, but he had managed to structure his schedule so he could complete his first semester of senior year—also football season—on campus, and then do his spring semester at an internship where I was in school. *Perfect plan.*

We had a church, a reception location, and a bridal party. I had my dress. My bridesmaids had theirs. The invitations were made. There was just *one* big problem—me.

About a month after we got engaged, I panicked.

I started to question the *too good to be true.* Nothing in my life had ever made sense or felt so right. No one had ever really understood me the way he did. So, clearly, this *had* to be too good to be true. Why did *he* get me when no one else had? Why did he choose to love me—through my traumas and insecurities? *What was the catch?* I had so much fear. I was, essentially, terrified that every day, the worst-case scenario was going to happen.

That I was going to lose him—and everything else.

There would be good days when I could just let myself be loved and believe that I deserved as much happiness as anyone else—because why wouldn't I? We would plan our wedding on those days. And then there were the bad days.

On the bad days, I would pick fights just to cause trouble. Dane, unlike every other man in my life, just listened. He didn't fight back because he never took any of it personally—he understood what was going on. To my traumatized mind, this was infuriating! Why didn't he want chaos? Why did this seem so good? How could this perfect person love me? When was Ashton Kutcher going to jump out and tell me I'd been punked?

He just stayed patient and kind—and somehow, he loved me even harder.

When I started medical school, I went back for his football games and got excited when our wedding bands were finished. One day, I actually wore his wedding band to the field along with mine because I just had to show him—that was a good day. Within a couple of weeks, however, I would have the worst day.

Completely out of the blue, with absolutely no precipitating factors, I called him and ended it. His response was, "What the fuck, Heather?" My response to that was, "Where was that this whole relationship?"

I somehow convinced myself that I ended things with him because he didn't fight with me—because he made things too easy. Too good to be true and all. A couple of weeks later, we sat down to talk. I was heartbroken (by my own doing) and wanted nothing more than to ask for forgiveness and for him to take me back. But I didn't tell him that. I didn't think I was worth forgiveness or second chances.

So instead, I tried to make up a story about cheating on him, hoping he'd be mad at me so it would be easier—but he didn't believe me, rightfully so, since I hadn't. He knew me. He *got* me. He loved *me.* I still couldn't ask for forgiveness, though I'm sure he would have given it. I apologized, but I didn't try to fix it because, in my mind, he deserved far better.

People are always surprised when I tell them I was engaged in college. I don't like talking about it. I don't like admitting that I let go of the greatest guy ever because I didn't think I was worth it. I didn't know how to live in a world without turmoil and chaos. Once we got engaged—when my life was happy and good and I had a true love who *chose* me—I just didn't know how to feel. Yes, things had been amazing and happy and committed before, but an engagement sealed the deal. Who was I to think I deserved that?

I don't know what's harder—knowing I had such low self-worth that I didn't believe I could be loved the way I actually *was* loved by an amazing human who understood me, cared about me, and was there for me, or knowing that if we had gotten married, I probably would have destroyed not just us, but *him*. I'm not trying to say I martyred myself for his sake. Rather, I hurt him to avoid getting hurt myself.

They say that in our healing process, we are supposed to forgive the younger versions of ourselves. We are supposed to love them because they—*we*, in essence—did what they had to do to survive. We're supposed to imagine that child who went through so much trauma and love her because she never thought she deserved it.

This is not easy.

I look at 22-year-old me, and I am mad. I am sad. I am frustrated. I am angry. My heart *breaks* for her. She didn't ask for the things that happened to her—the things that made her feel less-than and unworthy. She didn't *want* to live in chaos, but she knew no other way. All she ever wanted was to be loved and accepted for every single part of her. And when she had that—*all* of that—in the absolute greatest, God-sent form, it didn't bring comfort. Instead, it created the opposite because the fear of losing it all was greater than the *known* feelings of chaotic isolation and loneliness.

That is the thing about trauma. The situations, people, and things that are *supposed* to bring comfort, joy, safety, and stability instead result in anxiety, panic, fight-or-flight, and fear. And the things that *should* raise red flags—the things that *should* cause fear and anxiety—end up feeling comfortable and secure.

So yes, I look at 22-year-old Heather, and I am heartbroken. She had everything—and she threw it all away.

What does it all mean? If God has some great plan and purpose for our lives, then clearly, that was all supposed to happen. I obviously can't go back to being 22, nor can I even imagine what the last couple of decades would have looked like had I made a different choice. I can't live with regrets. I also can't live without my kids; so was all of that supposed to happen for some greater purpose?

This is one of those things in my life that I struggle with. Some things just make zero sense—or at least, they make zero sense for a very, *very*, *very* long time.

I do have a rule in my life, though: I *can't* have regrets. Regrets eat at you and do no good. I am heartbroken and sad that I made that choice back then, but again, I can't regret my kids. I can't regret some of the parts of my life that came after.

Dane got married. He has his own kids. His own life. As far as I know, he's happy—and ultimately, that's all I can ask for. More than anything, I hope he got the happy, healthy, stable, *perfect* love he deserved.

The thing is… I deserve that too.

Chapter 13: The Sign of the Timing

The weekend I moved into medical school was rainy and cold. Maybe that was a sign that things were about to go poorly—and soon. I, on the other hand, was very excited. Ron and Nancy helped move me into the servant's quarters of a very old mansion that was rented out to medical students. It was amazing!

Don't think it was fancy by any stretch—it wasn't the actual mansion. **But** it was in a great location. The retired ENT doctor and his wife were incredibly kind, it was right next to a stream with a fun running and hiking trail, and it was my first actual apartment. It was the first time I had chosen to live, be, and exist alone!

A couple of weeks later, the actual storm hit. After my very early-in-medical-school self-destruction with Dane, I quickly started to spiral. Breaking up with Dane was a major turning point in my life—or rather, a boiling-over point.

For the six years since my mom died, I had been living in what felt like an invincible, superficial, yet empowered and independent world—one where I could handle anything. I had no choice but to deal with everything that had happened. I had no choice but to 'adult.' And I ran with that—proving, once again, that I was fully capable of doing anything and everything and excelling at it all.

All of my emotions, all of my pain, all of my confusion—everything that a normal person might have processed in the moment—I had no choice but to bury. I shoved it deep into the recesses of my mind, locked away in those toxic oil barrels. Some of those barrels had started to shake and surface when Dane and I got engaged. But overall, I was still the strong, capable, independent Heather I needed to be.

When I ended things with Dane, one of those barrels exploded. Its contents—everything I had avoided feeling—came rushing out, and I had no idea how to handle it. I didn't even realize what was happening. Back then, I didn't understand those barrels, and I couldn't believe I was anything other than the strong, capable person I had always seen myself as.

I thought I was *fine*. Yes, I had insecurities like anyone else, but I lived by 'fake it till you make it.' And in a way, I believed that faking it would eventually erase the buried truth of my traumatized inner self. The self-sabotage with Dane and the truth behind why I did it began to crack this illusion. But I wasn't ready to unearth everything, nor did I quite understand the magnitude of all I had buried. Instead, I convinced myself that if I just faked it harder, I could hold it all together.

Now, many years later, I can clearly see how that moment—giving in to the belief that I didn't deserve a life with Dane—set off a chain reaction. It ignited actions, behaviors, choices, and trauma-driven responses that shaped the situations I found myself in. For the next twenty years, unfortunately, I lived not as the person I truly was but as the person I thought I should be. It's like I seemed to keep faking it but never making it, at least not as the true me. I molded myself to fit what I believed everyone else expected of me. I played an Oscar-worthy role, presenting an exterior of strength, capability, resilience, and confidence—a person who, on the surface, could and did do everything for everyone. I was an imposter.

Yet, I received so much positive reinforcement for this role that it almost became my truth. I almost convinced myself that I had expertly navigated my life's trauma and truly embodied all those admirable qualities. Most of the time, I handled it well. Most of the time, the attention was enough. Most of the time.

Over the years, however, the cracks in that facade deepened. The real me—the scared, alone, abandoned, and never-quite-worthy me—began to surface. It happened at random times, often triggered by feelings of rejection, of my emotions being dismissed, or during major life changes, especially pregnancies. When that version of me tried to voice her needs—to ask for love, for reciprocity, for safety—she was often shut down, further rejected, misunderstood, or ignored altogether. It was brushed off as I was being dramatic or emotional or, better yet, in a mood. That only led to more walls, more compartments, and more resentment. It also led to me becoming someone I'm not proud of—a person who made many poor choices, blinded by one desperate need: to be loved and wanted.

The rest of this book is the story of those buried emotions finally exploding—and the eventual, intentional, self-unburying of the ones that remained. It's a story of healing from trauma, of learning to nurture oneself toward acceptance, self-love, and forgiveness.

Starting medical school, ending an engagement, and living alone did not go well. Stress was high, emotions ran even higher, and isolation was deafening. I was not good company for myself. My mind did not do well alone. I needed something. I should have been working on myself, healing my wounds—but that was terrifying. So, unfortunately, I looked outward for fulfillment, a pattern that would continue until my ultimate awakening decades later.

Our first date was actually fantastic. It's the one date I can look back on as being completely happy, exciting, and free of any underlying pain. We went to Applebee's and then back to his house, where we spent hours watching the music channel on TV and talking. And when I say "music channel," I don't mean MTV or music videos—I mean the kind that just displays the song title and artist on the screen. The irony of that is not lost on me now. He was never a music person—unless we're talking oldies—and he refused to go to concerts (well, with me, anyway, as I would later realize).

The point is, we talked. A lot. He knew nothing about me, and, as always, when I shared parts of my story, I appeared confident and strong. (I supposed a big important thing to note is that I shared *parts*. I couldn't share *all* because that would truly scare anyone away). I seemed intriguing. I didn't "suck." No one, after all, shares their pain and sadness right away. No one wants to look weak. It wouldn't be until fifteen years later that a therapist would point out how unhealthy my storytelling was. It wasn't what

I said—it was how I said it. The complete absence of emotion was concerning to her. A trained professional saw what others didn't: my monotone retelling wasn't a sign of strength but a sign of deep pain, compartmentalization, and a sad, abandoned little girl. But we'll get to that.

Anyway, after several awkward hours, I finally kissed him. And that was it.

Two weeks later, right after we received our white coats in medical school, we had a conversation. It went something like this:

"I just got out of a serious relationship with my girlfriend, and you just got un-engaged, so I don't think we should date. We should just be friends and get through the first year of medical school."

It felt like a breakup. Or rather, it felt like our first date had been fine, but now he wasn't interested. The reason he gave was, actually, very fair. But to me, it was just rejection. Regardless, after that conversation, we weren't together. We weren't dating. We also were eons, eight or so months, away from the end of our first year of medical school.

A few weeks later, I spent time with a different guy from our medical school class. No big deal. We studied, hung out, and drank champagne for no real reason—other than celebrating the fact that we weren't out in the cold, deer hunting like most of our classmates. One thing led to another, and yes, we had sex.

I think, more than anything, that moment was about release—about letting go, being present, not overthinking, and simply giving in to desire. And really, consenting single adults don't need a reason. But this was when I apparently misunderstood what "just friends" actually meant.

This is where I will preface with a disclaimer: although I will be very honest about my traumas, choices, and marriage, I cannot include every detail. I will take ownership of my actions and will not place blame. The following events are from my perspective only. I, again and redundantly, understand that there are multiple views and interpretations of situations, but I can only share my truth, my reality, and my feelings about what happened. I will not attempt to analyze what Carson may or may not have been thinking or feeling—only what I experienced in those moments.

Please also respect the fact that my marriage gave me the four most amazing children, and for that reason, I will always love my ex-husband. We may not have been right for each other in the long run, but we will always be connected through our children. It took a significant rock-bottom fall for me to gain perspective on everything that happened.

Before I go further into this part of my story, I want to say that I am sorry. Looking back, I can see how broken I was and how the weight of my struggles kept piling up. The perspective I have now on my situations with Dane and Carson only came to me long after the events had passed. In hindsight, I realize I was in no position to be in any kind of relationship—I should have spent years working through my trauma before even considering one. I never acted with malicious intent. Yes, I will reach a point in my story where I justified, rationalized, and ultimately caused a lot of pain, making poor choices. But I never intentionally set out to hurt Carson or anyone else.

This is the story of my relationship with Carson, my ex-husband.

A couple of weeks after sharing champagne with Jeremy, Carson found out. No one had been keeping it a secret or trying to be deceptive—it simply wasn't anyone else's business. However, when Carson learned about it, his reaction was intense. I can't say he was entirely wrong, given his beliefs, but his beliefs were different from mine, and I was told, definitively, that I was in the wrong. After a month of silent treatment, he told me we could never be in a relationship because, in his view, I had betrayed him. He couldn't understand how I could sleep with someone else—nearly a month after we had agreed to be just friends— after I had wanted to date him.

In truth, we probably should have ended things then, remaining only colleagues and friends. We had been on one date, and we had already reached an impasse. Yet, to me, this almost felt like a challenge—because if it was a challenge, then it wouldn't be the outright rejection that it was. His emotions during that conversation made it clear that he either truly cared about me or was deeply hurt by the idea that I had moved on. I chose to believe the former, but in hindsight, I'm not sure I was right.

That Christmas—about three weeks after the silent treatment ended—I somehow ended up spending the first week of Christmas break with Carson's family. Holidays were complicated with Ron and Nancy because of Brandon, my high school boyfriend and their nephew, so I always tried to be respectful and keep my distance to avoid discomfort for everyone. Ultimately though, I had an incredible week with my soon-to-be in-laws.

Carson's family was amazing. I baked cookies with his mom, went sledding with his brothers, and laughed and joked with his dad. His father reminded me so much of my own that it stirred up mixed emotions—we bonded instantly, but something about it also felt strange. He had just moved back home after his own interpersonal struggles, and I think my presence, being 'new,' was a welcome distraction for everyone.

Carson and I didn't spend much time together over break. We were only ever going to be friends, after all, and he had his lifelong friends to catch up with. Still, I ended up going to Christmas Eve at his dad's family's house, and that night sealed everything for me—I knew I needed to become part of this family. Christmas with them felt like home. They reminded me of the kind of happy childhood I had only seen in movies. They were warm, welcoming, and kind.

On the way to midnight Mass with his parents and brothers, we even sang Christmas carols in the van. Every part of my walled-off, abandoned inner child was begging to come out and be a part of this. I needed this.

I was supposed to leave that night but ended up staying until Christmas morning. On Christmas Eve, Carson changed the game. He told me that *maybe* we could have a chance at some point. We slept in the same bed that night, but only as friends. I was fine with that—I had a chance.

During presents the next morning with his family, he sat behind me in a comforting sort of way. Things shifted even more as he leaned forward to whisper in my ear or touch my arm. Although I was confused by this complete pendulum swing, I was happy. At the time, I neither needed nor wanted to know why I was suddenly *worth it* when just three weeks prior, I was not. I easily boxed off those feelings of rejection and inadequacy, choosing only to see what I wanted to see—and what I wanted to have.

When I left to go back to Ron and Nancy's later that day, he gave me a hug and said we would talk in a week when we were both back at school. He still insisted he didn't think we would be a good couple, but he admitted he was confused as well.

When I arrived at Ron and Nancy's, I found out that Jeremy had planned a beautiful Christmas surprise for me that week. He had arranged everything down to the smallest, sweetest detail. He picked me up, and we went ice skating and out to eat. He even tolerated it when Nancy pulled out my wedding dress and showed it to him, saying, "Do you like Heather's dress? She's supposed to be getting married in one week." (To Dane.)

Needless to say, I felt like I was in the middle of a very large triangle, refusing to lean in any direction. We had a great day as just friends. One major difference—one I sadly see only now—is that I was pulled toward Carson's corner because of the welcoming love from his family, whereas I was drawn to Jeremy because of *him*. This subtle but oh-so-important distinction, had I recognized it at the time, may have completely changed the course of everything.

Meanwhile, while Jeremy was making grand gestures, Carson was back home, hanging out and sledding with his recent ex-girlfriend—something I would only learn about later when I saw the pictures. Clearly, we were both being pulled in different directions. On top of that, I was doing everything possible to avoid noticing what week it was, because I was, indeed, supposed to be getting married. I still hadn't healed or processed any of that.

On New Year's Eve, Jeremy planned another big event back at school. I knew Carson and I were going to talk the next day, so, once again, I kept my distance and made sure to clarify that we were just friends. Midnight found me in the bathroom stall. Jeremy, as always, was incredibly respectful.

Carson informed me of his plan when we met to talk on New Year's Day. His plan was that we would finish the first year of medical school as friends and *maybe* start dating in the summer. In six weeks, we had gone from the silent treatment to being "just friends" to "maybe more at some point." This cycle fueled the fire of my traumas, pulling me back to the abandoned three-year-old on the snowbank and the eleven-year-old whose father had disappeared. The hope that *maybe* I would be good enough at some point was all I needed to comply—with a smile. Another He, I now see.

Why can we only recognize our traumatized, self-destructive patterns after the fact?

There was a catch, though. I was expected to spend most nights at his house, especially on weekends, but nothing physical was ever supposed to happen. *Lay in my bed, but don't come near me*—the proverbial carrot, just out of reach. He said it was my responsibility to ensure we followed these rules because *I* had hurt *him*.

Such logic. Such manipulation.

By keeping me at his beck and call—knowing I would do, and did do, everything for him—he ensured I wasn't seeing anyone else. And yet, we weren't even together.

Meanwhile, Jeremy was understanding, patient, and supportive. He told me I needed to see things through with Carson before moving on to him, otherwise, I'd always wonder. Jeremy was, essentially, the doctor version of Dane.

What if I had self-worth and self-value? What if I had realized that this "arrangement" with Carson wasn't healthy? What if I had recognized that, yet again, it was *his family* that pulled me in and not necessarily him?

There are times in our lives when we make critical choices—defining moments that alter our entire trajectory. I can look back and identify that moment clearly.

Yes, it is strange that I had another one of these moments so soon after ending things with Dane. Or perhaps that entire block of time was *one* defining moment. Regardless, on January 1, 2006, I made a choice.

I want to tangent on the word *choice* for a moment.

As an addiction doctor, I spend a lot of time discussing the disease-versus-choice concept of addiction, but these ideas can apply to many aspects of life where it *appears* a choice is being made. Choice involves higher-level thinking—the ability to evaluate multiple sides of a situation logically, without emotional interference, to weigh risks and benefits, to use reason.

Disease, on the other hand, is *not* a choice. It is something we have little to no control over. We can't logic our way out of cancer, for instance. Disease is innate. Certain actions—things we do without thinking, like breathing—fall into this category.

That day, on the surface, it seemed like I had made a choice. I wasn't under the influence of anything, nor was I being physically tortured or coerced.

But after years of reflection, trauma work, and simply the maturity that comes with age, I now see that I wasn't *thinking* from my rational, adult brain—the higher-level areas of my prefrontal cortex. No, that day, I was responding from my primitive brain, the part triggered by fight, flight, freeze, or fawn.

I wasn't *responding*. I was *reacting*.

Had I been thinking logically, I would have seen that, on paper, Jeremy checked all the boxes. Mentally, I *knew* he was the healthier choice for me. But when we are in a state of heightened emotion, our prefrontal cortex essentially *shuts off*.

If it didn't, humans would have been eaten by saber-toothed tigers long ago.

The more trauma a person experiences—especially in childhood or adolescence—the longer the prefrontal cortex stays shut down in these moments. We react based on what feels safest, even if it makes no logical sense. The good news? Trauma healing can change this. We aren't lost causes.

Carson's actions so closely mirrored my father's that I reacted in the only way I knew how: fight harder, work harder, care more, love more, prove yourself, Heather.

It doesn't make much sense to choose *more work*. But to my traumatized brain, that felt safer.

And so, I chose Carson.

Not because he was right for me. Not because I was right for him.

But because it felt familiar.

Jeremy was scary—much like Dane. Since I hadn't processed that situation yet, I hadn't learned from it. Instead of growing, I simply added another layer.

Was Carson the right fit for me? No.

Was I the right fit for him? No.

Did it feel safe and comfortable? Yes.

But over time, I have come to understand that *this* kind of safe and comfortable was different from what Dane had given me. This was not unconditional, reciprocated, raw, genuine love.

I shaped myself into what I thought Carson wanted and needed. That wasn't his fault, but it wasn't mine either.

He never pushed to truly *know* me. And I never pushed him to listen—because deep down, I feared he would reject the real me.

I created a version of myself that fit into *his* world because I loved him—or at least, the *idea* of him and his family. I wanted to belong so badly that I never realized it wasn't *me* that belonged.

"There's just something about him."

I have learned that is not enough. Not for either of us.

I needed and deserved more.

And maybe, so did he.

He had every right to walk away.

I needed to be loved in the way I *needed* to be loved. And when I wasn't, I tried to be okay with that. But deep down, I knew he didn't have the capacity to love me that way.

And it wasn't fair of me to expect him to.

There were many times when I should have stood up for myself or when my voice should have been heard. There were red flags on both sides that neither of us truly saw. I am sure he would have recognized them if I had shown him my true self. I withheld a lot about myself because I didn't think he would understand, and that wasn't fair. I was afraid of how he would perceive my eating disorder, how he would react to my chaotic childhood if I gave him the full story, and how he would handle so many aspects of my past. Instead of telling him everything and giving him the option to accept it or not, I wasn't transparent. I was afraid of being rejected for who I was. I carried so much shame about where I came from and parts of myself, that I convinced myself I could spend my whole life playing the role of who I thought I should be, and maybe one day I would actually be that person I created. Again, that is on me. I can say that I didn't feel safe because I feared he wouldn't love me if he truly knew me (which is how I honestly felt), but the reality is, I was so afraid of not being good enough that I never even gave him a chance. So, I gave the right answers, said the right things, and, for him, I was good enough.

I know he loved the me I created—my therapist even confirmed that—but I also know that he didn't really know me. For a long time, I almost perfected the art of keeping my trauma locked away, and I loved the life I had. When I look back at pictures and memories, my heart breaks because I truly loved so much, and it hurts to think about what happened, especially to our kids. But nothing stays buried forever. Even without realizing it, I was building resentment, and my inner self was suffering deeply. The barrels started to crack and seep.

I won't and cannot take full ownership of everything, though. When I did try to open up and share, he didn't respond or even want to know. He was too afraid for himself to even try—his words, not mine. We hit an impasse too great to overcome, or maybe we were too emotionally heightened at the time to even try. I will always wonder: What if we had separated, worked on ourselves, and then came back together? Could we have made it work, or was there too much pain to forgive and move past? Was there even a choice at that point? And if there was, did we make the right one? I'm not sure, but it's too late to change it now.

The process of molding me into what he wanted and needed happened quickly, and I was far too willing to comply. Eventually, my opinions weren't even asked for, if they ever actually were.

I had dreams of going to medical school to become a high-risk OB doctor (perinatologist) or an infertility specialist. I wanted to live in the suburbs, like the environment I grew up in. At one point, I even envisioned Dane and me living in downtown Chicago to be close to his brother. Carson, however, made it clear from the start that he would only live in a rural community—specifically, his hometown. I never argued, even when we found ourselves buying land there, far from anyone I knew. This became a lasting source of resentment in our marriage.

He wasn't wrong in saying that I never pushed for what I wanted, and I wasn't wrong in saying that he never even asked. Because of that, I lost the opportunity to pursue the high specialties I had gone to medical school for. I settled on becoming a general OB/GYN, but when he decided to forgo orthopedics (his original plan) in favor of family medicine, my career choice came into question. He never outright told me I had to switch to family medicine, but he also never encouraged my own goals. Instead, he focused on all the ways my original plan would be difficult "for our family."

This decision—changing my entire career path—still creates moments of sadness for my younger self. Even as a physician, I couldn't make my own dreams come true. For years, I convinced myself that this was my choice, and in theory, it was. But when I look back, I feel heartbroken. I wasn't encouraged in a true partnership to follow my dreams; I was encouraged to make something else work instead. I spent a lot of time resenting him for this, blaming him. But ultimately, I could—and should—have fought harder for where I wanted to live and for the career I wanted. But I didn't.

Would we have stayed together or even gotten married if I had? Honestly, I don't think so. And yet, I can't truly regret any of those choices because of our kids. I'm just sad for my younger self.

That being said, I was a very good girlfriend and wife, no matter what others might say now. Just before Thanksgiving in our third year of medical school, we discovered that Carson had a brain tumor. It was a terrifying ordeal, made worse by a series of botched medical decisions. We were assured that the tumor would never become dangerous, that it wasn't cancer, and that it had likely been there since childhood.

I never wavered in my commitment to him, even when Ron pointed out how this could change the course of my life. When Carson asked Ron for permission to propose, Ron even questioned him about the tumor. My grandpa and my dad had their concerns, too. But in the end, they all trusted me and gave their blessing, even though they saw through the situation. They believed I could handle it. And I did—until I couldn't.

One illogical but deeply important goal of mine was to get married before I graduated from medical school. I didn't want to be Dr. Sieben, and I think that played a huge role in my eagerness to get married when I did. The truth is, neither of us was truly ready for marriage and everything it entailed long-term. Between school, residency interviews, planning a move—and a brain tumor diagnosis on top of it all—we never really had time to date and deeply know each other.

We functioned well together in day-to-day life, and there was a magnetic pull between us, which seemed like enough. We never had time to question it. Unlike with Dane, I knew the proposal was coming. Carson used my ring from Dane, with minor adjustments, and we had already discussed wedding timing based on his uncle's deployment. But the actual proposal was beautiful. His mom and brothers were involved, he created "our spot" in his parents' woods, and it happened on Christmas Eve, just before his dad's family Christmas—the night that had, two years earlier, solidified our relationship, well in my mind.

Unlike with Dane, I didn't panic after we got engaged. I was comfortable in my role, and I knew that as long as I kept up my part, I would always know what to expect. Wedding planning was easy and fun. Our wedding day was perfect—except for one moment the night before, when Nancy questioned whether I was losing myself in the relationship. But otherwise, it was perfect.

For years, people told us it was the most fun wedding they had ever attended. I have never laughed, cried, or danced so hard. But the only problem was that I wasn't being honest—with myself or with him.

There were moments in the week leading up to the wedding when I was alone, scared, and anxious, and I questioned it. But I assumed that was normal. People talk about "cold feet," but no one explains what that actually means or what goes through someone's mind when they feel it. I questioned whether my mom would have liked him (I even said so in my vows). Would she have accepted him, or would she have seen what others did? I wondered if I had lost myself and if I would ever truly matter in this relationship—or if I would always be the one to conform.

Still, I believed that the benefits, for me and for my future kids, would always outweigh my fears. Now, I feel selfish for not voicing those concerns to him. I feel selfish for not holding up my end of the promise.

So yes, deep down, part of me knew that maybe this wasn't right. But I also thought that if I just tried harder, I could make it perfect. I thought I was the problem—that I needed to change, to fix myself, rather than ask for anything that might seem "unrealistic."

When we started residency—the same program his mom had attended—I struggled more. It became harder and harder to be "not me." My advisor had been his mom's advisor years before, and he called me by her name the entire time I was there.

My identity quickly disappeared.

And then, just a week after medical school graduation and six months after we had gotten marriedI found out I was pregnant.

Chapter 14: Till Death (or Divorce) Do Us Part

When we get married, that is what we commit to—well, the "death" part, not the "divorce" part. I had personally lived through three divorces by the time I got married: my mom and dad's, my mom's second marriage and divorce, and my dad's second marriage and divorce. I saw the blessing of divorce when it was necessary. I also saw what it did to me and my sisters. Nonetheless, going into this marriage, I was determined to be different. I knew what not to do, which meant I knew what to do—be perfect. I had essentially perfected this in my life; I just had to keep burying the barrels and be what I needed to be.

Carson grew up with two parents who, I believe, got married because they had him in high school. I loved both of my in-laws very much, and still do to some extent, although clearly, the dynamic has changed—some ways more than others. But they are very, very different people. I don't know if I ever saw them as a genuinely happy couple, even superficially, but what did I know? Again, this is my story, so I won't pretend to understand or know the intricacies of anybody else's life. What I observed, though, was two people who cohabitated with the understanding that Mom was in charge—she was the doctor, the one who made the money, the one with the attunement and amazingly loving connection to her sons. Dad did what he needed to do to maintain things and keep things in order, scare tactics and all.

The thing about both of them is that they are fiercely loyal family members. Even from that first Christmas when I met both sides of their families, I was in awe. Yes, they were very different, but they had family, unity, love, loyalty, and togetherness—something I had never truly experienced, even with my extended family. It was a dream to be welcomed as a part of both sides of Carson's family.

Nonetheless, Carson did not grow up in a house where a healthy marriage was modeled, and it seemed like he never truly acknowledged how that impacted him as a person and a husband. I never saw the concept of partnership, equality, friendship, or attunement to each other's needs and wants. I think he—and, in some respects, his brothers, especially the next oldest—wanted to marry a woman who was strong, intelligent, and very much like their mom.

I love his mom. She is one of the strongest women I have ever met—kind, caring, and willing to go out of her way for almost anyone, even at her own expense. She was also a very involved mother who raised her kids well despite navigating the imbalance in her marriage. She did the best she could, but her husband had a role to play too. The problem was that, although I believe Carson thought he wanted to "marry his mom," he also wanted full control and to have things his way all the time—much like his mom did. He wanted to marry his mom, but he also wanted to be his mom.

Over time, that proved impossible. His desire to be his mom eventually trumped his desire to marry someone like her. And in so many ways, I am like his mom.

I, on the other hand, was raised by a single mom who was as independently strong as could be. I was raised knowing that I needed to be able to do and be everything on my own—because that was what I observed. I did not witness any real partnership, equality, friendship, love, or companionship. (Mel and my mom had that, but it was so short-lived. And just when it was about to be "forever"—well, you know what happened.) My grandpa later became my father figure and was everything I could have asked for, but that came later. My male influence before that was my first "HE," whom I spent every day trying to be good enough for.

The merging of Carson's views of marriage and partnership with mine…

So here we were—just graduated from medical school, just got a puppy, peed on a stick that said "pregnant," and were now moving into our first house together to start something as "simple" as residency. What's that saying again?!

We had Isaac halfway through our first year of residency. This would be my first glimpse of realizing where I stood as a wife. While pregnant, I was reminded that I was "just pregnant"—therefore, I was not pampered or given any special attention or treatment. No grocery store craving runs, no foot or back massages, and the only appointment he joined me at was my ultrasound. My hormones were used against me. And we were very busy.

Isaac's delivery was a nightmare. Thank God my mother-in-law was there to support me and keep me calm. Isaac was a very colicky baby who did not sleep. Unfortunately, as I was frequently reminded, Carson was still a first-year resident and had to work, so I was on my own.

(My mother-in-law saved me when Isaac was a newborn. I actually bawled my eyes out when she left after being with us for several days because I knew I couldn't handle it all on my own. She came back a week later! I still survived and did, indeed, manage.)

I was told I needed to "just get over" my postpartum depression because I was "just tired and moody." Until you have lived through and experienced postpartum depression, you cannot truly understand it—especially as a man. My not getting the help I needed for my postpartum depression only made Isaac's colic worse, in my opinion, which made everything that much harder.

Regardless, we survived.

I also felt so alone. I had my mother-in-law for those short weeks, but I didn't have anyone else *for me*. The absence of my mom hit like a ton of bricks at random times but that void never fully left.

I got pregnant with Emmitt about a year and a half later. Emmitt had a heart problem in utero that required frequent ultrasounds for me and multiple ECHOs for him while he was still inside. Since Carson and I were both still residents during that pregnancy as well, he didn't make it to the ultrasounds. I went alone every couple of weeks and watched as Emmitt's heart condition worsened each time. Thank goodness for the kind ultrasound tech—and thank goodness for the miracle after he was born when his heart repaired itself.

As I just couldn't do it again on my own, my friend and co-resident secretly treated my postpartum depression. Things went better, and Emmitt was a much easier baby. The summer after we finished residency, I needed major surgery while we were preparing to move [back to Carson's hometown]. Despite doctor's orders, I still had to pack and clean just as much. I wasn't taken care of—again—but I handled it—again.

Unfortunately, as if residency, having two babies, moving, and beginning our practices wasn't enough of a test, everything was about to change… again.

By this point, right around Emmitt's first birthday, I started to feel a division between Carson and me. After two stressful pregnancies and postpartum periods, I felt like I had handled everything without the emotional support and care I needed. I started to resent—maybe that's too strong of a word—but I was genuinely hurt. I didn't feel the togetherness of new parents; I didn't see the awe in him for what I had been through delivering his kids. It just was what it was.

He was—and is—a good dad who loved/loves his kids, and we had his family and support. I also stayed on my depression meds, and we were finally settling into real adult life, with the stress of medical school and residency behind us. But I still felt, in a way, emotionally forgotten—or at least minimized. Living in his hometown did not help this at all. I was an outsider and *the third Dr. Bell,* I was starting to truly lose whatever identity I had left.

Then, right after Emmitt's first birthday in February 2013, my person—my grandpa—had a heart attack.

I need to take a tangent here to talk about my grandpa. I know I've mentioned him before, but somehow, I need you, the reader, to fully understand what this man was to me. He was, essentially, the only one who didn't abandon me when my mom died. Now, at almost 30, he was the one person who had always been there—always dependable, no matter what. By this point, I had Ron and Nancy, my 'bonus' family, but my grandpa was my foundation.

They say you should marry your best friend—that they should be your person—but I don't think Carson and I ever reached that point, either before or after marriage. Much of that I attribute to the timing of our relationship, the demands of medical school and residency, and having kids right away. We never had the chance to just be us, to enjoy each other, and to build a passionate foundation of our own.

Carson was more joy-filled, happier, and more excited during his weekly phone dates with his best friend than he ever seemed with me. It never even occurred to me that his best friend had always been his person. If I had thought about it, it would have been obvious, that I was never his best friend or person.

My grandpa, however, was mine—but in a different way. He was my safe place. But grandpa didn't get my tear-filled calls, my life-drama calls, or my requests for advice that weren't about logistical life things. He was my person in the sense that I knew I was safe with him and that he would always be there.

My emotional person? Nancy, in a way. Bobee, in a way. Miranda, in a way. I think I gave them each a part of that, but never one of them all of it. Part of that was not wanting to burden anyone, and part of it was that trusting someone with all of it would mean so much vulnerability that, if lost, I would be devastated. (Foreshadowing: I wish I had kept this practice going, because my soon-to-be best friends would prove all my fears valid.)

Anyway, grandpa had that heart attack, and everything changed. This would prove to be another defining moment in my life—and in my marriage.

Although grandpa had made it clear in his healthcare directive that he never wanted any type of procedure, he still somehow ended up in the Cath Lab, where they put stents in his heart. While the procedure itself was successful in a cardiac sense, what followed was a nightmare. At baseline, before his heart attack, he had been experiencing some memory loss and early dementia, and we were in the process of determining whether it was safe for him to remain at home.

Then, my aunt Candy magically reappeared in our lives, doing everything she could to get back in his good graces—meaning, back in his will. It was painfully obvious she was trying to take advantage of his vulnerable state even before his heart attack. (Thankfully, he never signed the new copy of the will.) That's all she wanted.

After his heart attack, my grandpa had to be placed in memory care. He also had to undergo electroconvulsive therapy (ECT), where they zapped his brain to manage behaviors caused by his dementia and underlying depression. This was neither an easy nor a quick process, and I had a hard time getting him situated and stable.

By the fall of 2013, we finally found him a stable place to live. For me, dealing with all of this in the first year of my career—with a 3.5-year-old and a 1.5-year-old—was overwhelming. Every time he had an episode and became belligerent, I had to drop everything and personally go calm him down. On top of that, I had to figure out what to do with his house—the home he had lived in for more than 50 years.

With Candy furious over the will, I ended up sorting through everything with Ron and Nancy. We cleaned the entire house and even ran an estate/garage sale—on my birthday, no less.

Carson's dad and a friend of his did go and paint the entire interior, but Carson himself never helped with this exhausting and emotional process. Yes, he was with the boys, but he never made an effort to be there for me—to actually help me. He could have found someone to watch the boys once in a while, but he didn't. No, I didn't ask—but in the state I was in, why should I have had to?

A couple of weeks after the estate sale, I could just tell something was wrong with Carson. This, again, is called attunement. I could look at that man and know almost exactly how he was feeling—especially from this point forward.

Just two months prior, he had gone in for his routine follow-up on his supposedly 'boring' brain tumor, and they had even said we could start spacing out his visits. But by late October 2013, I knew something wasn't right.

We were about to leave for the Bahamas—Paradise Island, Atlantis—for a medical conference that happened to coincide with our five-year wedding anniversary. For both of us, this was a dream vacation. After everything we had been through over the past five years—the stress, the chaos—we needed this. We were both so excited.

But he just didn't look or seem right, and I wanted him to get an MRI before we left. He refused. In a way, I do appreciate that—because he didn't want to ruin our vacation.

We arrived in the Bahamas a couple of days before the conference started so we could enjoy our vacation. The first few days were amazing! We went for runs together, sat by the pool, floated on the lazy river, walked hand-in-hand, and had fancy romantic dinners. We did everything Atlantis had to offer. It was a dream. I truly loved my husband, and in those few days—just the two of us—I believe we made real progress in finding our way back to each other. Unfortunately, I was about to prove just how much I loved him, in the worst possible way.

Around day three of our vacation, during our run, we reached our turnaround point, and he needed to take a break—something that was completely unlike him. In medical school, we used to run the trail by my apartment, which had a picturesque stream, rocks, waterfalls, and a bridge. From our starting point, the trail was all downhill, but the challenge was the return—running back up what felt like a mountain. It took over a year of pushing me before I could run the entire route without walking parts of the steep incline. The point is, Carson didn't take breaks. He was always fit, always more athletic than I was, and—almost unfairly—he always looked good.

That day in the Bahamas, as we reached the halfway point, I remember him leaning on the railing of a gazebo, staring into nothing. It wasn't a contemplative stare; it was a pained, fearful look. And that's when everything changed. He admitted he had the worst headache he'd experienced since his tumor was discovered. He described a pressure behind his eyes, a symptom he had never had before. Finally, he confessed that the headache had started before we left, but he hadn't told me because he didn't want to ruin our vacation. I think a part of him already knew it wasn't good.

His headache worsened rapidly. By the next day, he could barely get out of bed, let alone leave the hotel room. The only way to communicate home was via email, so I walked across the resort to message his mom, hoping she could arrange an appointment and an MRI with his neurosurgeon for when we returned. I went back and forth between lectures and checking on him, grabbing Starbucks box lunches for my dinner. Getting him to eat anything was another challenge.

After a day or so, it became painfully clear this wasn't going to resolve on its own. I spent three hours on the phone with the airline before finally getting our flights changed to leave a day earlier. (As a side note, I had NEVER purchased flight insurance before. But for some reason, when I booked this trip months prior, I had. Divine intervention.)

The bumpy van ride to the airport was brutal. The only thought running through our minds was: *We need to get back to the U.S.* We had a layover in Atlanta and considered going straight to the emergency room there, but since his mom had already arranged an MRI and an appointment for the next day, we decided to push through and get home. We also debated heading straight to the hospital after landing, but Carson opted to wait until morning. That night, we stayed at Ron and Nancy's. He was in agony—barely able to move, barely able to open his eyes from the pressure, and the headache was only getting worse.

His appointment wasn't until early afternoon on November 10, 2013. That morning, however, he begged me to take him to the ER. Since his MRI was just an hour away, we went early. I honestly feared they would rush him straight into surgery, so I tried to convince him to skip lunch. But rightfully, he ate, saying he wanted to see the boys just in case something happened. (We had only been gone a week, but the fact that he was that afraid—that he might die—added another layer to this nightmare.)

The MRI revealed that his "benign" tumor—the one that was never supposed to cause problems—had grown. Worse, it had expanded into his fourth ventricle, a fluid-filled space in the brain, where it had started to bleed. The brain doesn't handle blood well, which explained his excruciating pain. He was admitted immediately, and surgery was scheduled for the next day.

That evening, the boys visited the hospital. We have, arguably, one of the most emotional photos in existence—Carson hugging our boys before they left. (They were 1.5 and almost 4 years old at the time.)

On November 11—his mom's birthday—Carson had his first brain surgery. It was delayed three hours because another patient, undergoing the same procedure Carson was scheduled for in three days, was struggling. (We didn't find out how badly it went until weeks later—thank God.) The delay did nothing to ease our anxiety. Thankfully, my sister, with her relentless sense of humor, was there to keep us distracted, albeit annoyingly so.

During the surgery, they placed a shunt in his brain—a thin straw-like device inserted into a different ventricle—

to drain excess fluid and relieve some of the pressure and pain. That was just the first step.

On November 14, 2013, Carson underwent a posterior craniotomy. They cut into the back of his head, moved his cerebellum, and removed all of the tumor in the fourth ventricle—the portion that had bled. They also took a small biopsy of the original tumor. Removing the entire mass wasn't an option due to its location and the severe deficits it would have caused. (Again, it wasn't cancer.)

From the moment he was admitted, I stayed in his hospital room every night. The first night, I tried to go back to Ron and Nancy's, but as soon as I got there, I turned around. I couldn't leave him alone in that hospital, terrified. The night of his second surgery, however, I had no choice but to stay in a family waiting room. His aunt—my favorite—stayed with me all night.

Just before midnight, we went to check on him. It was the most alert he had been since surgery. I remember him distinctly asking, *What was it?* Heading into the procedure, no one knew exactly what they would find. We had been hoping for a random collection of blood vessels—not what it actually was. The fact that his benign tumor had grown was almost the worst-case scenario. (The absolute worst would have been cancer, so we counted our blessings.)

I looked at his aunt, who shook her head, signaling that we shouldn't tell him yet—he needed to rest. But I couldn't lie to him.

Right around midnight, now November 15—his 31st birthday—I had to tell Carson exactly what he didn't want to hear. It was devastating. I can still picture his surgeon pulling me aside, explaining everything with as much empathy as possible, fully aware that this wasn't the news we had hoped for. I was terrified of saying it *wrong*, of making it even harder for him to process. It was heartbreaking. I spent the rest of the night sitting in a chair beside his ICU bed, my head resting against his side, holding his hand. (Yes, I have a picture of me in that spot, just staring at my husband. Yes, you can *feel* the love in it.)

Ironically, by the next day, he didn't remember me telling him. So I had to do it all over again.

I wish I could say the rest of his recovery went smoothly. In terms of his brain healing, it did. He only lost a quadrant of his vision, which returned within a couple of weeks. I got to teach him how to walk forward and backward again, and, to this day, he still can't look up quickly without getting dizzy—but it could have been much worse.

The real problem was the pain. It was unbearable. He had to be heavily medicated, to the point where he started reporting the wrong pain score just to get more meds so he could sleep. The pressure in his head persisted, leading to multiple scans. Each scan required moving him between his bed, the elevator, and the scanner—every shift made him nauseous, and no medication helped. There was a lot of vomiting. (Side note: watching pink meal replacement shakes come back up into a suction straw while being the one holding the straw is *not* a highlight of marriage, nor was wiping his butt.)

Eventually, they placed another drain, this time in his lower back, and he spent Thanksgiving lying flat. It helped—enough that he was transferred to rehab. But that lasted less than a day.

The back of his head essentially *exploded*, leaking spinal fluid everywhere. He was rushed back to the hospital, where he underwent a third brain surgery to implant a permanent shunt, draining fluid from his brain into his abdominal cavity.

That was just the beginning.

Carson came home on December 8, 2013. This would prove even more impossible. The entire month he was in the hospital, someone stayed with him every single night. I had to go back to work occasionally, I had to spend time with our boys, and someone needed to be with him. We all somehow rearranged our lives and made it possible. I updated CaringBridge every single day, sometimes multiple times, because I refused to talk on the phone to anybody but his parents. I did all the Christmas shopping online that year. Much to Carson's disappointment, I bought a fake Christmas tree (rather than a real one), which the boys and I decorated during that month. I even managed to put the lights up on the house.

When Carson did get to come home, however, life got even harder because most of the help—okay, the level of help—disappeared. I had to care for an almost 4-year-old, an almost 2-year-old, and a 31-year-old who, for a while, was still hooked on pain meds. (On a positive note, he got himself off them, but that meant we also had to deal with several days of withdrawal. In the end, though, it worked out for the best.)

Physical therapy was a nightmare because everything they had him do made his head hurt and made him more dizzy. Even his "second mom" from childhood had to call me home from work one day to calm him down because she didn't know what to do when he refused to do anything due to his headaches and dizziness.

Christmas that year was also difficult because, at this point, he still couldn't do much but lay around, rest, and do PT—if he ever followed directions. The most exciting thing for him was getting his ice fishing clothes from his mom. For some reason, this destroyed my soul. He thanked me, and he was grateful for all that I had done, but it never seemed like it was enough. I didn't even get so much as a card, as selfish as that may sound.

Being the primary caregiver is so hard. Maybe part of me was very triggered because, once again, I was caring for someone I loved so much—like my mom—and there didn't seem to be an end in sight. It was hard not to, at times, be so angry because it just didn't seem fair. I do understand that what he went through as the patient was worse than anything most people will ever experience and that, especially at that point, I was exhausted, burned out, and probably taking everything too personally—being overly sensitive. His family was very supportive, and I am grateful for that.

Meanwhile, at this same time, my grandpa was still not doing the greatest in memory care. Honestly, looking back, I don't know how I survived. I was still his primary caregiver as well, and I had just recently elected to put him on hospice—not necessarily because he had a diagnosis like cancer, but because, with his level of dementia, he qualified for the additional services. And I needed help.

By March 2014, Carson was feeling better, so he had a neuropsych test done to show he could still work. (This test checks cognitive ability and several other things to assess for any disability. This included the ever life-changing moment when he received his "only average" IQ result. His direct quote: "I've never been average at anything my entire life.")

To me, the most important part of this test wasn't that, but the fact that he was even able to work again. I guess we had different thoughts on that. He went back to work for a couple of days a week.

At a follow-up appointment with his medical team, we were told that he should consider having radiation—not because this was any type of cancerous tumor, but because it had grown and bled once. There was always a chance of it happening again. Radiation wasn't a guarantee, but it was believed to be the best option to help mitigate the risk of recurrence. The type of radiation they recommended—proton beam, due to risks and complications—was still fairly new, so he ended up going to Massachusetts General in Boston for treatment.

On May 8, 2014, we flew to Boston to start radiation. However, I was a couple of days late on my period. That morning, I found out I was pregnant.

I had never experienced morning sickness until that pregnancy, which was made all the worse by the many flights back and forth between Minnesota and Massachusetts. I may have been miserable with nausea, but at least for the first half of radiation, Carson felt pretty good.

We were lucky because his mom's best friend from medical school lived out there, so he had a place to stay. However, getting to Mass General from her house involved a couple of blocks' walk, a bus, a train, and a couple more blocks' walk—approximately one hour each way. The actual radiation procedure itself took all of five minutes.

I was there for the first week of radiation, which went very well. We spent quality time together before the fatigue of radiation really hit, and we even did some sightseeing and took a trip to Maine over the weekend.

The day I was supposed to fly home, I got a call early in the morning from hospice. They told me I needed to come home right away.

After my car wouldn't start at the airport—and after having to get it jumped in the garage by a random stranger—

I finally made the hour-and-a-half drive to sit with my grandpa.

On May 19, 2014, my person died. He, of course, waited until about 20 minutes after I had left one night. I'm not at all surprised that he didn't want me there at that exact moment. And as much as part of me wishes I had been holding his hand, I knew he wanted me to remember him from before.

Luckily, earlier that day, both of my boys had gotten to go and see him. He was oddly alert for their short visit.

He didn't know about Carson, nor did he know I was pregnant. I knew, if anything, that would only worry him. And I also knew he wouldn't be there for any of it.

Although I knew it was going to happen, getting that phone call was devastating. Much like my mom, I knew this wasn't going to go any other way. And, also much like my mom, I got to say goodbye. Unlike with my mom, however, my grandpa dying opened a chasm inside me that my mom's death had only cracked in my soul. I had Nancy and Ron. That was who I had left—those who were mine. At the very moment of his death, and in the days leading up to the funeral, I believed I had Carson too. I also believed, to my core, that I had a supportive, unshakable family of in-laws. My wishes didn't quite match my reality, which did something else to my soul.

Some may see, as Carson seemed to, that my grandpa was 86, had dementia, and that his death was inevitable—

maybe even for the better. But even on his worst days, just being around him made my heart feel at home and safe. I can see now that it was a blessing for him to pass peacefully, but I realized I didn't have a person to fill that void.

Planning his funeral was interesting. I was in full compartmentalization mode and was "handling" things, so, emotionally, the planning part was fine for me. My aunt tried to play the part of the doting daughter—because, at this point, she didn't realize she had not been added to the will. Honestly, all I cared about was doing the eulogy. I told Carson not to fly home for the funeral because it would have delayed his radiation treatments by almost two more weeks. I had a two-year-old and a four-year-old who wanted their dad to come home, so a delay until July didn't make sense.

The day of Grandpa's funeral was rainy—torrential downpours and cold. I honestly don't know what I would have done that day if it hadn't been for my father-in-law. I was able to be present, physically and emotionally, for everything I needed to do while he looked after the boys.

What I don't remember are the exact words I said during that second eulogy of my life—the second eulogy for the other person, besides my mom, who had been there for me since day one. My last foundation person.

The actual burial, however, was quite eventful—if anything at a funeral can be. By that point, the rain had stopped, and the sun had come out. We had the seven-gun salute and taps at his burial, and it was beautiful… until one of the VFW members, just after playing taps, collapsed.

Through my tears, I quickly had to go into doctor mode. (The gentleman was fine; he had just gotten lightheaded and dehydrated. After the rain and cold stopped midday, it had become unreasonably hot and humid.) Once he was safely in the ambulance, I couldn't help but smile and shake my head. In that moment, it felt like my grandpa had orchestrated the entire situation as one last acknowledgment of how proud he was of me. It was as if he wanted me to show my strength and abilities even in that most horribly sad and painful moment.

When the day was over, I received one phone call from my husband. There were no flowers. No card. Maybe it's my fault—like he and his mom said—for telling him not to come home for the funeral. Maybe that was "permission" to completely disregard my needs and feelings on one of the hardest days of my life. My strength, for his need to be in Boston, seemed to tell him that I was, once again, fine.

His lack of acknowledgment, attunement, support, and understanding of the significance of that day to me, however, felt like one of the biggest abandonments I had faced in more than two decades. It ended up being one that my heart could not understand and still cannot forget. Yes, I know he was having brain radiation, and that trumped everything, as it always had. That damn brain tumor trumped everything. But I needed support that day. I needed my "person"—which he claimed to be.

The lack of support that day wasn't even acknowledged by him for years—until his best friend's grandma died.

"Seeing how hard it was for Mark when his grandma died, I can see how hard it must have been for you when your grandpa did."

Really? Mark had so many people. One cannot compare grief, but it took years for him to even acknowledge mine. And then, to just make it the same? That felt like a huge slap in the face.

Then, a couple of years after that, Carson's own grandma died. He had a difficult time going to see her when she was dying because it was "too hard." So he asked if I would go in his place, which I did. He also needed my support standing next to him on the altar when he gave her eulogy. But me? I had been alone. Again.

The last day of radiation, we celebrated. I flew to Boston with both boys by myself, and they got to help their dad ring the bell announcing his last treatment. On top of that, the Minnesota Twins were playing the Red Sox at Fenway that day. All seemed right in the world—on the surface, for inside, I was a shell

When we flew home, we had a big party for him. Everyone took a relieved—albeit cautious—breath, and we moved forward.

Kilie was born in January 2015. Carson still had a lot of fatigue, so it was good that I had a longer maternity leave this time. I did, however, have to have a C-section, which made the whole process more difficult for me to handle since Carson needed more sleep and was limited in his ability to help. But overall, things were okay. She even has a birthmark on her lower back in the shape of Massachusetts!

We had found a new normal and flow. Carson went back to work, the kids were doing well… until the mom who chose me—Nancy—decided to get a brain tumor of her own.

Approximately four years after I sat in the waiting room of the hospital, waiting for the neurosurgeon to save my husband, I was sitting in the exact same chair, waiting for the exact same doctor, to save my "bonus mom."

Once again, when he emerged from the operating room, that same look was on his face, and the news we were given was not what we wanted. Although this time, it was even worse. She, like my real mom, had something exceedingly rare. Nancy's was also very aggressive.

This was devastating. But even more so, my heart broke for what could have been an ultimately perfect pairing—Grandma Nancy and Kilie Nancy.

Less than a year later, on November 26, 2016, in a hospital bed in her living room, with all of us surrounding her, she took her last breath while I was eight months pregnant with her second granddaughter, whom she never got to meet.

By now, you can probably understand, assume, and predict that I gave a third eulogy. I wrote her the following poem:

The Mom Who Chose Me

You gave me your love right from the start,
Wide open arms and open heart.
A lost teenager you took in, faults and all,
You've always been there—to cry, hug, or call.
You never tried to push, pry, or demand,
Just a strong guiding force and a leading hand.
You were the one there for life's big events—
Graduations, a wedding, babies—you were heaven-sent.
I don't know where I would be if it wasn't for you,
The luckiest person I've been, with the greatest moms times two.
On my mind, in my heart, and an inspiration you'll always be,
Forever grateful I am for the mom who chose me.

After that first summer of living with Ron and Nancy, Nancy and I became inseparable. Nancy was as close to home as one could be. Nancy was my safety just behind my grandpa. Nancy was my *bonus* mom.

Eighteen years after I lost my first mom, I lost my second. Coincidentally, I had them both for sixteen years. None of this will ever make sense to me.

Carson was there for me that time around. I don't think he really knew, however, that Nancy was always mad at me for not marrying Dane. She, of course, like any good mom, supported my decisions. Although at this point, I can hear her saying a big, *I told you so.*

I cannot end like that. In truth, that wouldn't be fair, complete, or fully transparent. Throughout my healing, I have, of course, spent much time reflecting on this—my biggest failure—my divorce. I was so determined never to go through this one thing that I had already lived through three times with my parents. I never wanted that for myself, but even more importantly, I never wanted that for my kids. So why, then, did it happen?

I won't begin by pointing fingers—I have matured beyond that cowardly act. I can tell my story, as I have, and on the surface, it may appear that I am doing exactly that. But in truth, this is simply my honest account of events. Unfortunately, it is only when looking back that we can see the deeper, previously unknown root causes—causes that go beyond just "trauma." Rather, they lie in the actions that occurred between the trauma and the event itself. There's something we often overlook, something I didn't fully understand until I began caring for patients with opioid use disorder. And I didn't truly grasp its personal relevance until the "after"—after the papers were signed, after the marriage was over.

As is pretty obvious, I spent much of my life yearning for love and attachment. I clearly didn't recognize it in Dane, nor did I take the time for self-reflection and understanding after him. I was nowhere near where I should have been when I walked into my relationship with Carson. It was something we both should have acknowledged with actions rather than getting swept up in the early, rose-colored-glasses stage of a new relationship. The red flags—from both sides—were glaringly obvious, but we missed them. Neither of us, especially me, was ready for this relationship, let alone a lifelong commitment. I don't believe either of us truly understood what that commitment was supposed to mean—what unconditional love looked like or required at its core.

I had never witnessed unconditional love modeled in a healthy way, and I would argue that Carson hadn't either—at least not from his parents, who divorced at the same time we did. We both entered marriage determined not to repeat our parents' mistakes, but I see now that determination alone wasn't enough. One cannot simply avoid a behavior without first understanding its root cause. Nor can one embrace a desired behavior without fully comprehending what it entails. Years into the marriage, I think we both recognized these shortcomings, but by then, we had already lost sight of prioritizing each other and our marriage. Instead, we each viewed the problems as the other's fault rather than owning our own roles. Blame became the default, and any attempt to change that cycle failed—whether due to stubbornness, pain, or something else. The point is, neither of us was able to truly cherish the other for the sake of the marriage. And the longer that cycle continued, the harder it became to break.

From my perspective—though painfully clear only in hindsight—I married Carson's amazing family as much as I married him. I saw what I wanted and was all too willing to shape myself to fit into it. I didn't value myself. I didn't believe that I mattered. I convinced myself that I could, and would, be happy forever as long as I gave all of myself to him and his family—never asking for much in return. In the process, I cut off my own less-than-perfect family. That is completely on me.

I look back at the "sacrifices" I made—my career choice, where I wanted to live and raise a family—and I carry deep scars. For years, I placed all of that blame on him, failing to acknowledge my own role. I didn't fight for what I wanted. At the first moment of conflict, when he worried that my becoming an OB-GYN would negatively impact our family, I caved. Did he directly forbid me? No. Did he strongly oppose it? Yes. But did I advocate for myself at all? No.

We will never know what would have happened had I fought for my dreams. Perhaps it would have ended our marriage right then, or perhaps it would have led us down a completely different path—one that might have been better for us in the long run. But we can't go back. What resulted from my lack of confidence was years of internal pain and resentment. In turn, he was angry that I placed all the blame on him. My argument was always that he never even asked me what I wanted. He never encouraged my dreams or tried to find a compromise. And he didn't. That was on him. But it wasn't *all* on him. Neither of us handled that situation well.

I saw him as completely selfish for not offering love and support. And I wasn't wrong. But I also didn't give him many chances to show up for me in that way. Why would he, when I so easily gave in to what he wanted? We had that argument countless times—both of us failing to take ownership, neither of us truly hearing the other's feelings, and neither of us willing to forgive the pain for the sake of the marriage.

There were many situations like this—each following the same pattern, each leaving similar wounds, each leading to the same repetitive arguments. In the grand scheme of life, love, and marriage, these moments should have been opportunities for growth and connection. Instead, they only added cracks.

I still ask myself *why*. My heart still aches when I reflect from this different place. Could we have made it if we had both done the deep self-work and chosen each other, put our marriage first and now ourselves? I honestly don't know. I honestly don't know if I could have healed while still living in the pain. But what if we had truly honored our commitment and vows? I am ashamed that I didn't try harder.

He, our kids, and I deserved better—from both of us.

So why didn't I? Why didn't we? In learning and understanding my patterns—shaped by my history and trauma—I see how many walls I put up. I felt invisible to him and to everyone, and the moment I tried to voice anything, even when something wasn't exactly how I wanted it, I emotionally fled. My fight-or-flight response took over. (Yes, it was often preceded by an unproductive fight, but the longer-term result was my emotional withdrawal behind walls.) I wanted him to read my mind, to know that I needed affirmation and support, to pull me out from behind those walls—something he never tried to do. That, in turn, only made me feel more and more isolated.

Still, I loved him more than anything. I was committed to not becoming my parents, so I resigned myself to the way things were, focusing first on one child, then the next. That was, until I broke and just couldn't anymore—or, rather, perhaps I just chose not to.

You always hear about marriages that fall apart when a child gets sick or dies. That level of stress and trauma can be too much for families and marriages to bear. I never fully understood that. But you really can't unless you're in it. Oddly, when I was in it, I didn't recognize it. Truthfully, I didn't realize it until embarrassingly later—far later than I would have ever guessed. It wasn't until a patient told me a story about infertility that it all clicked.

Fred, Carson's brain tumor, was our proverbial child with cancer. Fred tested our relationship while we were dating, making his debut—ironically—a month before we got engaged. At the time, it seemed to bring us closer. Now, I see that it set a precedent and standard in our relationship that disrupted the balance of caregiving. I took care of him during that first event, and I did it well—so well that he praised me for it in his personal marriage vows.

For years, when we thought Fred was behind us, things seemed almost balanced. But we hadn't truly been tested under the same stress—both of us navigating medical school and residency together. When I got pregnant the first time, I didn't notice the imbalance until much later. At the time, I completely agreed with Carson's sentiment that I was "only" pregnant and didn't need any special attention or care. Because I was almost stubbornly independent—again, due to my childhood—I believed I could do everything while pregnant. So I did. (But I was still jealous when others were doted on during their pregnancies.)

Carson didn't lovingly choose to come to my OB appointments like some husbands did. He didn't rub my feet or talk to my belly. Over time, with each pregnancy, I grew to resent that lack of attention, compassion, and love. I felt taken for granted, as if carrying his children didn't afford me any special consideration.

When I struggled with postpartum depression or dealt with a colicky baby, he was far too willing to let me handle it alone. But I was also far too willing to handle it because that was what I had always done. I didn't know how to ask for help. But deep inside, I wanted it. I needed it. I wanted him to want to be there for me, just as I had been for him with Fred.

Again, a deeper rift formed. Again, we were both at fault.

But even that wasn't my breaking point.

When Fred returned and Carson spent a month in the hospital, then had to live in Boston for two months for radiation, I broke. I did it all, as I've laid out. All I wanted from him was appreciation—for him to go out of his way to give me even half of that energy and effort, to think of me, to put in effort for me. To ask someone to get me a Christmas card (not even a gift) the year he came home from the hospital. I knew he wasn't going to be shopping anytime soon, but why couldn't he have considered all I had done and gone out of his way for me? That put me 90% over the edge.

The final push was when my grandpa died.

Years later, Carson acknowledged how hard that was for me—which, in a way, only hurt more. Why hadn't he seen it at the time? Why, when he was in Boston, with me traveling back and forth, managing the kids, the house, my grandpa on hospice, and being pregnant—why couldn't he do anything for me when my grandpa died?

Is that all on him? Is it all on me?

I think, in the grand scheme of our relationship—roughly nine years at that point—we had set a precedent, an acceptable pattern. I had never held him to a standard where he had to go out of his way for me, in the way that I needed. So why did I expect that to change then, especially when he was solely focused on Fred, and his entire family was supporting that focus?

Once again, I hoped, *this will be the time.*

Once again, I set him up for failure.

Once again, I set myself up for heartbreak.

Fred, much like the high stress of a child with a terminal illness, became the center of our marriage. Even our kids took a backseat when Fred acted up. We didn't prioritize ourselves as a couple, because Fred truly eclipsed everything.

One could argue that it had to be that way.

But did it?

Shouldn't our marriage have always held the highest priority?

It may seem like semantics, but I don't think so. The way we frame these things—the way we live in the truth of them—matters. It impacts the balance, the very essence of commitment and vows.

My response to being broken was nowhere near acceptable. I was isolated, wanting nothing more than to be loved in the same way that I gave love. I lost all hope. Rather than addressing it immediately—which I owed to him, to us, and to myself—I withdrew even further, putting up a wall that was likely never going to come down while still living in the pain.

Everything that happens to us is connected, although we don't always see it at the time. Each event is intertwined, overlapping, and so dependent on the others that we cannot fully grasp the gravity of each moment or word until we are on the other side of it. When we are under trauma, we aren't thinking logically or healthily; we are operating solely in a fight-or-flight state, often doing whatever we can to protect ourselves at the time, no matter the cost. If we don't have a solid foundation or healthy coping mechanisms, we can end up causing more harm than good—hurting ourselves in the long run rather than truly protecting ourselves. It isn't fair, and I won't claim it to be, that those of us who have lived through trauma have so much more work to do just to be ready for unconditional love and commitment. We have to build our own foundations first. Those with stable, healthy upbringings get a huge head start. Unfortunately, it's often those of us with the deepest wounds who crave love and attachment the most, leading us to rush the process before we truly understand what we need. This, in turn, only worsens the underlying issues, further delaying—or even preventing altogether—the very thing we long for: real, unconditional love.

So where does this leave me now, months after my divorce was finalized and nearly two years after we separated? I have so many thoughts and emotions that I almost don't know where to begin. I suppose I'll start with embarrassment and shame. I cannot believe I am where I am, especially given how committed I was to not becoming another statistic. I cannot believe we were unable to humble ourselves and put our egos aside to follow through on the very vows we both wrote and agreed to. I failed myself, Carson, and our family—our kids most of all, we both did. None of us deserved this outcome. I am disappointed in myself for not recognizing things sooner, for not addressing them sooner, and for not coming from a place of love rather than pain and resentment. I regret not advocating for myself more and not trusting him to honor his vows as well. I am truly and deeply sorry for the pain I inflicted, for the mistakes I made. I did the one thing I feared most—the unforgivable thing. Forgiveness from him is something I can only hope for, not demand. I do hope he can forgive me, for the sake of our kids and our need to be in a healthy place for them. I forgave him, despite never being asked. We made four beautiful children, and I cannot regret that.

I am also jealous. I am jealous of the attention he gives his girlfriend—the things he does for her that I begged for over the years—the way he goes out of his way to show his love. Why wasn't I worth that? I am jealous that she gets the best of him when I committed to him for so long. There are so many thoughts and feelings. But most surprising, after all this reflection, self-work, and writing this book, I have found a different love for him

For so many years, I questioned whether I loved him and whether he truly loved me. I analyzed all our "good times," searching for the moment when we were most in love. Our wedding day was perfection, but I'm not sure I was fully, completely in love with him yet. At the peak of my pain, I convinced myself that I had loved him with all of me for so long but was too hurt by what felt like his lack of reciprocation. And then I'd wonder—had I ever really loved him at all? But that wasn't true either. The truth is, I probably love him now more purely and genuinely than I ever did then.

I love him now more for that time, as if I can bring myself back to each moment of our relationship and re-feel the love I questioned or doubted back then. If the version of me today—the one who has done the work, hit rock bottom so many times, and shed countless tears—could go back to October 25, 2008 (if that day would have even happened, if we had both been healed, matured, and truly chosen each other), my vows would have been different. They would have been less idealistic and naïve. They would have been direct, honest, and genuine. They would have come from a place of understanding that life is hard, that bad things happen, that love isn't always easy. They would have acknowledged my flaws and his, and they would have asked for acceptance of both. They would have promised to lead with love and grace, not with the fantasy of perfection. I would not have just promised "forever"—I would have understood what that actually meant and committed to it anyway.

All I can hope for now is that he and I can both heal, find a place of mutual respect and understanding, and be the best parents we can be for our children. And that, someday, we can each find the love we missed out on.

Chapter 15: Daddy Issues and The Ultimate Manipulator

I cannot pretend to be perfect, innocent, or the victim in my own story. What follows is not only a description of my discovery of my life's passion and the rise of my career but also the other side of the story—my [assisted] trip to rock bottom. I endured much in my life, which, as I have noted, led me to question why. Why did I have to keep handling everything? Why did I have to be "perfect" for everyone else? Why did my voice and needs get so easily overlooked? This questioning, however, was dangerous, as it led me down a deeply self-destructive path.

I will own my role; however, I will also tell the truth as I experienced it and as I have uncovered it. Hopefully, this will put things into perspective and show how I allowed myself to be manipulated and taken advantage of again—as I had not yet done the necessary work on myself. (No, I am not victim-blaming, nor am I blaming myself for what he did; I will own the choices I made regardless.) This part of my story makes me feel angry, ashamed, guilty, and embarrassed. And now that I have done the work, I also feel proud that I survived, came out stronger, and healed. I hope this part of the book will help others recognize the signs, understand their worth, and know when to speak up and get the help they need so they don't follow this painful path—for themselves and those around them.

I will start by stating, once again, that this is my story. What I will do is lay out my facts. These facts are based on emails, texts, experiences, and conversations. I will share my feelings, but I cannot speak to the perspectives of others. I can only say what he told me. Unfortunately, some of these therapeutic details were made public when my ex-husband stole my personal journals and then subsequently shared [selective parts of] them. The years that were shared covered the time around Alex's reveal, the time from September 2020 until March 2023. They do not tell the whole story, as there were gaps when I didn't journal, but they do show the pain I was in, the isolation and turmoil I experienced, my questioning of my worth and value, my sense of hopelessness, and my struggle—both logical and emotional—to understand the "Hes" who pushed me over the edge and to my own freedom. They lit the match that ignited the toxic barrels I had buried for so long.

That violation of my personal thoughts, feelings, dreams, realities, and self-care therapy elicited much inappropriate feedback on this time in my life, arguably the worst years in my life. Many people judged, shamed, questioned, gossiped about, and ridiculed me based on writings that were meant for therapeutic purposes—never intended for others to see. Their interpretations were one-sided assumptions. One cannot accurately interpret another person's inner monologue of rambling associations. I learned a great deal about people during this horribly painful time as they revealed their true colors—their lack of empathy, their pious natures, their hypocritical truths—and just how insincere most people really are. No one asked for clarification or my actual reality of my own experiences. I have owned my truth, I have faced my consequences, and I have worked tirelessly to clean up the mess that resulted. I no longer have toxic barrels buried, and for that reason alone, I am grateful for how things happened. As for those who shared my journals and gossiped about them—that is their story, their problem, and not mine.

The only supportive feedback I received from my journals concerned the worst decision I ever made—Jack. Every piece of feedback about Jack gave me further strength and validation, as others' perspectives and experiences with him now, surprisingly, align with mine, as I now see him.

It all began years earlier. I started my primary care career on October 10, 2012. On my first day, I was on call. Throughout the day, I received many refill requests from patients of my partners, who were off that day. This is a fairly common practice in primary care. What was not common practice—at least based on my training—was the extremely high doses, large quantities, and sheer number of opioid prescriptions I had to deal with that day.

That was my first experience with the opioid epidemic. I understand that pain is real and must be addressed, so that was never my concern. My concern was the toxic levels of addictive and potentially fatal drugs circulating in my community. I didn't refuse medications outright—I simply ensured that their doctors, who knew their full medical histories, handled their refills promptly upon their returns, thus filling only a couple of days' worth.

About a year later, Jack, 20 years my senior, joined our practice. He, too, was astonished by the prescription issue. However, he had no desire to fix it, as he was planning to retire soon and wanted to stay under the radar. I was approached to lead the group that would address the opioid prescribing issue since our clinic had received a grant for this purpose. Our clinic, however, was primarily made up of older white men who were never going to listen to the young female who had just started. Looking back, I made my first mistake by asking Jack—the only older white male who hadn't bought into the opioid-pushing propaganda—to join me in this mission.

We developed a program to examine prescribing issues and quickly found success in treating patients through alternative means, thus reducing opioid diversion in our community. The state took notice, and we were approached with additional grant opportunities to expand the program statewide. We received our first award a year later, in the summer of 2016.

However, that day was quickly marred by the overdose of one of my patients who had a heroin use disorder. At the time, physicians were required to take a course and apply for approval to prescribe the life-saving medication buprenorphine-naloxone (Suboxone®). His death ignited a new passion in me—a deeper desire to care for patients with substance use disorders. (I will dive much deeper into the world of addiction in, hopefully, my next book!)

With awards came attention. I didn't particularly enjoy the spotlight, except for the fact that it brought in funding, resources, and recognition for my patients. Jack claimed to feel the same way, but he clearly liked the attention. He liked to tell people about the program *he* developed and how *we* were being approached by state entities and legislators. However, when it came time to actually meet with legislators, testify, or help write the grants, he played ignorant.

The rapid growth and success of our programs, the awards, and the opportunities to present on big stages became an addiction of their own. Standing in front of an audience—whether a dozen people or several hundred—was exhilarating. Winning an award brought the same rush, even when the true purpose was to raise awareness and educate. As attention grew, Jack insisted that everything we did had to be done together. We couldn't present individually because, in his mind, the attention had to remain shared. He often reminded me, *"We are a team"* or *"You need me."*

At first, Jack seemed like a considerate, caring friend and colleague. He encouraged me and acknowledged my skills as an advocate. But now I wonder if that was, as I do suspect, just grooming. Within a year, our professional relationship shifted. He began sharing more of his personal life with me—stories of heartbreak and betrayal. He played the role of the emotionally wounded husband, claiming his wife's *emotional affair* (though he didn't believe it had been *only* emotional) had nearly driven him to suicide over a decade prior. He shared this with tear-filled eyes, insisting he had never told anyone else.

He told me stories of growing up insecure, of idolizing his best friend's father, of harboring an unspoken crush on this same female friend. His vulnerability was always paired with gratitude—gratitude for being part of something that helped so many people, for being pushed into this program, and for finally feeling understood. He confided that he had never experienced this level of confidence or appreciation before. No one, he said, had ever really understood him the way I did.

Not long after, he began to take on a protective, hero-type role. As I shared my own insecurities and struggles, he analyzed my life, dissecting my choices—pointing out where I *should* have done things differently. Then, after unearthing these wounds, he emotionally supported my healing process, making me believe that he alone understood me. That he alone could help me through it all. That I needed him for this too.

You can probably guess what happened next—the inevitable next step in the grooming process. The declarations of *"I am in love with you."* The *"I've never felt this loved, heard, understood, or cared about before."* The *"You are the greatest thing that has ever happened to me."* And I fell for it. Hook, line, and sinker. And yes, I felt love, too. I felt heard, too. I felt like I mattered—until the moments when I didn't.

My marriage at this time was already struggling—there's no escaping that fact. The constant travel, the endless conversations, and then the *love* Jack gave me all came at a time when I was drowning in vulnerability and loneliness. I had just survived Carson's brain tumor and radiation. My grandpa had died, followed shortly by Nancy. I was emotionally exposed. And I told Jack everything, as he had told me everything. He knew more about me than Carson did—because he asked because he *listened.* He knew about Alex. He knew about my dad. He even knew about my eating disorder. (*We bonded over that—he confessed to having significant body dysmorphia due to his cross-country running and obsessive training... unless that, too, was just another carefully placed connection.*)

He pointed out how awful it was that I had to endure so many hardships alone. He emphasized how Carson *wasn't there for me.* He told me how strong I was to have survived it all. Slowly, he played deeper into my vulnerabilities, using my weaknesses as a means to pull me closer.

A self-proclaimed very private person, Jack seemed to have no trouble sharing emotionally difficult stories from his life, even beyond Karen's affairs and his deep depression. His stories weren't quick overviews—they were detailed, filled with so many specifics, and not just about himself. Sadly, I was told far too much about his wife. In hindsight, I believe most of it was lies meant to make me feel sorry for him. He, of course, prefaced each of these stories by insisting, again and again, that he had never told anyone else before. Apparently, I was "special."

Through my own self-growth, I've learned that when someone tells you that you're *that* special and they've never told anyone else what they're telling you, it's usually a manipulation tactic (psychologists call it "love-bombing"). If they say things like, *"You're so different from anyone else," "I've never felt this way before,"* or *"There's just something about you,"*—run. And if this all happens in a matter of *months*, especially with a man who had been married for more than three decades [and 20 years your senior]—run even faster.

At the time, though, I was in a vulnerable state. Everyone around me was dying, I felt emotionally isolated, and I never had the self-worth and value I should have had. So, I kept falling for every single thing he said.

After telling me about his wife's affairs, he would say he hadn't felt loved since the day he found out and questioned whether he had ever felt loved at all. He claimed he stayed for his kids, that she was a great mom, and that his love for her existed only because of that. He shared details about their conversations, counseling sessions, and the years that followed. He often admitted that he regretted staying because it meant he could never have a true, happy love story.

The next major red flag, which I completely missed—likely because I felt so bad for him, genuinely thought I loved him, and because he made it sound ok—was what he did in response to her betrayal. He told me that, despite not loving her and feeling hurt and unloved by her, he still needed to show her that she was *his*. For the next twenty years—until he met me and finally felt "loved" for the first time—he made her have sex with him every other day because, in his mind, she *owed* him. What the hell was I thinking!? He said he didn't even like doing it, but it was the only time he felt any connection to another person. It was the only way he found self-worth, all the while, essentially, sexually abusing his wife.

He would tell me that he wished I was older so we could have met years before. He said it was amazing to finally have someone who understood him and with whom he could have deep, intellectual conversations. He insisted we were something special, proven by the awards we were receiving. He told me we were good for each other, that we helped each other, that we *needed* each other. And so, we made a deal.

Our affair began shortly after his emotional confession, built on the premise that we both had a lot to lose and we needed each other for our programs. Part of the deal was that if one of us wanted it to end, the other had to accept it without argument to prevent any negative impact on our careers. He made sure I understood that this would be difficult for me, because, to him, I was apparently the weak one.

As our programs grew more successful, we gained more attention and traveled more frequently. Work trips were the only time we were together. At the peak, we traveled every two to three months, staying for one or two nights. It was thrilling, fueled by the fact that it was so wrong in so many ways, and yet, somehow, our chemistry only seemed to make our programs more successful. It became a toxic storm of secrecy and success.

Whenever I questioned anything—whether because I wanted to work on my marriage or because I was uncomfortable (see the journals for proof of this)—he quickly reminded me that we were a team and that we needed each other, no matter what. He insisted that our chemistry couldn't be affected because we were the *Jack and Heather show.* He even used the overdose death epidemic to keep me enmeshed, ensuring I wouldn't disrupt the dynamic that made our programs thrive. He used our programs to keep me enslaved. My ego became entangled in it, and fears crept in.

To the public, we were exceptional.

Jack also said all the loving, supportive, caring, and encouraging things that my husband didn't. Of course, everything was always on *his* schedule. He used a secret email but required proof that everything was deleted. He would remind me of how difficult my marriage was, how difficult *his* was, and how much we *still* needed each other. At some point, I truly believed I loved him. And, according to him, he never thought a love like ours was possible. (Yet another red flag that should have sent me running.)

I believed everything he said. I felt like I *needed* him—not just because he told me I did for the sake of our programs but also because he gave me the validation I had been craving for years. If I could go back, I would have made so many different choices. I wish I had the self-love and self-worth to reject the illusion of what I thought I was getting from him. I wish I had told Carson the moment this all started so that he could have had the chance to be my knight in shining armor and save me from Jack. Maybe then he would have found a way to give me the kind of love I was missing. But I didn't.

After my grandpa died and then Nancy, I didn't trust that Carson truly understood what I needed emotionally anyway. I was afraid that if I confided in him, it would be misinterpreted and only make things worse.

When the Alex story hit the news in February 2020—about three years after the affair started—Jack was quick to say, *"I told you so,"* regarding the abuse Alex had inflicted on me so many years before. He never questioned much beyond expressing concern that Alex was five years older than me and that I was only sixteen at the time. (Ironic, considering Jack was twenty years older than me, yet he fixated on the fact that I was only sixteen when it came to Alex.)

But when the news broke, Jack said, *"I always thought something wasn't right when you told me, but I didn't want to hurt you by saying so at the time."* Smooth.

He was also quick to console me, playing the hero. He even accompanied me to see the detective to tell my story, conveniently coinciding with a separate meeting we had. But when I *really* needed someone when I testified or at sentencing—he, like Carson, wasn't there.

After meeting with the detectives in the summer of 2020, I started to withdraw from everyone, Jack included. I became very uncomfortable with the concept of sex. I began questioning every single decision I had ever made regarding relationships, sex, and men in general. I started to really see my "He" pattern. I wondered if any of it had been real, and I doubted my choices and actions when it came to all of it. One thing I realized was that because of that first time—that assault with Alex—my view of sex was different. I learned that I could get positive affirmations and attention because I had the ability to flirt and tease. This made me feel wanted, desired, and worth something. I was good at it and the attention affirmed that.

Luckily, I was also smart. Although I alluded to the idea that I would have sex with people, I didn't actually sleep with many. When, in 2020, I came to the realization that I felt the most validation from men through anything related to sex made me sick to my stomach. I felt deep sadness for the version of myself who had believed, for so many years, that was all she was worth. I was heartbroken that I had felt the need to flirt and tease because I didn't think I was good enough without it. I withdrew more.

I became almost hyper vigilant and paranoid, overthinking everything when it came to sex and relationships. Even though Carson and I were not very intimate at that time, I struggled with it. I knew—or at least thought I knew—that my husband loved me, so it wasn't about that. But I also knew he didn't know how to love me (or at least show me) in the way I needed. So, even sex with him felt one-sided because I wasn't receiving love in the way I craved and needed. Sex was not for me.

I also questioned Jack's motives. Luckily, it was COVID, and all travel had stopped. This made it easier to internalize, pull back, and reflect. I wish I could say it was that simple. He would remind me constantly that he loved me more than my husband. I think his charm and affection were laid on even heavier at that point for two reasons. One, because we weren't traveling, and he needed the affirmations of love I gave him. And two, because I had slightly more control over our programs due to job changes. He knew he couldn't manage them without me—he even said as much—so wherever I chose to work, he would have to follow, or he ran the risk of losing them altogether. And with that, he would lose his notoriety.

Ironically, years later, he did manage to convince others that he could handle everything without me. But by then, working with him had become so toxic, and the "others" had so many people involved in the things I had historically managed, that "losing" the programs was more of a relief for me. I knew they could handle it and that the remaining program would live on past me. But by that point, it wasn't worth it anymore—the harassment wasn't worth it.

Anyway, when we finally changed employers, and our travel schedules shifted—forcing us to travel solo—he became jealous of everyone. Over time, within a year, he managed to "encourage" me to leave that company as well to work for the organization where his friends worked, where he had a significant power advantage. Of course, I fell for that too. I always believed he had my best interests at heart. (There was much more to my decision to leave that company, but I don't believe I would have left as soon as I did if not for Jack.)

Throughout this whole time, however, I was still pulling further and further away—emotionally and in terms of my connection with him. (If my honesty is being questioned at all, everything is very well documented in my infamous journals!) Jack became moody and started to pull my “best friend” Emily, into the situation. Meanwhile, the Alex legal situation was still ongoing.

By the fall of 2020, I needed to be done. This did not go over well. From then until mid-2022, it took him this long to realize I was serious, I just kept pulling away. The “deal” we made somehow evaded him, as he never believed I would be the one to end it. We would get into loud and aggressive arguments over the “programs,” but that seemed to be more of a cover for the emotional rollercoaster we were on. The more I pulled away, the harder he pushed. I just couldn’t do it anymore.

In June 2022, Alex was sentenced and I finally found my full voice and inner strength. That day in court, giving my victim impact statement and watching Alex walk away to prison, made so many other things click.

I was so indifferent to Jack and reminded him, again, of our deal, the one that said that when one of us said we were done, we would remain professional colleagues for the sake of our programs. He began setting up meetings within our organization without me, notifying me only as they were starting so that I either couldn’t attend or would be late. And every single person bought it. (This was his good-ole-boys-club organization that he had managed to pull me into.)

But that was just the beginning of his version of "remaining professional colleagues." The fall of 2022, we had a work trip to Nashville to meet and interview one of my favorite and most influential people—advocate and author Sam Quinones. We reserved an Airbnb with two bedrooms and a large common space for taping and interviewing. The night before our flight, however, we stayed at a hotel closer to the airport. In true Jack fashion, we had to go to the bar when we got there. He ordered an IPA; I ordered a small margarita with chips and salsa. When I got up to use the restroom, he ordered me a second margarita—this time, a large one. He also ordered himself a second IPA, but when they "brought the wrong one," he ended up with two more.

This turned into an emotional apology—a monologue about how good of a team we were, how we needed each other, and, more importantly, how all the people dying of overdoses needed us. He reminded me that he had never been loved the way I had loved him. He was so sad because he knew that *someday* I would get divorced, *someday* I would meet someone else, *someday* I would be happy—and he never would. Ever again.

It kept going. He insisted on following me into my room so he could continue to apologize. He *needed* a hug. He *needed* to know I forgave him. He *needed* to make sure I knew that he would always love me and that I was the greatest thing that had ever happened to him.

And then he *needed* to force himself on me. To sexually assault me. To remind me that I was his—just as he had done to Karen so many times.

The next morning, I was sick—literally and figuratively. I was angry. If it weren't for the person who we were going to meet, I wouldn't have gone.

We barely spoke in Nashville unless we had to. I would go to my room and quickly lock the door behind me. He would knock, cry, apologize, and beg. The door stayed locked.

Two weeks later, he approached me at work under his self-proclaimed title of my Medical Director, using words like grooming, manipulation, and victim. (The topic of the conversation was based on a bad decision that I had made, I won't deny that and I have faced all of my consequences. The problem, however, was how it was brought to my attention, and the timing of such.) He, unprofessionally, used all my trigger words—ones only he would know when approaching me. He said he was just trying to look out for me and protect me. (When he took the leadership position of Medical Director six months prior, he had failed to disclose our previous relationship because his supervisor was a friend of his. When he stepped into the role, he also made it clear that he was "in charge"—something he and the organization now deny.)

He, however, managed to be the puppet master of the investigation—an investigation he acknowledged he shouldn't have been a part of. He twisted everything until he got exactly what he wanted: I resigned.

I disclosed everything to the organization—our past relationship, the conflict of interest, the assault—and they disregarded it all.

(Concerning the topic of the investigation, again, I faced my consequences and I became a better person because of it. It is over.)

Did I make a bad professional choice? Yes.

Did I deserve to work in the toxic environment that led me to resign? No.

Did far worse things happen in that organization, even before my indiscretion, and get overlooked for financial reasons? Yes.

Did they do everything they could to silence me and try to ruin my career? Yes.

Does telling the truth still sometimes lead to horrible consequences? Yes, sometimes the truth doesn't win.

Is medicine still a business, first and foremost, with employees and patients reduced to mere numbers? From my experience, yes.

Does gender harassment and discrimination still exist in medicine—especially at the professional level? Yes.

(To cover my bases: I will not take any further action—legal or otherwise—with my knowledge or experiences. I have moved on.)

I have tried and failed to find my voice in that arena. All I can do is control my actions moving forward and hope that, at some point, positive change will come. But society isn't, unfortunately, ready yet. And, much like drug dealers, if you remove one harassing, gender-biased, hypocritical leader, another will take his place.

I have found my healing, my peace, and my forgiveness for them all. I am just sad for the patients who have suffered as a result.

Unfortunately, it isn't just men in leadership. Women, too, often sabotage each other—whether out of fear, self-preservation, or manipulation. Jack informed our grant managers (all women) that I had too much going on in my personal life and he was worried about me—this was even before divorce proceedings started. They approached me, sympathetically offering me respite.

I *needed* a break from Jack, so I took it.

Did I know this was his way of pushing me out of the programs I had worked so hard for? Yes. But I also thought I would be respected by these same managers. That I would have the opportunity for a conversation.

I was wrong.

Once again, he got what he wanted. I resigned from my programs—for my own mental health. And that, in the end, was for the absolute best. I needed to fully remove myself from any situation involving him.

Unfortunately, Emily was part of that latter organization. She chose Jack, too.

I have found my own path, my own voice, my own dreams, my own purpose. For once in my career am not tied to another person. And because of it, I am far more supported by my colleagues and friends.

Some people, however, evade consequences. Some people thrive on hurting others. Some people enjoy all the riches without any strife. Some people put on a great façade—pretending to do the right things for the right reasons when in reality, it's all for the wrong reasons.

These people are not genuine.

I share the title of *Doctor of the Year* with Jack.

The award itself humbles me. But it also makes me deeply uncomfortable.

To me, it represents the people I was too late to save. The sadness and pain of others.

But it also makes me smile when I think of the patients whose lives I was honored to be part of.

The nomination statements make me smile, cry, laugh. They remind me of the genuine, good people in the world.

Sharing that award with Jack, though? That hurts.

I had *29* nominations. Jack had *one*—from Emily.

I will forever have him as part of the best, most humbling, and most rewarding years of my career to date.

Despite my childhood traumas, despite my teenage traumas, Jack was the worst of all of it. He knew my weaknesses. He knew my trauma. He knew my triggers. He knew *everything.*

And he preyed on every single part of it. He is the worst kind of monster. Yes, I chose some of my own self-destruction. I was also a victim of his ways.

Because of Jack, I was silenced. I wasn't believed. I made choices to survive emotionally. I dug my rock bottom. I didn't dig it alone. At the bottom, though, I grew a strength they all tried to silence.

No one should have to be manipulated for someone else's benefit. All I can do is shine a light on the truth. If it helps even one person ask more questions, see the red flags, be less quick to judge, or recognize their own worth, it will have been worth it.

I made bad choices during that time. And I know some people will still judge me for it. But I am human. I am not perfect.

Regardless of my story with Carson, he didn't deserve that. My kids didn't deserve that. My pain and hurt in my marriage do not excuse it.

It has been hard to forgive myself. And it is hard to ask for forgiveness.

I will forever live to earn it back.

Because what *happens next* is what truly matters.

Living better.

Doing better.

Being better.

Jesus did not sit in the palaces of the righteous. He sat with the sinners—the ones society looked down upon.

The ones who repented. And then *did better.*

Chapter 16: Saved by Seven Teenaged Girls

Just two months after my Mississippi nightmare with Alex, seven teenage girls saved me, and they didn't even know it. You see, these seven high school girls came forward together, setting in motion the end of Alex and the beginning of my crumbling into the hardest years of my life. They recognized the grooming that I didn't. They recognized the inappropriate behavior that I didn't. They understood the nature of the monster that I didn't. They ended it, and I didn't.

During the initial investigation leading up to Alex's arrest and the news story on February 6, 2020, they recognized the depth of his manipulation and charm. As the investigation continued, it got so much worse. There were many victims between me (1999) and the seven girls, but I was the first.

The word *first* brings up several sensations—winning, being the best, the head of the pack. But this was a *first* no one would want. This *first* carried shame, guilt, and a sense of stupidity. For goodness' sake, I work with victims of abuse. I teach trauma. And yet, I didn't even recognize my own. I let him hurt others because I didn't see what he was doing.

This *first* also forced me to question everything and brought to light painful patterns. Therapy helped me recognize that I had developed patterns of isolation due to abandonment, that I was starving for love, attention, and a sense of being chosen. That made me the perfect, naïve victim for those all too eager to take advantage of my blinded willingness. And then I had to ask myself: *Can willingness truly be a choice, as many would say?*

These girls saved me. Now, I can recognize the 16-year-old vulnerable me. Now, I can recognize the grooming. I can name the pain and the hurt. I can free myself from that ownership.

For those who don't understand this, I envy you.

I was *in love* with *my Alex* for 20 years because he groomed me to be. He knew how to make me be. He preyed on me, and he did just enough to keep me there—to keep me questioning, to keep me believing that I was special, that I was different. Stockholm Syndrome is real. It creates an emptiness, an isolation, a disconnect from others, and an inability to know, feel, and understand true love and connection.

That was *my Alex*, this *he*, for decades, guided me out of the safety of healthy relationships and into other manipulative ones. Relationships where I would never be valued or respected. Where I would always *need* Alex, and so many other *hes*, in some way. Where my worth was dependent on others.

And now, because of seven strong teenage girls, that would all change.

The process of walking Alex off to prison took two and a half years. Just over halfway through that time, in October of 2021, a judge questioned my relevance to the case of these seven brave, courageous girls. I walked into a courtroom, sat in a witness stand for several hours, and was interrogated and re-victimized over the entirety of my Alex story—with Alex sitting a mere 20 yards away, facing me.

I would love to say that I was strong, brave, resilient, and empowered that day. But that would be a lie.

I was almost those things. I wanted to be those things. But I wasn't. I walked into that courthouse alone but not empowered. I hadn't yet healed from my need to be supported, despite my lifelong façade of doing everything on my own.

My husband chose to know nothing. He was not there that day.

That day, just a week before our 13th wedding anniversary, he only knew that I had met with Alex in August of 2019 (the down by the river meet up, under the guise of the drug talk). He didn't want to know what happened that August. He didn't want to know what happened in 1999. He didn't want to know what happened when Alex got home from deployment. He was too afraid of what I might say—too afraid of being hurt. Too afraid for himself, so I was forgotten.

He didn't understand grooming. He didn't believe in Stockholm Syndrome.

The night before I testified, he said he wanted to be there, but *how*? How could I testify to the details—down to what was on the walls and the very description of everything—with my pretending-to-be-supportive yet oblivious husband sitting there? If he wanted to support me, he would have asked to hear the story in the nearly 2 years since the ball was set in motion.

Honestly, the very idea of it made me feel even more rejected and isolated. He had no clue.

Jack, who *did* know it all, who had told me *I told you so* many times, who claimed to be my hero and savior, who touted how different he was from Alex—he refused to be there, too. *How would that look?* Oh, the optics. What if our affair somehow became known just because he supported me while I testified against my rapist?

Yes, Jack, you were *so* different from Alex.

Oh, Jack—my what, now fourth *he*? I think I lost count.

Anyway, I walked into that courtroom alone and went straight to the bathroom, where I anxiously vomited. Then, I was taken to a holding room, just outside where Alex was being held, so he couldn't see me until I followed him into the courtroom.

Ok well, I guess I *did* have support that day.

Krista, the victim advocate, and the prosecuting attorney were there. Two strangers who, truth be told, were paid to support me. Who needed me for their case. But still—they were there. They said the things that helped.

After vomiting again, this time into a garbage can in the holding room, they had me *confident, strong, and empowered.*

(Okay, that was an Oscar-winning performance.)

Yet still, I wondered—in perfect Stockholm Syndrome fashion—*What if I'm making a mistake? What if I really was/am different? What if, what if, what if...*

So, I made a deal with myself. At some point while on the stand, I would look at Alex. I would *look at him*, and I would *know* if I was different.

After the standard *state and spell your name for the record*, I glanced up.

What I saw was not *my Alex.*

What I saw was the mugshot. The monster by the Mississippi.

The man who had ruined my life by introducing me to this horrible pattern of choosing manipulative men—men who used me for their own benefit, only to discard me when I found my own voice or when they didn't *need* me anymore.

I would love to tell you that the judge sided with me and the prosecution, that he added me to the case of the seven girls.

But he didn't.

Because the seven girls had recognized the grooming and stopped it, my case—being a higher degree of sexual assault—would have to be its own, if it was ever brought forward at all.

My entire motivation for coming forward, the reason I called the police on February 6, 2020, was twofold:

1. To give longevity to the story of the monster that was Alex.
2. To do whatever I could to prevent those girls from having to testify against him, to stop them from having to sit in that stand and be re-victimized.

And now, I felt I had lost that. That I had let them down.

I was devastated.

Until March 2022.

Days before jury selection for Alex's trial, days before those seven courageous girls would have had to testify, I got a call from the prosecutor.

Alex was going to plead guilty to all seven charges. No alterations. And the girls wouldn't have to testify.

Under one condition:

That I, his first victim—nearly 23 years after that day at the pool when I was covered in blood—never charge him with my sexual assault. (The statute of limitations in 1999 would still allow me to charge him.)

Alex *knew* I would agree. He *knew* I would protect those seven young women. And, in doing so, he would get less potential prison time. Alex would win. Alex would have the upper hand. He managed to manipulate me one last time.

But this time, I had a choice.

I chose the girls who saved me.

On June 24, 2022, Alex was sentenced. I still wasn't part of the case, but I would get to meet my heroes.

My husband, the man who supposedly *loved me more than anything*, my for better or for worse.

Notably absent.

When I arrived at the courthouse, Krista approached me and said the judge had given her blessing—I would be allowed to read a victim impact statement.

And so, I did.

6/24/22: Victim Statement (Directly from one of my infamous journals. Ironically a part of my privacy that Carson didn't care to share with the world. I wonder if he even read it.)

I have been very good at separating, at dissociating, at living, in a way, two separate lives. Being here today, hopefully, is my next step in stopping that. For 21 years, I lived the life everyone saw—the student, the doctor, the wife, the mom—while also living as the "love of Alex's life," just waiting for the time to be right. Waiting for the five-year age gap to not matter, waiting through deployments and receiving all the love letters home, waiting through school, then marriages, then kids. We bonded over the less-than-ideal family lives we had and planned for a happily ever after.

Then, one day in August 2019, his lies and manipulation cracked, and my whole life no longer made sense. And yet, I still *loved* him—until I saw the news and learned about seven extremely brave and strong women, all the same age I was when I was groomed into being his victim for so many years. The seven of you saved me, changed me, and have given me the gift of my life back—my whole life back.

Despite this double life of manipulation by a monster, I have succeeded. In my career, I care for patients with substance use disorders, most of whom have traumas like mine or worse. I did this despite the fact that this person used and took advantage of a 16-year-old girl who had just lost her mom—yet I didn't even realize I was a victim, too.

But today, thanks to you seven amazing people, I get to stand here and say it's over.

Mr. Fowler, Alex's attorney, mentioned, *"This isn't the worst sexual predation, so please respect that"*—in reference to what Alex did to the seven girls, because they stopped it before it got worse. Well, by Mr. Fowler's scale—if we're somehow minimizing any type of sexual predation—I was his *worst* sexual predation.

I want to address my background and career as an addiction physician in response to Mr. Fowler's statement concerning PTSD. First of all, my rape predated Alex's deployments and law enforcement career—it predated this PTSD of his that you ask for leniency over. For him to request leniency due to his PTSD shows further manipulation and a complete disregard for others. My whole life has been impacted by this trauma—that is PTSD. These seven young women? PTSD. And all of his other victims in between? There are dozens who live with PTSD and will for many years. Concessions for a monster, in spite of and with disregard for victims, only further victimizes many.

In manipulating this plea deal and silencing my story from being heard publicly, you may have thought you won one last power play over me. But in reality, you are getting what you deserve, and I—and these young women—will live our lives with strength and power.

That judge, this *amazing* human, then did something unprecedented. She left the courtroom after three victim impact statements—mine, the mother of one of the girls, and one of the seven girls herself. We were not allowed to move, Alex included. When she returned, she actually gave Alex *extra* time beyond what was originally presumed, based on our statements. Regardless of what was in her mind when she made that decision, I got to have a voice that day.

Even more importantly, I got to meet most of my seven heroes. We all cheered and cried and then cried some more. We had *won*, but had we, really? We all get to live our lives with this history. As strong as we had become by that point, we still had to *experience* the nightmare. They thanked me, though I still don't quite understand why. *They* saved *me*. They are the heroes.

Later that day, I journaled again:

6/24/22

Well, it's *over*. Everyone keeps asking me if I have closure. *Seriously?* I have closure in my questioning myself, in my truth, in my reality.

When you believe something for 21 years, then spend 2.5 years isolated, embarrassed, and ashamed—you can't just accept the reality of your truth overnight. Honestly, even this morning, I was still questioning his love. *What if I really was different? What if I was special?*

But today did something. It solidified the truth. It helped me *appreciate* my truth—it made it fact instead of doubt. There will still be bad days, but I can start to rethink, to reprocess the last 23.5 years.

It's overwhelming. I am afraid, though. What if I can't get there? What if I always question every move, every statement, every action I make? How will I ever truly be the *real* me versus the person who was created as a victim?

I am so good at *speaking* about it. At *counseling* others in similar situations. But how do you truly get there and just *be*?

I feel like a fraud. A cheap imposter.

It feels so much like the eating disorder—I *know* the how, the why, all the pieces. But the reality of *living* through it? The actuality of healing? I need time. And I *hope* those around me can give me grace and time.

That day, I now see, I did it alone.

The people who claimed to love me and support me just continued to show me I was never worth it. Eventually, I found my strength, and yet at the same time I realized something painful: *even those who claimed to love me were just as bad.*

They all used my pain and vulnerability for their own benefit—each in different ways—but they all, in some way, followed the same pattern. And what they did, in reality, hurts even more than what Alex did.

But I have risen above it.

I'm not sure if, or when, I'll ever be able to fully trust anyone again—not just because of Alex, but because of *them*, too.

But I *hope* so.

I hope, and I have faith, that in all of my self-work, I have gained *enough* self-worth to recognize the good people in my future.

Chapter 17: Worth

Louis Pasteur once wrote, *"Let me tell you the secret that has led me to my goal. My strength lies solely in my tenacity."* This was the first sentence of my personal statement to get into medical school. It also happens to be the word—*tenacity*—that I have tattooed on my body. I chose that statement because probably 45% of me believed it. Maybe not even that much.

People ask me how I survived, and I usually hesitate. Depending on who I'm talking to, I choose my answer very carefully. For the nuns I used to see in the clinic, I would quote the *tenacity* line. They were close enough to God that they could joyfully accept that answer. But when I speak to patients struggling with substance use disorders, I choose something else—something that, if I'm being honest, probably accounts for more than 50% of how I survived: *spite.*

Spite is not an acceptable answer when talking to nuns. I can already imagine their responses—*Oh, sweet child,* or *Please come to mass*—which would have inevitably lead to a conversation about God, forgiveness, and all the things that, at the time, made no sense to me. But spite? Spite makes a lot of sense to a person sitting in an exam room, someone who has been in recovery for maybe a day, maybe a month, maybe a year—someone still working through everything they pushed aside with drugs, and everything the drugs created. When they struggle to find their own purpose, their own reasons, *spite* resonates. And in that, I can completely relate.

Worth.

Such a weird-sounding word if you say it over and over. I'm guessing most people haven't thought about that—let alone fixated on it as much as I have. There are a lot of ways to define worth. We can have *self-worth.* We can have *family worth.* We can have *societal worth.* And there are probably other variations, ones that could fit into these categories or stand on their own. But for now, I'm going to stick with these three.

Let's start with the big one—*self-worth.* It's probably the first thing that comes to mind for most people, including myself, when the word *worth* is brought up. I'm sure Webster's Dictionary has a perfect definition, but for me, self-worth is the value a person believes they bring to situations. More than that, though, I think it's about the confidence in that value—a confidence often marred by shame. Or maybe it's guilt. Differentiating the two is challenging.

Recently, I heard someone describe it well. Guilt is something we feel internally when we violate our own morals, ethics, or core beliefs. Shame, on the other hand, happens when we stay true to our own values but go against what external forces—family, friends, society—expect of us. Shame is that feeling you get when you know you did what was right by your own standards, yet you still disappointed someone else. When you didn't meet their arbitrary expectations, despite the fact that it's none of their business.

Where's the fine line between guilt and shame? It reminds me of the concept of boundaries—specifically, *healthy* boundaries. The problem is, no one really teaches you how to set them. Maybe it's easy for some—those who have always been reserved, moral, ethical, or naturally more of a follower. But for people like me—and, I assume, many others—boundary setting is difficult. We're outgoing. We pursue justice. We stand up for ourselves. We see problems and want to fix them.

I imagine that for many of us Type A personalities or firstborns, we all know them, setting boundaries doesn't come easily.

The real challenge is this: no one teaches you how to come back from having minimal or *grey* boundaries. And when you try to set them, society has a way of placing shame on you for even *trying*.

Both guilt and shame do play a role in self-worth however. But somehow, *society* holds even more power in shaping it.

If someone violates both their own ethical standards and society's, they experience both guilt and shame. But what I find interesting is this—if I don't violate my own morals and ethics, why should I have to carry the shame imposed by *yours*?

A slight tangent: I personally believe that ethics, morals, and values are fluid. They can change. Big T Traumas—especially in certain situations—can blur the lines of morality, ethics, and boundaries. So much so that if a person violates a previously held moral or ethical standard, they *should not* automatically experience guilt or shame. They should experience grace and given a chance to heal and remedy, but that's just me.

I also believe that if someone *doesn't* feel guilty, they shouldn't have to feel shame.

OK, back to *self-worth.*

Yes, guilt and shame play into it. If someone constantly feels guilty, they're probably going to have low self-worth because they're violating their own standards over and over again. But what about someone who isn't guilty—yet carries an overwhelming amount of shame? They'll likely have low self-worth too, not because of their own failings, but because of society's judgment.

Family, friends, and coworkers also influence self-worth. Having people in your world who make you feel safe, protected, and loved creates a stronger foundation. A person who feels these things is far more likely to develop high self-worth.

I believe that no one ever has high self-worth if they don't feel safe or loved.

Now, let's talk about *worth* in another sense. Maybe we should call it *foundational worth*—or the worth assigned by the core group of people who chose to bring you into the world and/or raise you.

Ultimately, it doesn't matter what you call it. Family dynamics are always interesting.

One key factor in evaluating *family worth*—at least in my opinion—is birth order. And to complicate things further, there are blended families. No matter what kind of family you come from, every person in your immediate circle, regardless of how brief their presence may have been, has played a role in shaping your worth.

It's like the Chicago Bulls during the Michael Jordan and Scottie Pippen era. Dennis Rodman's role was primarily defensive. He had worth to his team based on his role.

So, in a family system, should there be assigned roles? And how do those roles—essentially *forced* upon us—impact us in the long run?

How we end up in these roles is another interesting question. Is it determined by birth order? Personality type? Circumstance? Or is there some greater force at play?

I think family worth depends on your arbitrarily defined (or forced upon you) role and, in essence, how good you are at it—or rather, how well you accept it. I would like to roll my eyes at this. Sometimes people *get* the role of peacekeeper. That's a thankless job with a lot of pressure if you think about it. If there's any type of upheaval in the family, the peacekeeper has seemingly no choice but to step in and then inevitably holds guilt or gets shamed—either for not foreseeing the upheaval and preventing it, for not stopping it immediately, or for personally causing it because they hit their breaking point.

The peacekeeper really doesn't *get* to have an opinion or feelings, because then it throws off the balance, and the rest of the family system seems to completely fall apart. Assignment of this role seems to just happen, with no choice at all. That person tends to be the quiet one, the meek one, and they may be the middle child. Okay, I have seen them be the oldest and firstborn, but rarely. My mom was the peacekeeper to the extreme. Case in point: when she died—or, as you saw, when that awful "family conference" to determine her fate happened—everything fell apart. Yes, of course, it is more complex, as most things are, but having witnessed her role for 16 years, it was heartbreaking at times. What is the self-worth of a person who is the peacekeeper? Do they have worth only when everybody is communicating well and there's no turmoil? Does their worth depend on someone actually acknowledging and appreciating them?

There are so many other study-defined family roles that I will not dissect, but if we all think about what our family role might have been—or is—how did we feel valued? What was our role? What did we do for that role? What happened if we didn't want to do that role or if we stepped outside of it for a minute? How did we NEED to feel loved within our family structure based on our role? And how did it impact us if the others didn't know—or care to know—how we needed to feel loved and appreciated?

Next, we have the catch-all bucket of worth: the societal worth—work worth, club or membership worth—but really, it seems to be the catch-all for everything that isn't directly self- or family-unit-based. Much like your role within your family, we seem to all have a role within society. Who decides who is worth more than others in society? Is there even a difference? Or should there even be a difference? But ultimately, who gets to decide it? Shouldn't the person who chooses their role in society get to determine if they feel worth in that role?

What kind of feedback does that person get—or need—to feel worth in society? And the million-dollar question, especially in what I do for a living, is: What happens when your role within the societal structure comes crashing down, regardless of the "why" behind the crash?

There seems to be an interplay between one's role in society—based on their job, occupation, vocation, trade, stay-at-home parenting, or volunteering (we could add to this more by adding race and historical trauma and so many other forms of discrimination, but I'm keeping this very high level)—and their personal relational standing as an outwardly projected version of themselves and their significant other [or their whole nuclear family]. What happens when both crumble? What happens if they crumble due to an outside force or the impact of an outside force's manipulation of the inside force—or both inside forces?

Okay, wow, that was a lot. You may need to read that again—I promise it does make sense!

Does one get to have more pull or say at any given time? And does this change over time, or should, in an ideal world, all be equal? One might ask: Does it even matter? I would argue that the only worth that should matter is self-worth, but I think the rest of the universe feels the need to have way more say over everyone else's life. Society, tends to judge everything about individuals—good or not—so then what happens to one's self-worth when society talks? Why does society get to have a say anyway?

Do we give society a say because it's hard to have and develop self-worth in a world full of judgment and hierarchy? Maybe the interplay between what society says and what we feel inside only highlights the inherent shame and guilt most humans focus on way too much. What if a person followed all their own morals and ideals and therefore had no guilt, but for whatever reason, society placed a lot of shame on them anyway because "they" didn't agree with what the person valued? Honestly, I think the people who place the most shame on others are actually those who feel threatened, are naïve, are hypocritical, or are too afraid to examine their own inner selves—and are, actually, just projecting.

In my opinion, none of it should matter. A person who is truly in one's "inner circle" should respect those boundaries and not cast shame—even if there was some type of negative effect—for grace would, okay, should, be the first response.

Okay, so then why did I start my personal statement with the quote about tenacity when I really didn't have any self-worth or believe my own strength? The easiest answer is that I was probably in a really good mood that day, was very confident in myself, and believed it all. Dang it, I deserved to be in medical school! In that moment, I was able to take all of my traumas and see them as things I had overcome. I was able to look through my compartmentalized lens and see what, perhaps, the average outsider would see. But in reality, I hadn't overcome any of it—I had simply barreled through and buried it all deep inside. What I had actually done was survive.

In writing that personal statement, I equated survival and handling what was in front of me as tenacity. My issue with this is, frankly, that at that point in my life, it just wasn't true. To me, tenacity implies an inner drive for goodness—an inner drive to take what one has been through and use it for the positive sake of others or oneself. To me, tenacity implies healing, growth, acceptance, and self-forgiveness—none of which I had at the time I wrote that statement, in the spring of my junior year in college.

(Okay, yes, I had an inner drive to care for others, but not because I was drawing on my own strength or healing from my past.)

What I had was spite (glad I didn't tattoo that on my body!). I survived it all, so that was enough! I can now say, acknowledge, and take pride in the fact that, years later, yes—I survived it and I can acknowledge my strength. But putting myself back into that 21-year-old's shoes, what I really did was handle, compartmentalize, dissociate, hate, and was driven by revenge. I had a "watch me prove you all wrong" attitude. It all felt like a dare.

I had handled my life, that is true—because I had no choice. So, in my mind, I couldn't have chosen the right path because I had no choice in what led me to that time. I had to prove everyone wrong. That right there is the definition of spite.

My entire place in my completely fake, arbitrary "family" seemed to not matter—I was erased so quickly and easily. Turns out, my place and the family's stability were all dependent on my mom, the peacekeeper. I was seemingly disposable—I was the scapegoat (another official role in a family). I was the easy one to blame so no one had to internally reflect on who they were, what their roles were, what their worth was. No one had to find their own strength while my mom—and her reassuring ways—was dying. They didn't need to find strength because the blame for their lack of strength was all on me.

I was too strong. I handled it too well. I did not have enough emotion due to compartmentalizing and dissociating. I was the easy one to remove—and remove me they did. All but my grandpa and my nine-year-old sister.

So again, fast forward to this personal statement, written five short years after the glue of my family died, when I had zero family worth—how could I have had true tenacity? That might sound like an overgeneralization, but that was how my reality felt to me. Without my grandpa, I likely wouldn't have had any worth whatsoever.

Can I describe "that" spiteful version of myself as having high self-worth? Absolutely not. What I can describe her as is lost and scared—because that Heather had no clue who she was. And as a result, she had very little self-worth.

Chapter 18: Toxic Boats and Treading Water

When thinking about worth, especially self-worth, the concepts of safety and comfort come to mind. If we are to feel safe and comfortable in any relationship or in life, we must first have some understanding and grounding in our own self-worth—or lack thereof.

In the book of Matthew 14, Jesus challenges one of his disciples, Peter, to walk on water. Peter, however, is afraid because—duh—it's a deep sea in the middle of a big storm. I'm not turning this book into a Bible study, but this story resonates with me. Although I've heard it many times, like most people, it's only recently—after my free fall into rock bottom—that I've really thought deeper about it and what it seems to be saying.

The whole idea of the story is to get out of our comfort zone. Several of the disciples, including Peter, were professional fishermen—or whatever that meant back in the day—and, in theory, they shouldn't have been panicking and struggling so much in the middle of a storm. In the story, Peter, while in the boat during the storm, looks off into the ominous distance for a sign, for reflection, or for whatever reason any of us looks off into the distance when we're afraid. He sees Jesus walking on water. At this point, Peter was becoming somewhat of a leader among the disciples. (He was originally named Simon, but Jesus changed his name to Peter, meaning "rock" or "stone.") Many looked to him for guidance.

After Peter saw what seemed like a mirage of Jesus walking on water, he got a bit testy. He had just gone through a personal trauma of his own, and he, too, was questioning why Jesus didn't prevent his sadness and pain if He was who He claimed to be. For some reason, this prompted Peter to test Jesus by asking Him to prove His power by allowing Peter to walk on water as well. Why on earth Peter wanted Jesus to prove Himself in that way is beyond me. I was a swimmer and love the water, but in the middle of a storm, there's no way I'd ask a visual hallucination to help me walk on water—just saying. (To be clear, I'm not claiming Peter was hallucinating, as I don't believe he was, but I personally would think I was hallucinating if this happened to me tomorrow.)

Regardless, in the story, Jesus urges Peter to get out of the boat, essentially taking the challenge. A few things stand out about this moment. First, Peter has to step out of the boat on his own while his lifelong friends and family loudly urge him not to, questioning his sanity. He has to find his own strength to follow his belief and faith in order to make the right choice for him. He needs the self-confidence to do it. Once out of the boat, Peter must believe that he will actually walk on the water rather than drown—the more likely scenario. He has to keep his eyes on Jesus and maintain his faith. The moment he allows fear to take over and looks down, he starts to sink. Despite the worsening fear of the reality—sinking in the deep sea—he must redirect his gaze back to Jesus, refocus, and believe. (All ends well, of course.)

The whole idea and message of this parable is that the boat represents safety—it's Peter's comfort zone. As a professional fisherman, even in the storm, the boat is known and familiar to him. At that moment, he and the disciples are afraid, but the boat still feels safer than walking on the open sea. (Again—duh. Hence, the disciples yelling at him to stay in the boat.) At the same time, Peter is going through emotional turmoil and questioning his faith. The idea of stepping out of his comfort zone, into something unknown and terrifying, and trusting in something he's actively questioning is striking. Why on earth would you do something when your last experience with it was so deeply negative?

Like anything we become proficient or comfortable in, our surroundings and routines become second nature, like muscle memory. They feel safe, regardless of the actual situation. (That boat, in that storm, was filling with water and nearly capsized more than once.) Even when there are slight shifts in "normal," we still feel comfortable in that place. But stepping out of that place—our "boat"—especially into something unknown and terrifying, triggers fear. That fear is essential to survival; it's at the root of our fight-or-flight response. Fear is meant to protect us from harm. Peter's fear of walking on the open sea was legitimate—drowning was a much more realistic outcome than walking on water. In the context of this story, stepping out of the boat, far from shore, in raging water, didn't appear safe—it looked terrifying.

We all have our comfort zones, and leaving them is scary. Trying something new, like skydiving, bungee jumping, or downhill skiing, gives us that anxious, excited fear in our stomach. We know or hope that, in theory, it will be fun. The fear is short-lived, and the experience could end up becoming our new favorite activity. Overcoming fear in those moments requires weighing risks and benefits—especially with safety measures in place. Typically, the benefits outweigh the risks. The same concept applies when encouraging a child to try a new food. We might say something like, "What if this becomes your new favorite?" (Though I still don't understand why my mom made me sit at the table, gagging on Brussels sprouts for hours. There is no way in the universe that Brussels sprouts could actually be someone's favorite food.)

Trying new things is necessary for growth, but it's a continuum—anything but black and white—when it comes to deciding what we should or shouldn't *have* to do. It's especially hard to step out of our comfort zones—our "boat"—when we know it could be dangerous or worse. Think of Martin Luther King Jr. He knew the risks of what he was doing, but without his bravery and belief that things *should* be better, where would we be now? (Even though we are still nowhere near where I can only assume he had hoped we'd be by now.) There is a balance. We won't all go down in history as one of the greatest humans of all time, but we still have to take that first bite—even if it's Brussels sprouts.

These examples are easy to grasp because we've seen their results or are still seeing them unfold. We've all discovered new favorite foods. But what does it mean for us to get out of our "boat" in the big moments—like Peter was challenged to do? How do we know when to trust and have faith in the force (or Jesus hallucination) calling us to step out? And how do we know when to listen to our fears and stay in the boat where we feel safe? In each situation, how do we decide which should "win"—faith or fear?

The *hypothetical* boat in our lives can be the security of a job. I had what I described—and still describe—as the perfect job. I absolutely loved each and every one of my patients, from newborn babies to nuns, from adolescents to Medicare recipients, from pregnant women to those struggling with substance use disorders. I mentored and taught. I had *the* perfect job.

Then, in what would be my last year of that job (overlapping with COVID in 2020), things became toxic. Leadership changes at both the local and national levels turned my dream job into something unrecognizable. My boat hit the storm. It wasn't just COVID—it was a shift in mission. It seemed to go from patient-centered to business-minded (as much of medicine has, unfortunately). Every single day, I threw up in the parking lot before going into work. I was sick all day. *Every. Single. Day.* For more than six months. My perfect, dream job was making me sick. (This was in addition to what was going on with Alex, Jack, and Carson.)

Then, amidst the turmoil, an opportunity arose to transition my addiction practice to a larger health system nearby. It was a complicated shift, but at the time, it seemed like an exciting and positive one.

But how could I leave my patients? How could I leave the known?

I had the perfect job, after all.

An aside: I wasn't the only one struggling in the toxic environment, so the organization brought in people to try to remedy the situation. I had been verbally harassed by my boss, and I had proof that things were being withheld from me to "blackmark" me in a way. I felt like the focus of a witch hunt (later confirmed to be true), but they claimed they were working on a solution to improve the work environment.

Turns out, they completely ignored my concerns and complaints. My "family-like" coworkers chose to protect themselves and their old white male buddies rather than tell the truth, and I looked crazy because of my—albeit very legitimate—accusations. Their supposed attempts at remedying the situation were just a cover; the toxicity was never truly going to end. My strengths and contributions to the organization, the patients, and our community—including the fact that I was Doctor of the Year and had brought in recruits—meant nothing. The health system cared about one thing: making money. And to do that, they needed to be able to control their employees. In big-business medicine, employees who make waves for the actual well-being of patients are nothing more than disposable black flies. Business trumped patient care—as the following years have shown, with the declining quality of healthcare in my community and many community members traveling elsewhere for better care.

I tell this story because, looking back, it connects to the idea of getting out of the boat. It was so obvious what I should have done months sooner, but I was scared. Just three weeks before finally resigning, I went on a wellness retreat to one of the most amazing places on earth—Canyon Ranch in Tucson, Arizona. While there, I met with life coaches and spiritual advisors, had acupuncture, and even had tarot cards read, of all things. But it was hiking in the mountains that gave me more clarity than ever. Looking back, I guess you could say it was my "seeing Jesus walking on water" moment—asking Him, like Peter, if I could walk on water… in the mountains!

After just one day there, I had complete conviction that I was going to resign, get out of that work boat, even though it had been my perfect job. The signs were obvious once I was removed from the situation for even a short time. But when I returned and went back to work that first day—my first in a long time without vomiting—the emotions quickly became mixed. I liken it to the moment when Peter looked down while walking on water, and fear made him sink. I was ready to leave, ready to keep walking on water—but then I saw my patients and I had just gotten the perfect nurse. I looked down. Within two days, all my convictions shattered, and I went back to the boat. It still seemed safer. (Yes, I started vomiting again.) Somehow, I convinced myself that the known—even though toxic—was still less scary and less stressful than getting out of the boat.

When I finally did end up getting out of that boat, I was pushed. It's interesting—and sad—because if I go back and look at my journals from that time, my struggles before and after being pushed were so real. I, however, didn't fully grasp the severity of the storm until I was pushed into the raging sea, left to tread water—because by then, I no longer had faith in walking on it. I stayed, and I got resigned because here's the truth of what happened just two weeks after I returned from Arizona: I walked into a room filled with suits—businesslike old white men (plus one brand-new-to-her-role white woman)—who disregarded all my positives and contributions and told me they no longer needed me in their boat. A boat that was already struggling to find enough providers for our community. But because I wouldn't just sit quietly as patients were mistreated—as I was mistreated by the very people in that room—I was out.

The organization I had planned to transition to, which was nearly a done deal, suddenly changed its treatment of me after hearing about the situation at my "perfect job." And just like that, everyone around me—including my "friends"—disappeared. The business of medicine, I learned the hard way, is actually one large, chaotic, toxic boat—interconnected by the boat lines of golf course handshakes and unspoken agreements among those in power. Competitors in name only, the good ol' boys' club of decades past still thrives.

Although my patients, at that time, were left to drown and tread water along with me, getting pushed out of that boat was exactly what I needed. After my "100 days of hell" treading water, I found a new passion for correctional medicine—something I would never have realized without being thrown overboard. The company I joined was perfection.

(The downfall of that company is not my story to tell, nor do I agree with it no longer being around. I will say only three things:

1. Once again, Jack convinced me to leave at the end of my first year under the guise of "the programs." I was ready to give up the programs, but what Jack really wanted was to keep me at his "beck and call." He knew his fame would lessen if I stayed and he left, so he convinced me that if I stayed, my career would be ruined.

2. If I could have bought that company to save it, I would have. Looking back now, I see that I should have stood up for myself—without Jack—and never should have left. I should have done whatever I could to find financial backers.

3. Again, I won't speak on what happened, but that company was truly a gold standard in county jail healthcare. Our county jails—and the patients in them—are now truly missing out on great care.)

Okay, that really had nothing to do with getting out of the boat, but the point is: I needed to be pushed out of that "perfect job" boat to find a career path that, much like falling into the addiction field, became a huge passion of mine—one I would have never known if I hadn't gotten out of that boat.

I always describe these times—after getting pushed out of the boat—as feeling like I am treading water. Unfortunately, in my case, I didn't have the faith to walk on the water and trust that it was where I needed to be. My faith was non-existent and so I was stuck treading water between the known, yet toxic, boat and the faith-led unknown.

The next example of fighting to stay in a chaotic and toxic boat was the job that followed the correctional company. Ironically, it was with the very company that had heavily recruited me before my resignation—only to later treat me so poorly. Of course, I was manipulated and pulled into that trap by Jack. Looking back, I should have known better. I did know how they had treated me just a year prior, but I was convinced it would be different because *promises* were made.

By that point, my trauma bonds were so ingrained and strong that I didn't—and couldn't—remember my own inner strength and, instead, I followed what sounded like good promises, rather than seeing patterns of actions. I lacked support and encouragement at home, and I didn't have the self-confidence or self-worth to recognize that I didn't need Jack, or anyone else, to live my truth. I hadn't yet done the work to be confidently me. I don't blame anyone for my choices, as I have to own my insecurities, fears, and lack of self-worth, but I also won't take ownership of the manipulation.

While working in that position, an even bigger corporate medical company, I quickly realized that words are just words to get you in the door. I learned there is a hierarchy based on specialty and on who you knew the longest, who was your student, or who was your mentor—nepotism at its finest. There was a brotherhood that protected the "fight club." Everyone knew it existed, but just like in the movie *Fight Club*, as Tyler Durden (played by Brad Pitt) says, "The first rule of Fight Club is you do not talk about Fight Club. The second rule of Fight Club is you do not talk about Fight Club." This behind-closed-doors brotherhood couldn't be exposed in a way that would bring about real change, and none of them would ethically do the right thing for fear of being pushed out of the gang. The Club was too big and engrained and no one was willing to be the person who brought it down. That had to come from within.

At this point, as the Alex situation was coming to an end, my marriage was at the brink of separation, and the Jack situation was reaching the level of sexual assault, I was starting to see what was actually in the boat with me. I no longer saw just the external storm of fear—I started to look around the boat itself. What I saw was even more terrifying than the sea. I saw manipulation, puppeteering, and realized I wasn't safe with any of them.

My response to this realization, however, was anything but appropriate. Rather than looking out onto the sea and having faith that I could stand on my own and walk on water, I leaned on unknown others to get me out of the boat. I still didn't feel strong enough to stand—let alone walk—on my own. This will be further explained shortly.

There are many more examples in my life where I should have gotten out of the boat but needed to be pushed. In a way, my marriage was one of them. Although I personally took the steps to get out of the boat, I can guarantee that if my ex-husband hadn't stolen my journals and strategically shared only parts of them, or hadn't strategically shared only the hard parts of our marriage, never acknowledging my positives, I probably would have gotten back in. Another part of my comfort in the chaos of the boat was that at least there were people there. In other words, being in the boat—even with people who were trying to throw me out and drown me—at least gave me the illusion of belonging. (I would, in all likelihood, have gotten back in for my kids.)

With my years of abandonment—from my dad, to my mom dying, to Nancy and my grandpa passing—not having people is nearly paralyzing. Treading water alone is just that—alone. If I stayed in the boat, even with those trying to push me out, I wasn't alone. And I was really good at managing and handling the chaos, even though part of me knew it wasn't real and that the people in the boat didn't actually value my presence.

This was never more evident than during my divorce. Staying in the boat of my marriage was known chaos. Between us, there was a lot of hurt, pain, miscommunication, and lack of attunement. The things I needed and the ways in which I needed to feel loved were seemingly not understood—and therefore not attempted or given. I was met with the statement, "You knew how I was when you married me."

Yes, that was true. But we were supposed to be in a partnership, growing and evolving together, supporting each other through sickness and health, for better or worse. I was very good at adapting to his life, his family, and his wants and needs. I took care of him when he nearly died several times. Yet, when I needed him—for the Alex situation for example—I had never felt more alone, even in his boat.

I thought that if I threw every shower, helped orchestrate every get-together, and made sure we attended everything for his family, I would be appreciated and loved. However, over time, I felt taken for granted. The effort was not reciprocated. I had a role in the boat, and I needed to accept it.

I was okay with my position in the boat until I finally asked for exactly what I needed and wanted. The moment I found my voice and started to see my value, I was rejected. Rather than continue to push for myself, I simply found my seat at the back of the boat. I chose the boat over everything else.

I knew what to expect in the family and in my house—I knew the boat. I knew date night would never be planned. I knew the weekend away that I requested would never happen. I knew that my accomplishments would never be applauded like those of my sisters-in-law. And yet, I also knew that I would still plan and coordinate things, keep the calendar, and remember all the details.

That was my comfort zone. But *I*, Heather, was lost.

For years, I did it—because it was comfortable and known. I was suffocating in the boat. Or maybe I had only been treading water alongside it the whole time. But I knew that if I got out of the boat—if I let go—I might truly drown.

And when I did finally get out of the boat, as I realized I wasn't modeling strength and worth to my kids—I barely kept my head above water.

Now, out of the boat, it has never been more obvious why I stayed in it for so long. There is no one out here. I don't have a mother's shoulder to cry on or someone to ask for help. My kids don't have nearby grandparents who can come over for supper, take them to the cabin, or go for a walk in the woods. I can't offer them cousins to play with or the big family holidays that I miss so much. The normal is different, but that doesn't make treading water alone any easier while looking back at the boat, the life raft hanging there, unused, because I wasn't worth the effort.

That sense, or illusion, of belonging in the boat made all the red flags with Carson easier to overlook from the very beginning. I felt like I was part of something, and even after getting out of the boat, there are moments when even the illusion of belonging seems better than treading water alone. But in my downfall, amid the chaos of work, Jack, and Alex, Carson threw me out of the boat—not by force, but by failing to see me and by choosing not to be the person he had promised to be. I have chosen to stay out of the boat. His sharing of my journals, a betrayal as equally heinous as mine, has, in some ways, been a gift. It has made any chance of reaching for the boat—or clinging to the illusion of belonging—in my moments of deepest fear while drowning, no longer a possibility. I am finding my strength in the raging sea, in the wake of the boat, where the harshest and biggest waves are.

Now I ask myself, after years of self-reflection, self-care, trauma work, and healing, why did I struggle so much to get out of the boat when it turned out to be exactly what I needed to do—so many times over? The answer is sad but simple: I never trusted myself, my worth, or my why. When I got out of the boat at work, I didn't have a plan—not at that point, at least. There were so many unknowns, and after being in control of everything important for so long, the unknown was just too much. Even though everything was toxic, I knew how to survive in chaos. In reality, there was no comfort in that boat—except the comfort in the chaos, which, to me, was the very definition of safety. The idea of leaving the boat—even for the possibility of something safe—was more terrifying than the familiar chaos I knew. Prior to years of healing and trauma work (a never-ending process, of course), chaos was my safe place. When given the choice, I always stayed in the boat to avoid the pain of being alone. And in the end, all my worst fears—the ones that kept me in the boat for so long—came true. Even worse than I could have imagined.

Leaving the boat of my marriage made me realize, more than ever, my lack of foundation and the absence of a true home. Getting out of the boat—alone, in the middle of the ocean with no land in sight—has been my reality, all while holding four kids above the water as I gasp for breath. I have had to take many swimming lessons in life while treading water. But I know now, without a doubt, that I am a better mom out of the boat.

Like Peter, I had no choice but to discover my faith—to believe and to have hope that as I continue growing into who I am, I will find my own foundation with my kids, showing them that they, too, deserve to be seen, to be loved, and to be safe.

Chapter 19: The Lost Sheep

I have, for all intents and purposes, never been a "religious" person (yes, I know there are several references in this book already). I have questioned religiosity, its meaning, God's meaning, and the hows and whys of it all—both scientifically and spiritually. I have asked, "Why me?" and struggled to make sense of everything.

However, from February 2020—the day I saw *that* news article—I felt as if I had no choice but to revisit all of it. From that moment on, absolutely nothing in my life made sense, and I began questioning everything with even more intentionality and depth. No, the revisiting didn't go well for a long time, and yes, I probably still have more questions than answers, but the process at least deserves an entire chapter.

I am also at a point in my life where I have started to deeply question my purpose. My son's favorite quote is, *"The two most important days in your life: the day you were born and the day you discover why"*—Mark Twain. (To be clear, the exact original author of this quote is widely debated, but Twain is the one most often credited.) This is not to say that I haven't questioned my life's purpose before—many, many times—but during the most pivotal, impactful, traumatizing, hope-inspiring, motivating, and life-changing years, I have reflected more deeply. I'm sure that's when most people do.

Did I wonder if this was just a *midlife crisis*? Well, yes. But transformation can happen at any time, and the timing is irrelevant. The purpose of this chapter is to explore my faith journey and how I have, now, come out the other side—although, again, that statement could be an oxymoron. The word *journey* implies an ongoing process, regardless of the rest stop we find ourselves at in any given moment.

I started doing a Bible study with a friend, and I kept asking *why*—trying to justify my skepticism. Within the first few days, my typed-out "my thoughts" section turned into a phone call. That conversation made me realize that this was not the beginning of my faith journey at all.

As a child, I was *raised* Catholic. We were *holiday Catholics*—the kind who slipped into the pew at 11:55 p.m. on Christmas Eve for midnight Mass, where I would proceed to sleep on my mom's lap. Then we'd hit up Easter as well, cashing in on the egg hunt that surely followed. We didn't regularly attend church, partly because my mom worked in the hospital every other weekend, and when she wasn't working, she admitted she just wanted to sleep in and not *have to do anything*. That was fine with me. We prayed at every meal and at bedtime, but I'm not sure I really *got it*.

When she got sick, however, something changed in me. I felt an urge—a need—to go to church. Not *our* church, though. Instead, I tagged along with a friend and her family to their Lutheran church nearly two towns over. (A fact I still don't understand, considering how many churches we passed on the way, but that's beside the point.) That choice—and that church—changed me for several years.

Everyone in that church seemed engaged, not just with the church itself but with their faith. They had a golf cart to pick up older adults from the assisted living center next door and bring them to Mass. They had a youth group that went on long-weekend canoe trips. They had a true dedication to their community and, even more importantly in my opinion, to the youth and the future of their church. They didn't preach fear of God or focus on rules—they simply *lived* Christian.

Attending with my friend and her family, I joined the youth group and participated as if I had been a member forever. At 16, I enrolled in confirmation classes. I had some catching up to do, but when you're *me*, that was simply a challenge I was more than willing to accept. I remember doing the 24-hour fast and the confirmation retreat. I was hooked.

I hadn't thought about this next part in years—until I was talking to my Bible study friend recently—but after that retreat, my faith changed.

You see, I had wanted to be a doctor my entire life (after my mom convinced me I *wasn't allowed* to be a nurse). But after that retreat, I started having doubts. I even questioned whether I should become a minister. At the confirmation service, we had to stand up and recite statements about what confirmation and faith meant to us. (I *wish* I still had what I wrote.) I was so moved that I cried—something significant because I *never* cried like that back then.

I had found a comfortable and safe place in that church and in my faith. It carried me through so much that year.

I didn't become a minister, obviously, but just remembering now that I *once* had that fleeting thought gives me pause. It makes me reflect.

Aside from the retreat and confirmation declaration in front of the congregation, whenever there were five Sundays in a month, the youth ran the mass. Typically, the message, homily, or sermon was still done by the pastor, as that's a big ask of a teenager (like writing a paper and publicly speaking about what you wrote—oh my). I, on the other hand, loved the idea of this. Over the couple of years I attended that church, I gave several sermons.

Sunday, January 31, 1999, was the fifth Sunday of January and also Super Bowl Sunday. In true Heather fashion, I was not only going to give this sermon during youth service Sunday, but I was going to push every single boundary while doing it. We all wore our favorite team's jerseys (don't hate, but I was proudly wearing #21 of the Dallas Cowboys, Deion Sanders! I was a HUGE Cowboys fan! For those who might question church attire and say it isn't appropriate, I will argue that Jesus doesn't care what you wear to mass, just that you showed up).

My two closest friends in the youth group were quite hesitant when I told them my plan. I started mass with some arbitrarily named run play up the aisle of the church—a mild, "church-appropriate" boundary push. I gave a sermon, but the big bang came at the end of the message—I threw a "touchdown" pass from the altar, all the way down the center aisle of the church, to my friend at the back. I HAD to throw the perfect spiral, as it was a fairly long aisle (at least in my memory), the church was packed, and he HAD to catch it. It would have been very bad if we broke something in church while playing football during mass.

Anyway, the point of the sermon and why he had to catch that ball was simple—it was about faith. Faith in the hard work preparing for the Super Bowl, faith in one's abilities and performance in the game, faith in one's teammates and coaches, and just faith that things would be as they were meant to be. If anything was forced, if anyone tried to stand out as the star, if anything interfered with the process, turmoil would ensue, the ball wouldn't be caught, and so on. Having faith as a player in the Super Bowl was a very simple parallel to having faith in one's own life and situations, like Peter's faith to walk on water.

Sunday, January 31, 1999, in Super Bowl XXXIII (33), the Denver Broncos defeated the Atlanta Falcons. I don't know if this was how it was "supposed to go" based on Vegas odds, nor do I even know the specifics of the game, but what I do know is that in mass that morning, that football was caught, and I nearly changed career paths to become a minister.

This faith of mine, however, would be significantly tested a couple of months later.

The phone call in early 1999, when Mel and my mom talked all night and she, floating on the clouds, told me they were getting married when he returned from Colorado—then, several hours later, when the phone rang again, telling us he had died—just didn't make sense. What? Are you kidding me?

My mom had never looked more despondent, sad, devastated, or ill. The world would never be the same. I knew, in that exact moment when she told me what happened, that she would no longer win this fight against her illness. I wouldn't say she "gave up" because I don't believe she would ever do that, but I just somehow knew that her destiny was not what we all wanted.

Over the next couple of months, her illness worsened and worsened. She did all the things, followed all the recommendations, but she still looked empty. When the time came to make the decision to let her be comfortable or to hope for a miracle, not only did I make the right choice based on the medicine and facts, but a part of me also knew she deserved—needed—to be happy, healthy, and at peace... with Mel.

Although I struggle to understand Heaven and Hell and how that all works, I do firmly believe that my mom and Mel are, and have been, together since April 16, 1999. I knew there was a bigger force at work.

Even knowing that, I still questioned the great faith I had developed over the prior year. I would go to chapel during college when I was feeling stressed out or had a big test, but I wasn't engaged, and I wasn't really believing. My thought was—if there was a God, then why this? Why me? Why did my mom have to go through that? Why did I have to go through that? Why, why, why?

I just did what I needed to do to survive. I had no "choice." All the things that had happened "to me" since my mom died made no sense. It seemed like I could depend on no one else but me—and I was good at it. I continued this very firm stance for a very long time. It is what ended my engagement to Dane, and it is what drove me to stay in chaos.

In medical school, I started to struggle more with anxiety and feeling overwhelmed, so I would attend morning masses and listen to the rosary, somehow managing to find a sense of calm and peace. I wasn't necessarily going because I believed in what was being said, but because it was peaceful and quiet.

Can I reflect now and see that perhaps my soul knew there was more to those moments than just calm and quiet? Yes. But at the time, I really didn't understand or believe. I just kept having more and more questions than answers. I was asking for answers and never getting any. I would ask for miracles, but the opposite would happen.

Things that were good in my life (like Dane) I destroyed—because why would I deserve the good? It was far easier to create even more isolation because I knew how to live that way—again, in my proverbial boat of chaos.

I knew how to need only me. I knew I could depend on me. I was my safety.

Throughout my marriage, this only continued to worsen. I saw so many examples of "strong Christians" who lived anything but— even in the close-knit family I was part of. Righteous people who didn't understand love, comfort, or forgiveness—who lived as "better-thans" rather than givers. I found even less calm, peace, quiet, or comfort, so I questioned everything even more. I rationalized with myself, citing time, work, and babies. Whenever a morsel of an idea of God would surface, I would ask the "prove it" questions, find satisfaction in the fact that no one could answer them, take that as proof that I was right, and move on. As a result, I kept hardening myself more and more against any outside force, idea, or comfort.

I trusted no one except myself. I relied on no one except myself. Whenever I did "try" to let others in, something even worse would happen, which only proved me right—I had just me to depend on. And, darn it, I was so good at it.

All the while, in the very brief and infrequent moments of quiet, I would feel this urge to ask the questions—not just to hear my own self-fulfilling ideas but to actually hear the answers. I wanted reassurance and guidance. I wanted to hear what I should be doing, who I was. I wanted that reassurance from God, the universe, or whatever was out there.

Canyon Ranch was my sanctuary, and I was back where I felt I needed to be. But then, yeah, we all know what happened…

What does that all mean now, though?

I came across the story of "The Good Shepherd and His Sheep"—John 10:1-21—and my faith journey started to make some sense. I feel as if I've spent much of my life jumping over the fence of the pen, led astray by fear. When something bad happened in my world, rather than finding comfort in the pen, in the safety of the Shepherd, I would seek another archaic way out. I would find another rocky wall to climb, another tunnel to burrow through—another treacherous way to navigate back to "me," the only dependable place I thought I had.

I had full confidence in my own ability to handle all the routes alone because, in many situations, I had to. To survive, I had to be strong. I had to be resilient. I had to be smart. I had to be able to handle everything. In a way, though, I got too good at it—to the point that I just knew I could do it all and let go of the very idea of the Shepherd's comfort.

From 1999 to nearly 25 years later, the times I found my way back through the gate became more and more spaced out. Meanwhile, life grew increasingly challenging, stressful, and lonely. The climb—while continuing to stand alone—got steeper. The routes got more treacherous. My arms grew sore. My body became exhausted from always "having to."

Some may say I had a husband and a family who wanted to support me and be there, and, at times, I did feel it. The problem, however, was two-fold though as to why I couldn't just let go and accept, embrace, and release. I was, admittedly, a huge part of the problem. I had so much fear, distrust, and my triggers were quick and many. I didn't advocate for me out of fear of rejection and I really wanted to be normal and not difficult so badly. On the other hand, I didn't feel love the way I needed, I wasn't met with grace or a curiosity to understand, I never felt like the true me, the deep down scared me, was ever encouraged to be known, I never felt safe enough to let her out. Over time, I felt more disconnected and rejected, the very thing I feared anyway, and when I finally tried to voice this all, it went the complete opposite of what I needed and wanted. Escape, therefore, was the only action I had.

Clearly, however, escaping the pen to do life my way was not sustainable. It's exhausting. And lonely. I didn't have faith in anyone or anything but myself.

I now realize that every time I felt that calm in the church or that longing for peace, it was me hearing and listening to my name being called back—I just didn't yet understand. Listening to that voice requires a willingness to hear rather than speak. But, even more importantly, it requires faith—to follow rather than lead oneself.

I now see, believe, and know that in my life, I need to throw that football down the aisle and have faith that it will be caught—and by the right people. I need to have faith that the right people will want to know, understand, comfort, and provide the true unconditional love and safety that I, too, deserve. I've thrown it to the wrong people many times and have made many bad choices as a result.

But, as the Book says, "There will be more joy in heaven over one sinner who repents than over ninety-nine righteous persons who need no repentance."

I now see—and anticipate that I will continue to see—that I am okay. That all my bad choices—and there have been many—have been forgiven because I have repented and continually do the work to better myself each day.

I can "explain away" the whys and hows that led me to what I did poorly in my life. I can give my reasons—my excuses—for the pain I caused, the lies, and the deceit. But I now realize my explanations are unnecessary because everything is already known by the One that matters.

My explanations reflect my fears from the past—my longing for safety and guidance. But where there is fear, there cannot be faith.

My defense against an outside world, so quick to judge and gossip, does not lead to healing or growth. It is not my place to direct or correct the misguided "others" or the half-truths said about me. The outside world's opinions are not the full truth—and they are burdens that are not mine to carry.

Their intent and choices—their beliefs and actions—are not mine to control. I am not the final judge, and their destiny is not mine to guide.

I have acknowledged my part and my role, and I have been forgiven in the way that truly matters. I have apologized to those I have hurt—those willing to listen with grace rather than offense.

(If we're looking at this through the Alcoholics Anonymous lens, as so many of my patients do, I have worked through all of the steps—a never-ending process—but this one being Step 9, which also states that if apologizing to the one you have harmed may result in further harm, it is acceptable to repent to a higher power instead.)

I see now that I have been a lost sheep far more times than I probably even realize. And that's okay.

Because who I am now is a far better version of me than I ever thought possible.

An aside—or perhaps a sign I recently discovered—or, as I see it now, a higher power's message to me: I remembered the year of that Super Bowl Sunday when I threw that football during Mass. What I didn't remember—or even likely knew at the time—was that it was Super Bowl 33. Ironically, my basketball number changed from #21 (Deion Sanders—that was intentional) to #33. I had absolutely no reason for choosing #33, except that I couldn't be #21 in high school.

Now, I have #33 spray-painted on my driveway next to my son's basketball number, and my daughter wears #33 for her sports as well. Little did I know that, all these years later, I would recognize the significance of that number in relation to throwing that football down the aisle—and that my faith journey would rise from the fog.

(P.S. Jesus also died when he was 33 years old. Take from that what you will.)

Chapter 20: Lost At Sea-Part 2

In some ways, I just get madder… Where would I have ended up? Would I have stayed with Brandon for so long? Would I have ended up at Gustavus? What then about Dane, and then medical school, and then Carson, and, and, and... Who and where would I be now if I had accepted the safety and love that Dane offered? Even better, what would life look like if my mom was still here?

As much as these last many years and decades were never easy and never fully safe or secure in love, I, in essence, became me. There are parts of me I can admire and parts of me that have positively impacted so many. So, in the 're-writing' of that time in my mind, I cannot fathom what the me now would be if it didn't all happen the way it did.

The summer after Carson and I separated, I got a phone call. That phone call put into perspective everything that happened after Susan told me she couldn't take Molly and I. Even though Susan had lied to my mom and couldn't take us, even though my reality was that we were completely rejected, there was, I learned, more to the story. My mom's best friends were fighting for us, wanting both Molly and I to not only stay together but to live with one of them. That phone call was a game changer.

As I walked away from the baseball field, trying to comprehend the call for what it was, I felt completely opposing emotions. I felt comfort in hearing that I was actually wanted after my mom died, but I also walked away feeling confused and hurt, pondering the 'what ifs.'

The 23 years before that phone call, I had felt so much abandonment that I couldn't even comprehend, after the call, what it would be like to un-feel and un-experience the world the way I actually did. I cannot look back and tell myself to get over the years of pain and feelings of abandonment just because I now heard that I was wanted. You can't just un-feel the actual experiences out of a new hearing of a reality that never happened.

We cannot take information—even comforting information—and re-write our real-time experiences with their real-time feelings. We cannot take things we learn later and apply them to the past when we didn't know them. And we cannot judge ourselves or others based on this either.

I say this because that's what happens. We get called 'dramatic' or 'extreme,' or we're told we're 'feeling sorry for ourselves' or 'see, it wasn't that bad,' or to 'get over it,' because of information gathered later. It doesn't work like that.

Did I have a momentary sense of peace and warmth? Yes. But it also made me sad for the 16-year-old me who didn't have the privilege of that knowledge at the time.

Several months later, I would have another experience that fit into this category and made me question many things. I found myself standing in my kitchen with my dad and my brother, during my first Thanksgiving separated from Carson.

My dad and I had just reconnected, bonding over my divorce of all things, after he was 'banned' for roughly eight years by Carson for not being 'appropriate' or a 'good example' for our kids.

I wish I could remember how that conversation started so I could put the whole moment into perspective, but I can't. Somehow, though, we started talking about my emancipation at 16—from this very dad standing in my kitchen with me.

Here's my very vivid memory of that day... emancipation day.

My grandpa told almost-17-year-old me that we had to go to court — the fall of 1999, after my mom died — so that my mom's life insurance money wouldn't be 'stolen' by my dad. He was convinced that my dad, who my mom had left on the policy as the executor in the event that I inherited it as a minor, would take the money and run.

I had seen him all of one day — my mom's funeral — since he disappeared when I was 11. And my grandpa was my world, so I went along with it, never questioning it.

(The very fact that my mom left him on the policy made me wonder later, though, if she really was okay with it. I mean, she got so many other things in order — I just cannot imagine she didn't think of this. But, regardless.)

I was quite removed from everything financial and logistical after my mom died, outside of the normal bills, so I really had no idea what was happening on that front.

The night before court, my [paternal] aunt — whom I now lived with — told me that I needed to ask the judge if I could be emancipated when I was inevitably asked if I had anything to say.

Honestly, I didn't even know what emancipation was. I told her I didn't think it was necessary since my grandpa said court was a formality and that the lawyers and judge had it all situated. Not to mention... can you imagine doing that in front of your dad?

She said I needed to do it anyway.

The next day, I walked into my second courtroom— the first being when my mom and Molly's dad got married in front of the justice of the peace. This was so different. Did it really need to be an actual, directly-from-the-TV courtroom to discuss one life insurance policy?! My grandpa, "my" lawyer (whom I met all of five minutes prior), and I sat on the plaintiff's side, while my dad sat on the defense side. So awkward.

I had no idea what was being said back and forth. It all happened super-fast. Like I said, was this even necessary? My mind was too distracted by the beige and brown and all the wood. I was doing everything I could to avoid looking across the aisle at my dad. I didn't want to look to my left at the stuffy old lawyer, nor did I want to look to my right at my grandpa. Even the idea of asking to be emancipated felt like a betrayal—not to my dad, that was just awkward—but to my grandpa, since he didn't even know I knew what emancipation was. This was going to blindside him. No, it didn't directly impact him, but my grandpa, like me, likes to be in the full know.

So, I sat there, alternating between staring down at the table and the reality TV-style microphone in front of me and looking straight ahead. The judge was slightly to my left, but the interrogation chair was directly in front of me.

The entire time the life insurance policy was being discussed—a policy I didn't even know existed until days before—I was imagining how many people had sat in that witness box, with their hand on a Bible, swearing to tell the truth, the whole truth, and nothing but the truth... and then still lied. My mind went down quite the rabbit hole that day.

Anyway, they eventually got to the end, and the judge looked at me and asked, "Heather, is there anything you'd like to say?"

I kind of shook my head and, in very un-Heather fashion, looked down, all pensive, and quietly said, "No."

The judge raised an eyebrow and said, "Are you suuuuure?"

I turned and first caught sight of my grandpa, who looked confused. The lawyer looked irritated, like I was wasting his time and he just wanted this to be over. Then I turned all the way around and looked at my aunt, who was sitting right behind me. She nodded and softly said, “You need to do it.”

Okay, for real, my first thought at that moment was whether or not the judge was going to yell at me or shout “Order!” or some other legalese thing since I turned around to "the gallery." I mean, come on, isn’t that what happens in the movies?!

Anyway, I turned back around, took a deep breath, leaned into the microphone, made eye contact with the judge—essentially pleading with him to read my mind—and whispered, “I want to be emancipated.”

Needless to say, the judge got quite the smile on his face, either because he actually heard what I said or because he *did* read my mind. Unfortunately, the court reporter (who has to type out every word spoken in the courtroom) and likely everyone else in the room didn’t hear me.

The judge said, “What was that?”

I felt the biggest knot in my chest as that wonderful wave of anxiety ran through me, top to bottom and back. I probably rolled my eyes in a "You've got to be kidding me, you're making me say that again?" kind of teenaged girl way. I took another deep breath, sat up a bit straighter in my chair, pulled the microphone even closer, and thought, Well, damn, if I have to say it, I may as well own it.

So now, in true Heather fashion, I very precisely annunciated, on the louder end of necessity, "I WANT TO BE EMANCIPATED."

The judge grinned even bigger, took a breath (for dramatic effect, I think), and, casually—like he was sitting in a beach chair—leaned back in his seat, raised the gavel, and said, "DONE."

Wait... what? That was it? I was so confused.

I turned around and looked at my aunt, who smiled and said, "See? Good work."

Then, in slow motion, I turned to my grandpa, who, for some reason, looked a bit shocked and taken aback—likely because I hadn't talked to him about this beforehand, which wasn't like me since becoming orphaned.

While I was giving him this wordless, facial-expression apology, desperately seeking his approval and acceptance, "my lawyer" mumbled a bunch of things along the lines of: What are you doing? We didn't talk about this. How dare you. Who do you think you are? Etc. etc.

Though, honestly, I'm not sure exactly what he said because, frankly, the tone just screamed, *You stupid little girl.*

And that's when, with the reassurance from the judge and the newfound confidence in myself, I did what I thought was right.

I looked at him and said, "You're fired."

And just like that, in my mind, I became an adult.

I'm not exactly sure when that "adulting" moment happened—when I yelled into the microphone, when the judge said "done," or when I fired my lawyer—but it doesn't matter. I became even more *me* that day.

Fast forward nearly 24 years later...

I was sitting at the kitchen counter with my dad that Thanksgiving when my emancipation somehow got brought up.

And that's when my entire perspective changed.

What I didn't know before that stressful day in court was that, for weeks leading up to that court date, my grandpa had been meeting with his (my) lawyer several times, discussing the life insurance policy.

They had even met with the judge privately to discuss everything—a meeting where, apparently, my dad was supposed to be invited as the current executor.

Except... someone forgot to notify him.

Yet, by whatever forces, my dad found out and showed up, unexpectedly, to everyone else.

According to my dad, the judge rightfully (from a legal perspective) asked him what he thought—since he was, after all, my remaining parent.

And this is what my dad told me, over Thanksgiving weekend, decades later (and I'm sure these weren't his **exact** words):

"Well, the way I see it, Heather has been taking care of her dying mom, raising her sister, getting straight A's, managing all her sports, and whatever else she's gotten herself into this past year... so really, I have no reason but to allow her to be emancipated."

Apparently, this was a huge shock to everyone—my grandpa included.

It seems my grandpa had perhaps wanted some kind of guardianship so he would have control... while my dad would be "out."

But instead, my dad's words took away everyone's power... and essentially gave it to me.

This news eventually got back to my aunt and uncle, which is why she told me to ask for emancipation that day.

For some reason, though... she never told me that she already knew my dad had signed off.

Hearing this information all those years later, I felt happy, mad, uncomfortable, confused, played, stupid, and so much more. Why on Earth did they ALL put me through that day in 1999? Did they not consider the psychological trauma this would, or at least could, have on me—having to sit in a courtroom, nonetheless in front of my dad, who I had worshiped for SO MANY YEARS, only for him to disappear off the face of the planet?

Although he had, once again, abandoned me at age 11 and wasn't seen or heard from again until just a few months prior—at my mom's funeral—he had been my hero and everything to me. He was high on that pedestal, and despite how I 'should have' felt about him and the abandonment, anyone who knows anything about psychology, especially regarding the not-yet-developed frontal lobe of a teenage brain, would understand that seeing him again would instantly bring me back to that place. It forced me to grapple with the tug-of-war between hero and villain, a theme that would continue to weave its way throughout my life.

The very act of putting me through that—especially when the decision had essentially already been made—set me up for a pattern of attachment and trust issues that would last for decades.

The other source of anger comes from the so-called 'well-intended' reason behind their choice. Apparently, making me do that in the courtroom that day was a 'test' of sorts. The judge, in his well-intentioned, old white male, likely not-trained-in-psychology mind (especially in 1999- a time not versed in trauma informed anything), felt that if I was truly ready to be emancipated, I needed to 'prove' myself. How backwards is that? Especially since I wasn't even aware this was happening until the night before, when my aunt broke the news.

Perhaps the judge didn't really want to grant the emancipation and knew I wouldn't be familiar with the concept. Maybe this was his way of easing his conscience. I don't actually believe that, though, given the way he kept repeating, "Are you sure you have nothing to say?" But still, it was a possibility.

So, instead, let's flip that narrative. What if, in that courtroom, they had all—since they (the judge, the lawyers, my dad, and my grandpa) already knew this was the most likely outcome—just granted the emancipation without forcing me to say anything?

(Although, maybe that wasn't the outcome my grandpa and 'my' lawyer actually wanted. I guess I'll never know.)

To me, looking back now, with 24 years of hindsight, I truly feel that I would have gained more empowerment and self-confidence if they had just done that. Instead, I lived over two decades with a mixture of guilt and uncertainty—some pride in my 'ballsy' nature for even asking the judge (with gratitude for my aunt)—but the negative far outweighs the positive.

It also led me to believe that my dad simply didn't want me.

Why didn't he fight against me that day? Why didn't he argue for me, proclaiming his love and his desire to keep me?

Well... because he was proud of me. He acknowledged my intelligence, my maturity, and my responsibility. He was actually giving me my own voice. It just didn't look, feel, or seem that way in that courtroom that day—because all of those affirmations were said behind closed doors, among four men.

Yes, I was given that voice. But at what cost?

Two major events from my adolescence, following my mom's death in less than a year, had profound impacts on my life and who I am today.

What if they had realized I was only 16, that I had just lost my mom, and—unbeknownst to them—had just been raped and was in a physically and mentally abusive relationship? What if they had set aside their "we know best" egos and actually thought through the long-term effects that year had on me?

What if they had done the right thing—by showing me love and affection directly, by including me in these life-changing conversations, by allowing me to hear those affirmations with my own ears?

Where would I be now?

Would I have spent my whole life searching for some holy grail of belonging?

Or would I have simply known that my remaining, although-absent, parent—the god-like figure that was my dad—actually believed in me and trusted me? That he didn't just want nothing to do with me. That he was, in fact, honoring all the strength I had already shown.

Chapter 21: To Eat or to Run

My name is Heather, and I have an eating disorder.

These words were difficult to think, feel, or hear. It was even harder to be told exactly what I had. I had considered myself a bulimic for most of my adult life—except during pregnancy or breastfeeding. On September 20, 2022, the first day of treatment for this very disorder, I was told I was also, and primarily, anorexic. A flood of emotions surged through me—overwhelmed, scared, anxious, mad, irritated, defensive, relieved, and so much more. But sitting in a stark, clinical exam room, staring at a tall, thin, beautiful woman more than a decade younger than me, I felt stuck. Trapped. I had to follow all the rules and do everything right, or else I would fail this trial—my one chance at treatment on my terms. Every other facility I had contacted had insisted on inpatient treatment, but I had been granted this single opportunity. And now, I was being given a diagnosis I didn't fully agree with—at least, not at first.

By that point, I had been battling my eating disorder for two-thirds of my life. When exactly it began is debatable. Much like my first experience with abandonment, the timing wasn't black and white. I would say it started when I began college, but every eating disorder specialist would argue it started long before that. A few red flags in my childhood stood out—one being my grandmother's comments about my swimsuits and my love handles.

I have vivid memories of being as young as eight years old, wearing a two-piece swimsuit, and hearing my grandmother tell me that since I was "bigger," I had to be careful because the bottoms of a two-piece made my love handles more noticeable. I disliked one-piece swimsuits, believing they emphasized my lower stomach. She reassured me that "all women carry more fat there to protect their babies someday, so it's better to see that than love handles." Even now, every time I put on a swimsuit, those words echo in my mind.

When I discovered online shopping, it felt like a blessing—I could order a bunch of swimsuits, try them on in private, and return the ones that didn't work. The humiliation of trying on swimsuits was then reserved for moments of personal strength, without the overhead glare of fluorescent lighting. I could choose to try them on first thing in the morning, on "good" days, when I woke up feeling less disgusted by what I saw in the mirror.

At eight years old, my solution was the trendy, in-style (thankfully) two-piece swimsuits with side attachments. While my mid-back, mid-abdomen, and upper stomach were exposed, my love handles were hidden. And since the bottoms started just below the stomach cutout, I felt that the "fat to protect my future babies" was less obvious.

When I began competitive dance around age ten, we were weighed weekly. To this day, I have no idea why that was ever a thing. I understand needing costume measurements for proper sizing—I actually handle that for our figure skating club—but making preteen and teenage girls stand on a scale in front of their peers? That was never going to end well for most of us.

To make matters worse, I was always moved up a level—not because of my stellar dance skills, but because I was tall. In those preteen years, I was placed in older age groups simply because I towered over the girls my age. So not only was I already considered a “chubbier” and “bigger” girl (as if "big" meant only tall), but I was also thrown into a room full of teenagers—many of whom had already gone through puberty.

I’m sorry, but the stereotypical 16-year-old dancer’s body looks *very* different from that of an awkward, prepubescent, chubby 11-year-old.

Then, in high school, Brandon would make off-handed comments, like telling me I shouldn’t wear jean shorts with a T-shirt because it made me look too big. I still struggle with this wardrobe choice. My legs have always been way too long, and I have nearly no calf muscles, so when I wear shorts, my legs sometimes look like toothpicks. Unfortunately, I also have very broad shoulders and somehow lack a narrow waist (picture linebacker rather than hourglass), so when I put on a T-shirt that isn’t fitted—because, obviously, a fitted shirt would show the rolls—it creates a very Frankenstein-rectangle shape on top of toothpicks.

Another conundrum from those days involved the lack of pant sizes for females with long legs. If I wanted to wear jeans, I had to wear men’s jeans because they came in different waist x length sizes. At the time, there was no such thing as short, regular, or long for women, and definitely no waist x length options. Needless to say, I hardly ever wore jeans! I lived in leggings before athleisure was even a thing—leggings often paired with baggy shirts. Looking back, I have no idea how I ever managed to get dressed! That is, until the store *Tall Girl* opened at the Mall of America.

Walking into that store for the first time, somewhere around age 15, already nearly 5'9" and standing next to my 5'2" mom, I was in heaven. I finally felt like I had clothes that actually fit me!

I was always tall, and I was always bigger than most, but I was never "fat" if you look at pictures. Even I can admit that now. But at the time, I was just "big." So why do I say my struggles really started in college, when there are so many instances from my childhood and teenage years, like the ones above—even years where I used diet pills or laxatives?

Well, after my mom died, which coincided with Alex and then me moving in with my aunt and uncle, I began to isolate. I would retreat to my room with one of my cousins, where we would play Nintendo and mindlessly eat Schwann's ice cream. I'm pretty sure I lived on ice cream.

Everything in my mind changed, however, when I first saw a photo from my senior prom and then another from my graduation party. Yes, I had taken diet pills at times. Yes, I had tried to induce vomiting when I had overeaten (I attempted it about three different times in high school, but I physically cannot make myself puke—thank goodness, because who knows how my eating disorder would have progressed if I could have, especially in high school). And yes, I was never comfortable in my skin.

But I personally didn't think I had an eating disorder. I thought I just had body dysmorphia and significant insecurities.

When I first compared my junior and senior prom pictures, I was shocked—I was very obviously bigger my senior year. That realization led to more diet pills, but I still don't think the eating disorder brain changes had fully taken hold yet. Much like with people who have substance use disorders, I don't think my addiction switch had quite flipped all the way on. (*Side note: Both eating disorders and substance use disorders affect the same areas of the brain and alter brain chemistry in eerily similar ways.*)

Seeing my graduation picture a few months after prom, however, changed everything. That was 2001, at the beginning of college. Upon seeing that photo, I realized that somewhere in the previous couple of years, I had gained about 40 pounds. So rather than just using diet pills, I did what I thought everyone did when trying to lose weight—I started counting calories and exercising more.

The phrase *exercising more* is misleading. In high school, I was always active, participating in swimming, basketball, track, powerlifting, and dance. So when I say I exercised more, I mean it became something very different in college. I did track in college (okay, I was a thrower, so take the image of endless track workouts out of your mind), but that alone wasn't enough to make up for the lack of organized sports or the need to now lose weight. So, in my true *I'll do one better* fashion, I didn't just count calories and exercise more—I made sure the number of calories I consumed in a day matched the number I burned, according to the cumulative time I spent on the treadmill.

I exercised before classes, between classes, and after classes—pretty much whenever I could. I did nearly all of my studying in college while running or walking on a treadmill. Y'all, I can even read the fine print in *People* magazine while running on a treadmill—that's how much time I spent training myself to run and read at the same time. I also ate the same meal for supper every single night for roughly two years, eliminating choice as that could lead to a spiral. I even tried, once again, to make myself vomit like a *true* bulimic, but no matter what I did, I just couldn't make myself puke.

Then I met Dane. Since he was an offensive lineman, I automatically looked smaller standing next to him. My weight stabilized after losing the Freshman 30. My exercise routine eased up a bit, and I no longer had binge nights of ice cream. I was happy. My stress naturally lessened, and my need for coping and escaping from life nearly disappeared. The safety and acceptance in our relationship were unmatched—I hadn't felt anything like that in almost ever.

What didn't go away, though, was my acute awareness of what I was eating, how I looked compared to my friends, and the sugar or carb content of my food (or whatever the latest diet fad dictated). For roughly two years, my weight was stable. I was safe, loved, accepted, and embraced—Dane just loved me.

When I started medical school, as you know, I couldn't handle the persistent fear of the *non-chaos* and ended my fairytale with Dane. And when I met Carson my weight became an issue again. Carson is my height and very much *not* an offensive lineman. Suddenly, I looked huge again in pictures. His eating habits were also very different from mine, and I became self-conscious fast.

I managed to covertly continue my treadmill obsession, studying for medical school while exercising. Carson was either completely oblivious or, rather, encouraging—missing the extreme obsession and the motive behind it. My weight fluctuated within a ten-pound range, which I was always painfully aware of. My brother-in-law's dated small, skinny girls, adding even more pressure to myself.

Comments would be made by them—or Carson—often as afterthoughts or casual remarks, about how brother-in-law *X* wouldn't date girl *Y* because she was *too big* (even though she was quite average) or how they only ever dated super athletes or tiny girls. I felt emotionally smaller and more insecure, all while feeling physically bigger and more out of place.

Throughout all this time, much like in early college, I did everything but vomit. I took diet pills. I used laxatives. I exercised to the extreme. I would be *good* until I wasn't. *Bad* looked like a very large, stress-induced binge—an entire large pizza *plus or minus* a pint of ice cream, *plus or minus* so much popcorn, *plus or minus* sugary candy, *plus or minus* so many other things.

The frequency of 'bad' fluctuated. At the beginning of our relationship, up until I got pregnant with our oldest (a span of about three years), I felt like I constantly had to prove that I was good enough in all ways. Binges would occur weekly or more often, worsened by comments or feelings of inadequacy. These binges (always after about 4 p.m.) would lead to guilt, which would lead to more time on the treadmill or more time spent researching a 'better' diet pill. And thus, the cycle continued.

I didn't share any of this with Carson, which, in hindsight, I probably should have. He was always just so healthy, proud, confident, and, to so many, perfect. I felt ashamed and not good enough. I honestly believed that he would look at me like I was insane and that it would become an even bigger issue. I thought I'd be seen as weak and not worth the time. I feared rejection.

When we started residency, I was pregnant. In one month of my pregnancy I gained eight pounds. The day of that appointment, when I got home, I stood on the front step, crying hysterically over the weight gain. His response was to tell me to just not eat so much. I'm sure he meant nothing by it, but in a mind with an eating disorder, that comment never left me.

Throughout all my pregnancies, I had a goal: I would not weigh more than I did at my high school graduation, nor would I weigh more than Carson at any point. That was incredibly stressful (and, honestly, not something I had full control over). I still had binges during pregnancy and continued to exercise—though neither excessively—but I never took pills or laxatives. It helped that I was in residency and didn't have as much time, but the anxiety was always there, and, without me realizing it, it was only building and worsening.

I actually met with a dietitian once. Of course, I minimized what was actually going on and instead asked for advice on just small parts of a much bigger issue. The plan of action, based on what I shared, was to try to prevent a binge. This meant keeping cinnamon red-hot gobstoppers on my desk—so that even if I chewed through the whole thing quickly (not hard to do), my mouth would be burning, making nothing else taste good. The problem was that, in a binge, you only taste the first bite, so clearly, this didn't work.

The next solution was caramel apple suckers. Since they couldn't be chewed through quickly because of the caramel, they slowed down a binge. But that frustration only made me want to binge more by the time the sucker was gone. My underlying insecurities, self-doubt, lack of self-worth, anxiety, and whatever else my eating disorder brain was trying to escape from were not satisfied—if anything, they only worsened. It was much like how a person with substance use disorder turns to substances to escape emotional and physical pain. (Notice I said their brains are trying to escape, not the person themselves.) These 'solutions' were Band-Aids trying to cover a geyser.

Once we moved to Carson's hometown after residency, I made a bet with myself that I was going to be done. It became harder to hide my binges after getting married and having kids, especially since we always ate supper together. I was hyper-aware of my kids watching my eating habits, so I would always eat what they were eating. That created so much internal turmoil because I either didn't want to eat at all—feeling like I had been "bad" all day—or I wanted to binge everything but couldn't. So this move started a new motivation to be done. But, like nearly every person with an eating disorder, substance use disorder, or one of the many other brain diseases that lead to repetitive, maladaptive coping mechanisms, that bet lasted approximately half a day.

Again, the brain chemistry changes in a person with an eating disorder are the exact same as in a person with a substance use disorder. Both have the same risk factors. Both are amazing coping mechanisms—until they kill you. The problem is that, unlike a substance use disorder, with an eating disorder, you still have to eat. For a bit after the move, I tried to just be *good* and *control* my eating disorder and not *let* it get *too bad.*

I found an amazing group of running friends in our new town. I was building a positive, supportive community. In theory, this should have minimized the space my eating disorder took up in my life. At first, it did. I did 'well.' I was 'good.' Three days a week, we met at 5:10 a.m. and ran four miles. That was reasonable and healthy. However, I quickly realized I could get in even more miles—increase my purge—and no one would think much of it because four miles wasn't that many.

I started parking a mile away from our meeting spot at 5 a.m., running the mile to meet them, running the four miles with them, then running the mile back to my car—logging six miles three times a week. They thought I was crazy, but no one thought much of it.

But then, three times a week wasn't enough.

For a while, I added spin classes two other days a week. Again, no one thought much of it since several of them also did that class. The biggest difference was our motivation for being there.

(Okay, on extra crazy days—days when I had binged or was feeling extra anything—I would run to spin class, do spin class, then run home. That added just under seven miles of running to the spin days.)

And then when all the traveling with Jack started, running became about getting faster—because that was always his goal. He had a similar body dysmorphia. Historically, he only ever ran with one person—a friend of his—and, according to what he told me (though I have no idea if it was true), never his wife.

Again, I was special.

He would push me on these runs—but in a very 'loving' way—and I did get faster, only perpetuating all of this unhealthy behavior. I started to feel a rush of excitement for these secret runs with him (since I was to tell no one we ran together).

After having my oldest son, I started signing up for races. That gave me another excuse to run more. I got obsessed with training programs—researching them, analyzing them—and followed them like law.

Initially, I didn't care much about speed or time—it was just about the running. (Please note, during pregnancies, all of this slowed down, as my priority was always my baby. Pregnancy somehow managed to pause my eating disorder.)

But as I started to get faster and train with Jack, the training intensified. The races became an obsession.

(These habits all began after my last child was born.)

Binges happened whenever no one would notice, but the anxiety was always there, only intensifying over time. I hid snacks at work and binged in the afternoons or while driving, but then I would compensate by running. Sometimes, even six miles wasn't enough. If necessary, I would wake up at 3 a.m. to start my run, trying to balance whatever I had eaten the day before. There were days when I ran more than ten miles—all before 6 a.m.

Food was always an obsession, but my habits evolved. After I finished breastfeeding my youngest, I found a "manageable" food plan. Breakfast would be coffee with creamer, or if I was feeling daring, a latte. In my mind, the latte totally counted as a meal because of the milk. (According to my eating disorder treatment dietitian, it doesn't.) I just simply wouldn't eat in the mornings outside of my coffee. I realized that as soon as I ate for the first time in the day, I couldn't stop, and a binge would start. Lunch was a major trigger because it was usually my first meal of the day, but the longer I could delay eating that even, the better.

Intellectually, I knew my brain was starving and that the binges were my body's way of trying to get enough calories, but my eating disorder—much like addiction—was more powerful. The prefrontal cortex, the brain's executive function center, becomes altered in eating disorders, just as it does with substance addiction. The problem with this pattern was that a binge meant uninhibited eating—usually of food with no nutritional value, just a quick sugar fix. It didn't stop when I should have been full. My brain was so starved that it craved the fastest, easiest fuel: sugar. The intake became so intense that my normal fullness cues shut off completely. Not only did a binge consist of high-sugar, high-calorie foods with little to no nutritional value, but it also meant eating in excessive quantities.

The binge, however, did something else. It numbed my anxiety, insecurities, and pain (and so much more) because my brain had been so focused on starvation that, when it finally received food, it released a surge of dopamine—the same "feel-good" hormone released when substances are used. That dopamine surge brought happiness and relief, reinforcing the cycle. My brain remembered that moment and wanted to chase it again and again because, in that moment, there was no pain.

The problem was twofold. First, the binge felt like an out-of-body experience, where I had no awareness of what was happening. Second, the dopamine surge was short-lived. What followed was shame, guilt, embarrassment, anger, frustration, self-hatred, hopelessness—every painful emotion I had tried to escape came back tenfold. No matter how many times I told myself I wouldn't binge or be "bad," it just happened.

Delayed eating was different for me. Also known as restrictive eating, it felt like another form of purging. It was what earned me the label of anorexia. (Yes, you can have both anorexia and bulimia at the same time—a difficult concept to grasp.) Instead of purging, like I did with my morning runs, I simply avoided food, eliminating the need to purge. At least, that's how I rationalized it. Restricting made me feel in control of my "problem."

There are many theories about restrictive eating and anorexia. One common belief is that control over food—or the lack of it—acts as a coping mechanism for feeling powerless in other areas of life. If you had asked me between 2018 and 2022, I would have said that concept didn't apply to me at all. I had always lived in chaos, and by now, you know I'm good at functioning within it. The lack-of-control theory just didn't resonate. To me, restricting wasn't about controlling my life—it was about controlling my bulimia. I believed I was managing it because I could restrict my intake for so long. Of course, in reality, this didn't stop my binges or purging. But it gave me the illusion of control over my bulimia, which was enough to keep me hooked.

All of it consumed me. I thought about food and eating all the time.

That all started to change in October 2021. I signed up for a marathon last minute and without training—because that's what I did when I thought I needed to run more. I ran it with a girl I had gone to high school with. We had reconnected not long before, and on a whim, we decided to run together.

During the race, the topic of eating disorders came up—triggered by a conversation about tattoos, of all things. I had no idea she had gone through treatment herself. Her eating disorder, her trauma, and the life stress that had led to it eerily paralleled mine. I wished we had been closer friends back in high school. Regardless, during that run, she encouraged me to get help.

Eight months later—after Alex's sentencing, after I had finally ended things with Jack following two years of trying, and after reaching a point in my marriage where I questioned whether I could ever forgive Carson for not being there for me through it all—I finally realized I was worth it. I called and did an intake assessment at a well-known eating disorder treatment facility, the same one my high school friend had attended.

They immediately recommended inpatient treatment and refused to budge, even when I asked for a physician to review my case. I called another facility. Same response: inpatient. (The irony of my reluctance isn't lost on me, given that I'm an addiction physician. I have a newfound appreciation and empathy for my patients who take that brave step.) The third facility I called agreed to give me a chance with outpatient treatment.

So, on September 20, 2022—after roughly 22 years of actively having and hiding my eating disorder(s)—I started treatment.

It took a long time for me to realize just how sick I was. A couple of months into treatment, I started experiencing odd symptoms. More lab work confirmed I had refeeding syndrome. This condition isn't common, especially in outpatient settings. It typically occurs in people who are severely malnourished and have restricted everything. It happens because, after prolonged malnutrition, the body overreacts when it finally receives proper nutrients—sometimes dangerously so.

Thankfully, my heart echo and bone density scans were normal and my labs quickly improved with a few short-term supplements, and I didn't need hospitalization. My case was mild overall, but that moment was defining. That's when I realized how truly glad I was that I had chosen treatment, and myself.

The other thing about eating disorder treatment is that it lasts forever—because you still need to eat! My treatment team is amazing, and we have easily identified all of my triggers. Emotional stress is by far my biggest trigger.

This is not, again, unlike people with substance use disorders.

The problem with triggers, one must understand at the brain level, is that they are where the chemicals start to react. When we are triggered, the prefrontal cortex—the part responsible for higher-level thinking—*shuts off*, and the memory of the relief from the dopamine surge caused by the binge, purge, or substance use takes center stage. There isn't a choice, as many believe. Just as a person with substance use disorder doesn't choose to use a drug that can kill them, I didn't choose to nutritionally harm my body. My brain chose a behavior that would eliminate the pain in the fastest, most guaranteed way.

(Journaling the pain occasionally worked for me, but look at how that turned out. Talking to a support system can work for some, but I just didn't have that. For many, these so-called "healthy coping mechanisms" failed over and over and even worsened the pain—thus leading to the damaging coping mechanisms in the first place.)

Treatment has to essentially rewire the brain, a process that takes a lot of time, especially considering factors like the length and severity of the disease, the level of support (or, in my case initially, the lack of it), and many other elements. The brain's purpose is survival, and survival means avoiding pain, even if that avoidance is maladaptive. Learning how to cope is the answer—easier said than done—and for me, scheduled eating was the first step. I had to give up control and simply listen to and believe what they told me regarding my restrictive eating.

(Over time, I realized that those four years when I was restricting and thought I had control of my life, I actually had no control at all. Those four years paralleled my traumatic years with Jack. My brain, so manipulated and then malnourished, was in panic mode.)

I had to completely surrender control and just follow instructions which did, at first, actually create more anxiety.

I wish I could say that I can simply listen to my body, eat when I am hungry, and stop when I am full. However, one major problem I have after so many years of disordered eating is that I have no idea what it feels like to be hungry or full. My concept of fullness, after a binge, is feeling like I'm about to explode. This is well beyond a normal satiety cue of 7-8 on a fullness scale—it's more like a 20. It is difficult to practice mindfulness when I can't listen to or trust my own body to tell me when I'm hungry or full.

Over time, however, my body did start to adjust. Now, I occasionally experience hunger cues, though for me, this looks like extreme nausea. I say "occasionally" because now, I typically recognize when I'm about to be hungry and can trust myself to eat an appropriate amount. Fullness, for me now, is a strange aversion to food—where I can have just a bite or two of my favorite dish or dessert left and suddenly find it as appealing as a pile of manure.

Part of retraining my body included not being able to run, to purge. (Thankfully, I broke my ankle in two places right before I started treatment!) Since exercise was my primary means of purging, it was essentially forbidden. I had to train my body to be okay just existing—without compensating. Now that I'm in recovery, I can exercise again, but only as long as I remain very mindful of my motives.

I've learned several major things during this treatment process—some of which brought embarrassment and shame—because what I'm told in treatment is exactly what I tell my patients. (I have, however, gained some awesome new analogies and metaphors!) My treatment has also helped me in my addiction practice, as I now have a deeper understanding. While I don't know what it feels like to be on psychoactive substances, I know what anxiety, cravings, and triggers feel like. I know what it's like to question my own self-sabotaging behavior. I know the shame. I know the hopelessness of trying to will it to stop and *failing*. I know how maddening it is when people just tell you to stop.

Most days, I think about food at what I would consider appropriate times. In the past, no matter what I was doing, food was always on my mind—it was debilitating.

To circle back to the concept of control, especially with restrictive eating, I find it interesting because I've always been good at managing chaos. But maybe that was the problem—everything was chaos. It took starting treatment to learn how to calm the chaos, and as a result, my eating disorder symptoms gradually subsided.

I didn't realize that during those four years of restricting, I actually had no control over anything. And when I tried to have control, life only seemed to get worse and worse.

The timing of my decision to start treatment, at times, felt like it couldn't have been worse—because my first year in treatment was, by far, the hardest and lowest point of my life.

As opposed to the control aspect of anorexia, my bulimia—both binging and purging—was always my main and, for the most part, accepted stress- and pain-relieving coping mechanism (along with journaling). Once I started treatment, all of my coping mechanisms were taken from me. (Okay, the journaling part was taken from me by Carson, but you get the point.) I had no choice but to find new and healthier coping mechanisms at the hardest time in my life.

However, especially now, I can look at it differently. Maybe the timing couldn't have been better—because had it not been for treatment, I'm not sure I would have survived that year.

Treatment is much more than learning how to eat, exercise, and live healthily in terms of nourishment. It's about self-worth and valuing the whole self—body, mind, and spirit.

Chapter 22: Attunement... or Not

Attunement is a concept that I believe is key to every relationship—or rather, every healthy, sustainable, and safe relationship. This concept was beyond my comprehension until after I made many bad relationship decisions—okay, many **awful** life decisions—and acted in ways I am quite ashamed of. It took **time, several rock bottoms**, a **very, very good therapist**, and, in a way, writing this book to finally **understand** why attunement is the cornerstone for true connection, healing, and love.

So, what is attunement? Simply stated, it is the quality of being in tune with something—particularly, a person. This is often demonstrated through a mother's intuition with her baby. (I'm using "mother" because that is what I am and what is often depicted in this context. However, I fully believe this applies to any **parenting figure or caregiver** as well.) Each cry a baby makes is understood by the mother, almost like its own language. Yes, others can learn that language, but the mother **feels** it—sometimes even before the cry leaves the baby's mouth—as if there's a subtle shift in the atmosphere.

Attunement is when your husband walks into the bathroom in the morning while you're getting ready, and with one look, you can describe exactly how he feels. I could take one look at Carson and just know if he had a headache, where in his head the pain was, how it felt, how severe it was on a scale of one to ten, and whether he had other symptoms. I just **knew**.

Attunement is walking into the kitchen and immediately sensing which of your kids needs a hug, which one needs space, and which one you can joke with in that moment. And, wow—what a concept—**respecting** that. All the while understanding that it can change in a matter of seconds. I'm not saying you should **always** avoid engaging with the child who's giving off that "don't talk to me" vibe, but what I am saying is that by being attuned, you have a baseline. You can act, respond, and anticipate accordingly.

For instance, my oldest son is the easiest for me (and actually his siblings) to read. I can walk into the kitchen **ten minutes** after he wakes up—a time when **nothing could have possibly gone wrong yet**—and without any interaction with his siblings, he's already giving off that **"leave me alone, I need to eat, I'm not awake yet, don't touch me, don't talk to me, and if you try, my tone will not be great"** vibe.

It's not that I won't say "good morning" (to which he may respond or may just give me a look, or maybe nothing at all). But that's **not** the morning I'm going to walk up and hug him or playfully tease him about something. There are mornings when those things are welcomed, and I act accordingly.

If I ignore the vibe my child is giving off, I end up looking like I'm trying to create conflict or that I simply don't care about his emotional state. The teenager will then react—almost guaranteed—in a **not-so-okay** manner (i.e., with attitude or disrespect). This sets everyone's day off on a negative note—all because the parent couldn't simply **respect** the child.

Whose fault would that be then? Some might say it's the teenager's because of the disrespect and attitude that resulted. I would challenge that. I believe the **unattuned parent** is just as responsible, if not solely, for the reaction. No, I don't condone or tolerate disrespect. But what if the parent had been attuned enough to **recognize** it wasn't the right moment? The disrespect likely wouldn't have happened at all.

What I'm saying is this: as parents, we need to **understand** our children. Setting them up for an emotional explosion is simply not okay. (And again, yes, there are times when playful teasing is also okay.)

Attunement, in part, is simply the ability to **"read the room."** (Ironically, what the above said teenager would say.)

The better question, perhaps, is **why** attunement is so important—especially for someone like me. Someone who, essentially, has lived her entire life lacking true attachment and struggling with significant abandonment issues.

Here's a typical "me" scenario to help explain: I say something to you, my amazing "love of my life." My communication isn't clear enough, and you miss my point, doing or saying something that feels like the complete opposite of what I was trying to express. This leaves me feeling alone, unheard, and unworthy. My response? I put up a wall, get distant, or become outright mean. The end.

Yes, this sounds irrational, but from my perspective, this is what that scenario feels like: I ask you or tell you something (which, by the way, is a very new concept for me—asking for help. Even this kind of communication feels super vulnerable to me, meaning the stakes are high). I'm indicating that I need you to be there for me or help me with something. I've even gotten better at actually saying exactly what I need and want because, after many decades, I've learned that people cannot read my mind. And honestly, it's not fair for me to expect that. (Although, truthfully, I still feel like they **should** just know—because that would be 1000% perfect attunement. But apparently, that's not reality.)

Anyway, when you don't follow through or even acknowledge what I asked for, especially when I've stated it clearly, I once again feel completely abandoned and unworthy of the effort it would take to hear me and follow through. The feeling of abandonment is this deep, boiling, acidic ache in my chest that makes me nauseous. I can't breathe. It's almost like a panic attack, except it can last for hours.

My brain—the trauma part—takes over. The logical, rational side of my brain temporarily shuts down. The trauma brain tells me, once again, that I was right to believe I'm not loved, that I can't be loved, and that I'm disposable. I opened myself up to the concept of love and togetherness, and it failed. Or rather, **I** failed. Again.

My fight/flight/freeze brain then reminds me of everything I've survived—alone. So why even bother anymore? Because that feeling in my chest is unbearable. At this point, my trauma brain completely shuts down. I freeze all emotions.

On the outside, I look stone cold and capable—because I've had to handle everything alone for so long. But on the inside, I'm suffering, drowning, and feel like I'm trapped in a stark white room with no doors or windows. A vault slowly filling with water that I've been treading for years and years.

And that sensation—that endless treading of water—is the worst part. Because I am so **tired** of treading water alone. When these moments happen in close succession, I feel so emotionally and physically exhausted that I'm barely keeping my head above water, doing slow bobs, gasping for air.

That's what it feels like on the inside.

But how I present to the world looks more like this: I just handle whatever it was I asked for help with. You'll probably get ghosted or receive short, one-word responses. You'll be confused as to why my mood shifted so suddenly—because you won't yet know that you "completely let me down." (And yes, I fully admit, this can seem and be dramatic.)

I'll be mad and hurt that you don't even **realize** you let me down, which only deepens my sense of emotional abandonment and increases my frustration and anger toward you. The more you ask what's wrong, the more isolated I feel, and the deeper I sink. Until eventually, I explode—probably through a super long text message or a fast, snappy in-person "telling" of how I'm feeling, why I'm feeling it, and how, "See? You don't really love me."

(The freeze turns into flight—handling it alone—which then turns into fight.)

And from here, one of three things typically happens:

1. I've now triggered **you** with my response. You get defensive, and all hell breaks loose. We're both now defending ourselves, likely saying hurtful things in the process, until one of us walks out, goes silent, or completely shuts down.
2. You call me crazy and selfish. You might say, "See? Nothing is ever good enough for you. You only focus on the little things and miss all the things I do right. Nothing will ever make you happy."

And honestly, you wouldn't be wrong. I know I can be frustrating. But this response? It's the **worst**. Because it only validates the things I already believe about myself: that I'm not worth the effort, that I'm too difficult, that I'm disposable and unlovable. It doubles the feeling of abandonment.

3. The third (and rarest) outcome is this: You stay. You understand what I'm doing because you understand my

trauma and my fight/flight response. And you just hold me. (This is what I so much desire.)

This, at first, won't go well either, because my trauma brain will question the sincerity. (Especially because the people who were supposed to love me the most—my "foundation people"—lied about this too.)

But if you truly know me and have taken the time to understand all of this, my walls will eventually come down. And over time, responses #1 and #2 won't happen... at least not as often.

Now, to those who might say I'm just making excuses, looking for attention, or feeling sorry for myself...

Well, frankly, I'm sorry for **you**.

I'm sorry you've never had to build resiliency. I'm jealous that you never had to survive trauma. You should focus on being grateful that you never had to go through what I've been through. And with that in mind, you should withhold judgment—because you have no idea what this feels like. Yes, abandonment may sound like a strong word for a small-ish seeming situation, but to a traumatized brain, even the smallest things trigger the deeper traumas.

The caveat to all of this is that I **am** constantly improving and evolving. Getting out of the chaotic "known boats" was just the first step. Owning my mistakes and accepting my consequences with grace has allowed me to heal and forgive myself.

Healing from trauma is hard. But I've fully committed to doing the hard work. My triggers are lessening as the grace I extend to others grows, and as my faith leads me.

I'm not making excuses.

When this pattern of emotional neglect persisted in my marriage for years, I eventually shut down completely.

When I truly needed my person for the big things—and was rejected and left to handle them alone—I responded in a way I deeply regret.

It was only then, in that moment of complete emotional abandonment, that I found (or, more accurately, was groomed into believing I found) what I thought was love elsewhere.

Which, as you know, turned out to be the worst decision and the most awful "he" in my predictable pattern.

This was not the right response. It's one I'll regret forever. It's also one I've learned more from than almost anything else.

I firmly believe that one cannot have deep attunement with someone who has been through trauma unless they, too, have experienced some form of trauma. (This is my personal opinion, based on my own experience, and not a scientifically proven phenomenon. I will add that the person has to actually recognize that they went through trauma though.) That is where I have gone wrong so many times.

I've seen these ideals — what I've dreamed of — these 'perfect' loving families. I saw what I wanted and played the part, hoping that I, too, would feel that sense of belonging. The problem, however, is that I lost myself in the process. My needs, fears, desires, and emotions were buried so deep — in an effort to protect the 'other' from me — that I disappeared.

That is only sustainable for so long.

Like with my ex-husband, who wasn't in tune with me, I was living in an illusion of belonging. I don't blame him completely. It wasn't his fault that I tried to 'fake it until I made it,' while burying all of me out of fear that if he — and his family — truly saw me, they would reject me.

Except for my sister-in-law, none of them tried to understand when my world crumbled and I really needed people. But even her care and acceptance backfired in a major way, once again reminding me why trusting anyone was not a good thing.

I needed to first accept and love myself — through my trauma, despite my trauma — and find my own worth. Only then would I be able to recognize who was truly worth trusting.

Why attunement is so important is because, to truly attach and connect with someone, you must have that attunement. You must feel known and understood. That sense of being 'known' creates safety, and where there is no safety, true intimate vulnerability, and attachment, cannot exist.

Then there's atonement — the act of apologizing, amending, or seeking forgiveness. This, too, when it comes to matters of safety, trust, and love, requires attunement.

To atone for anything, one must first have attunement. Otherwise, the very act of repentance has no meaning or depth. How can someone truly atone for something if they do not understand the emotional state and traumatic impact of their actions?

And herein lies the word **capacity**.

This has become one of my favorite concepts as I've worked through my trauma and healing. It gave me the perspective I so desperately needed to find forgiveness — so that I could heal, more on that in a couple chapters.

It is not fair to expect someone to understand what they do not have the capacity to grasp. It is not fair to expect someone to have attunement when they lack the capacity — whether due to ignorance, selfishness, unresolved trauma, or simply their current life circumstances.

Some lack the capacity because they have no concept of trauma, resilience, or healing. They have no foundation from which to draw.

In my quest to create the ‘perfect’ family, I failed to recognize this lack of capacity for attunement. Or, rather, I **did** recognize it — many times — but I believed that if I was ‘good enough,’ or ‘perfect enough,’ or if I did enough and revolved my life around him enough, I could somehow **will away** my own need for the very attachment and attunement I was so desperately seeking.

Do I think he intentionally chose not to have attunement?

In some ways, yes. He told me, more than once, that I needed to accept that he wasn’t going to show me love in the way I needed. But do I also believe that, for whatever reason — whether nature, nurture, or both — the concept of attunement was something he was never going to develop?

Yes. (I hope, for my kids’ sake, that I’m wrong.)

I do seek forgiveness — for not being fully me from day one. For not having my own voice from the very beginning. For not giving him the chance to reject me from day one.

All of one’s trauma is worthy of attunement, understanding, and grace. But we must first recognize, and then attach to, someone who has the **capacity** to embrace and honor the beauty in the strength and resiliency of survival.

Chapter 23: "You've Got a Friend in Me"

Friendship is such an important concept, regardless of who you are. It's well documented that humans are social creatures who do not thrive in isolation; in fact, prolonged isolation can even shorten lifespans. Typically, most people have the benefit of 'foundation' people—families, whether by birth, adoption, or some other definition. But what happens when that foundation is absent?

I won't get into the 'in-law' variety of family because, as I've at least alluded to, no matter how perfect or welcoming they may be, their ultimate allegiance—rightfully so—will almost always be to their kin, not to you. This means you can never be fully and completely vulnerable with them, though I tried to be.

As you've already read, my 'foundation' people were nearly nonexistent after my mom died. Even during the last year of her life, my foundation lacked emotional connection. One could—and should—argue that a teenager should not have been responsible for all that I was in any way. I shouldn't have had to be my own foundation. So, my 'people' tend to die, or I tend to choose the wrong ones.

Many people, especially in this generation, consider their friends to be their family. They celebrate "Friendsgiving" and say cliché things like "friends are the family you choose." But what I've learned the hard way is that a chosen family can lead to even more abandonment issues than biological family—because they are chosen. In theory, they *should* be *better*.

The way I see it, friendships evolve, and it's no one's fault. Careers and schooling take people to different places, and when marriage and kids come into the picture, things shift even more. As children grow, our lives begin to revolve around them—whether that's right or wrong. Our friends become the people we sit next to week after week at a field, court, or school event. Long-term friendships can be hard to maintain, especially if you didn't grow up in a small town and stay there forever—or if you live far away.

And then, when you get married and have no choice but to move to that small-town, middle-of-nowhere place your husband is from, you become the outsider. There's essentially no chance of truly belonging as yourself because you're always just part of a couple, or you're "Carson's wife." And when you divorce the hometown son of a doctor—also a doctor—the isolation, loss, and gossip become nearly unbearable.

I have an amazing friend from high school. She and I have been through so much together, and I know without a doubt that she would show up for me no matter what. But it's difficult when you live hours away, and she—bless her—has a community and a neighborhood family that is wonderful. Miranda is a true friend, and I will forever be grateful for her and her family. Still, as happens, our friendship evolved due to all these factors. And so, while we can seemingly pick up right where we left off, she doesn't fully understand the nuances of daily life that become the big issues—and nor do I of hers.

Then there was college—I had the absolute best group of friends. As I've said before, my time in college was amazing. But then, of course, life happens. One friend moved to Maui, another to Nebraska, another to the Cities, and I moved three hours in one direction for medical school and then a state and a half away for residency. Suddenly, seven years passed. We each had kids. Maintaining friendships wasn't impossible, but it was hard. After residency—or grad school or whatever career path—we all found ourselves in different stages of life, which, at that time, felt like a massive gap. This is something I've been working to correct, thanks to my near soul sister from college, Bobee, who has always 'gotten me.'

Bobee and I are eerily similar in our pasts, but the difference is that she truly doesn't care what others think—she just does Bobee. I, on the other hand, have always lived in the need to prove myself, driven by my insecurities and my fear of not belonging. I can rationalize that this is because she married her high school sweetheart and always had her mother—who still is present and amazing. That makes a difference. I was so close to having that fairytale with Dane. I was right there. But, as his chapter lays out, I destroyed it beyond belief. Bobee, however, is constant. What separated us ended up being an ocean as she followed her childhood dream of moving to Maui. When my life began to spiral, however, it was she who managed to reappear, seemingly out of nowhere, and re-solidify herself as the one who just knows what I need to hear, as blunt as that may be.

I had a couple of great med school friends, but I was in the early stages of a very tumultuous new relationship with Carson, which took a lot of time and energy. I made all the effort with him—I always went to him, planned everything to make him happy, and prioritized his needs.

Those friendships, too, eventually scattered, as residency tends to create distance and leaves no time for anything outside of work. Medicine is difficult in that way—surviving on no sleep makes maintaining friendships outside of who you're sitting next to for daily lectures or rounding with on any given rotation nearly impossible.

Then came residency—Kim and Ellie. Honestly, the three of us were unstoppable, and man, we were so good at it! Kim, being from the area, had a whole circle of long-term friends nearby, but Ellie—an outsider like me (though her husband was from the area, but as a pilot, he wasn't home much)—and I had each other. As much as I really didn't want to move to Sioux Falls, I wish I had never left.

All those amazing friendships are with people I cherish and trust. The problem is, they are not here, in the town where I am neither wanted nor accepted. They aren't a quick after-work happy hour or a spontaneous coffee meet-up away. Although they can't physically be here, I cannot minimize the support they have given me.

What hurts the most in my quest to have that spur-of-the-moment friend group is that I almost had it—no, I actually thought I did have it. Welcome to small-town middle-of-nowhere, population ~9,000—hometown of my ex-husband, the son of a doctor in town, now a new doctor in town, with three younger, stud-athlete brothers (and he wasn't too shabby himself). I had impossibly big shoes to fill—or rather, I had to step up my 'acting' game. When I moved there, I had to prove to the town that I was good enough. That I was good enough to be Carson's wife, that I was good enough to be a doctor, that I was good enough to live in this town as an outsider. Even going out to eat, there were always eyes on me. But again, I was so good—always the wife who went to all the things, whether for brother-in-laws or fundraisers in town.

My husband had his small-town friends—a couple of whom still lived there. I had the girls I ran with, although many were at a very different stage of life than I was. I tried to get involved with parenting groups, but that was challenging since I wasn't a stay-at-home mom. Many of the other moms were from the town or had husbands who were, so even when I was invited to things (a big "if"), the sense of belonging was always missing. It has always felt like I'm just on the periphery—an afterthought on the invite list, if invited at all—or that, if I wanted to be involved, I had to plan it myself.

Yes, to an extent, this is dramatic. Maybe I *could have* or *should have* been less sensitive to it all. But unless you've been the outsider in a small town, you have no idea how awful it can get—especially when you divorce that "perfect doctor," and your journals are taken out of context and shared with everyone, and people believe every rumor as if it were the gospel truth.

That said, I did manage to find the *best* friends ever. One friend, Emily, joined our clinic, and she was the most amazing friend. She had her own traumas, so she "got it." She had made many bad choices in her past—and present—but she was, seemingly, a ride-or-die friend who never judged. I even went out on a limb for her a couple of times, helping her get and keep jobs.

That is, until she, too, decided to choose selfishness—or maybe self-betterment or self-preservation. Or perhaps it was because her truths caught up to her (that whole "misery loves company" thing). Maybe she was never actually a friend to begin with, just someone who took advantage of the situation. Regardless, when your *best friend* makes the exact same mistake as you, knows the real truths of everything, and still decides to throw you under the bus and cut you out of their life without any acknowledgment, it hurts.

My ride-or-die became the one who flipped the execution switch on me—more than once. She destroyed me and never looked back. And then, just when I could start to breathe again, she partnered with Jack to make it all even worse. This level of direct malice and rejection—from my chosen family—brought a new depth of distrust and isolation.

Emily shared the "bestie" role with my now ex-sister-in-law, Jennifer. We kept each other grounded and sane. We traveled together. We ran together. She knew my truths, and I knew hers—the good, the bad, and the ugly. She had supported me and stood by me, and I her. But the second I mentioned divorce, I became the common target. Our friendship was rejected.

Do I understand it? Yes. But there was no softening of the blow, no support, no check-ins.

These *best friends* of mine took my confidences, in some ways twisting them or exaggerating them, and showed their true colors and lack of integrity. Trusting people with anything will never be the same, if possible, at all. Did I, or our friendship, ever mean anything? Did they forget that I, too, know things about them? And yet, it didn't, and hasn't mattered. I won't say anything, nor will I try to defend myself against their betrayal, it wouldn't matter anyway.

I do have a couple of friends in this town. And while we don't have that deep, forever friendship, I know growth takes time. My ability to trust—through no fault of theirs—is nearly nonexistent. Lisa, however, was there through the worst four years of my life, and she didn't leave. Her son is like a son to me, and mine to her, and she brings a feeling of safety.

The most reassuring thing, though, has been that since my secrets and privacy were violated and shared via my journals, she and her husband haven't bought into the one-sided narrative. They understand there are always two sides. I haven't been judged for the things I've taken ownership of. It was so reassuring when she said, "It is so great to see you so happy. I never saw you like this when you were with Carson."

(Note: To avoid things being, once again, taken out of context—she was by NO MEANS saying she doesn't like Carson. On the contrary, she was acknowledging that we both seem to be better apart.)

There are—and already have been—others who have emerged, seemingly out of the blue, as true and genuine people. I am cautious. I overshare much less. I listen more. But I also know and believe that there are real, sincere people in this life. I have found an angel of a friend in BreeAnn. They say if we stop forcing and, instead, listen and have faith, God will provide. She sees the good in people—including, surprisingly, me. She does the little things and understands my isolation, both physically and emotionally.

After doing so much personal work and healing, I feel that I am in a much better place to be a friend as well, and as a result, I think I am attracting better friends. I don't need or want a sorority-sized group of friends; rather, I want a couple of genuine people to share experiences with and enjoy the small things life has to offer.

Ultimately, the point of this chapter is to emphasize the need for community, connection, understanding, meeting people where they are, and loyalty. Feeling like a disposable scapegoat does not feel great, and I hope that those reading this—whether I know you or not—keep that in mind.

I cannot even look back and pinpoint the red flags or the things I missed, nor do I want to. I invested. I trusted. And now, I question, I overanalyze, and—if I don't center myself—I can get paranoid.

However, because of my healing and my ongoing faith work, I must trust and believe in the good in people. Friendship is a special type of community—our chosen family—and, as such, can bring, and take away, the feelings of safety, comfort, security, and inclusion.

We never truly know someone's experience, and it is important to remember that there are always at least two sides to every story and situation. We are all imperfect humans on the journey of life and, as such, deserve a chance at forgiveness, grace, and respect.

Chapter 24: Forgiveness

I was challenged to do an exercise on forgiveness. Forgiveness has always been a difficult topic for me because I never understood how forgiving someone could free the forgiver—that it could be for the one who forgives, rather than for the one who caused the offense. I understand that holding onto pain and resentment isn't healing and only leads to more pain and resentment, but I struggled to see how forgiving someone who didn't believe they had done anything wrong was supposed to help me.

Then I realized that I cannot control another person's actions or thoughts—especially someone with a personality disorder—but I can control my own. Such a simple concept, one we teach preschoolers, yet even as adults, it's so much easier said than done. That shift in perspective changed how I saw forgiveness. I realized there were several reasons why I had been hurt by another's actions, and by reframing my perspective, I have been able to forgive. I've been able to open up space for happiness and joy where previously, pain and resentment had occupied.

Many times, we are hurt by inadvertent actions or behaviors. These are usually easier to forgive because they are unintentional, often easily understood, and typically met with an immediate apology.

Then there are the hurts that stem from a lack of something. This "lack-of-something" hurt might include a husband who repeatedly refuses to provide emotional support—even when asked—or a friend who forgets to invite you or involve you. These are not direct hurtful actions but, rather, a failure to act. These types of hurt can be tricky, as the lack of awareness surrounding the inaction can be a barrier.

Then there are direct hurtful actions—things that feel intentionally malicious. A sibling pushes you down, a spouse violates your trust, or a friend betrays you. These wounds cut deep because they feel deliberate. Even when apologies are given, they may lack sincerity—or at least feel insincere. In these cases, true forgiveness often requires the offender to demonstrate meaningful change, not just offer words.

So how, then, does one forgive, rebuild trust, and move forward—especially when an offender does not apologize? This is where *capacity* comes back into the conversation.

Capacity is crucial to understand—especially in situations involving "lack-of-something" hurts. If a partner lacks the capacity to understand the deeper meaning of these hurts, they may never get there. The hurt partner will either have to change themself or continue to feel disrespected. But can people build capacity? If someone truly cares and is committed, they can do the work to gain insight and grow in their capacity. But I also think there are people who will—or may—never have the capacity needed for another.

Curiosity—asking "why" and "how"—helps build insight and, in turn, capacity, but only if it's done with an open mind rather than a defensive stance. However, at one extreme, people with narcissism cannot build capacity beyond the superficial. They cannot—or perhaps actively choose not to, or both—see things from another person's perspective. What's even more frustrating is that some do have at least *some* insight in recognizing another's perspective, but they either cannot or refuse to translate that understanding into action.

They are the ones who will never understand the deeper meaning behind the "lack-of-something" hurts. Any hurts in a relationship caused by someone with narcissistic traits likely can never be fully reconciled or apologized for—because the very capacity needed for repentance is missing. They don't have the ability to recognize why they should take ownership of an insult, action, or failure to act.

This lack of realization doesn't make one forget the hurt caused—it simply shifts the burden of responsibility. It allows the person who was hurt to stop taking ownership of the offending action. Over time, a victim of someone who lacks capacity often ends up gaslighting themselves—constantly adjusting, changing, or molding themselves to fit the other person because they have been conditioned to do so. (They also often defend the other person's lack of capacity and their harmful behaviors in an attempt to keep the peace, rationalize for the benefit of the offender, and keep up appearances when not behind closed doors.)

A clear example of this happened with Carson and me when we discussed love languages.

My love language was words of affirmation. At one point, I explained that to Carson, along with what that meant in terms of what I needed. He dismissed it as ridiculous, saying I shouldn't need so much reassurance. He didn't understand—or didn't have the capacity to understand—that level of reassurance, because that wasn't his love language or what he needed. I explained that the entire point of knowing your partner's love language is so that you can express love in the way they need it. But his response? It was up to me to understand that words of affirmation weren't his love language and, therefore, he shouldn't have to give them to me just because they were my need.

He only felt comfortable giving love in the way he wanted to receive it. So, my choices were either to accept that I would never receive love the way I needed (which is what happened for so long) or to somehow change mine to fit him (which isn't possible—love languages are not something you can just choose to change, at least to the point of feeling unconditionally loved).

His lack of willingness to even try to understand my love language showed me that he didn't have the capacity to love me—not in the way I needed. Not only that, but he openly chose not to try.

Yes, it all seems so obvious now, doesn't it?

Now that I understand that I deserve to receive love in a way that fulfills me—and that his lack of capacity wasn't my fault—I can let go of thinking I was the crazy one for asking my husband to love me the way I needed. I can let go of the idea that I just had to accept "that's just how I am—too bad." I can let go of the insecurities that came from never feeling fully loved, and the anxiety and isolation it created. I am placing ownership back on him and his lack of capacity, intentional or otherwise. I no longer resent those statements, nor do I resent that he couldn't love me the way I needed. I forgive him. Forgiving didn't come because he apologized—as I truly don't think he believes he did anything wrong—but rather, forgiving came from my understanding of his capacity to love me. Those hurts no longer take up space in my heart or mind.

So, as I said in a previous chapter, I love him more now for the happy times we had than I did at the time, because I am freed of the resentments that I carried. I am able to understand his love from his capacity, rather than from my expectation.

Does it still make me sad? Yes.

Do I wish, more than anything, that things could have been different? Yes.

But do I still ruminate over it? No.

And, as a thought, perhaps neither of us really had the capacity to love each other. A relationship is two people, after all.

A more hopeful example is my dad. He set the standard for men in my life—the amazingly awful pattern that I am finally breaking free from. But how and why did he set that standard? Or perhaps, more importantly, did he even know he had set it?

When I told him that I was following in his footsteps—getting divorced—and that I, too, had done the most awful thing one can do in a marriage, he surprisingly stepped up. At first, it was very superficial, yes, but I hadn't expected anything, so it was significant to me. He drove nearly six hours to my house at the last minute to be there for my first big holiday with my kids and without Carson, so they could see their grandpa—two of them meeting him for the first time. Again, this may seem small, but to me, it was huge, as this, to me, demonstrated growth. His actions were actually louder than his words.

And then, the unthinkable happened—something I had long accepted as impossible so that I could heal. (I had accepted he, too, lacked the capacity to understand what he did.)

My dad apologized for everything. This wasn't a vague, blanket "I'm sorry for everything" statement, which I likely would have barely acknowledged. Instead, it was an insightful, reflective apology, specifically mentioning several examples, taking ownership of his actions, and acknowledging how they had impacted me—even if he didn't understand why some of his actions—and inactions—had affected me so deeply. In that moment, I experienced so much healing—an almost instant understanding and peace.

He had set the pattern of low self-worth and unhealthy relationships. He defined what I would tolerate from narcissistic men—my normal. What I came to learn, however, was *why* it happened. His why, it turns out, was very different from those who followed. My dad, at the time of his painful actions, was truly doing the best he could. Back then, he completely lacked the capacity to be what I needed. Now, so many years later, with more capacity for reflection, he was able to acknowledge it all. This was not driven by excuses or defensiveness—he had even initiated the conversation. Instead, it was filled with depth, insight, and ownership. As he spoke, I stood in shock.

Of course, this does not change my experiences. It does not erase the trauma, the patterns I developed as a result, or what followed with others. But it did change my perspective on him—and it opened up the idea of reconciliation and hope and an *almost* trust in people (I'm still working on this). My dad, despite his past limitations, had always noticed my strength and my ability. Even in moments when it was difficult to see, he had pride in me and confidence in me. Understanding his capacity, both then and now, shifted my past views of being unworthy or unwanted by him.

The others?

I have already forgiven them—not for their sake, but for mine. I can let go, knowing that they do not, and may never, have the capacity to understand the impact of their actions and inactions. Understanding capacity allows me to forgive, so I can be filled with joy and not pain, with happiness and not resentment, so I can continue to grow, freed from the chains of pain.

The challenge of this exercise in forgiveness was simple (this is also something used in AA): using "I" statements and feeling words, list everything. Get it all out there. Release it. Don't overanalyze, don't explain it for anyone else—just write it down, visibly, and then let it go. Then, write wishes for everything on the list. And finally—the hardest step of all—forgive.

Forgiveness Exercise:

I have anger toward my mom for not being able to form a true attachment to me from day one.

I have feelings of frustration and anger toward my dad for leaving so many times—for making me think I had a choice, for brainwashing me into believing I had a choice. For making me feel like I had to be perfect to earn attention, which I translated as love. For not accepting me because I am a girl. For modeling how to be loud and outspoken to a fault—forcing my opinions to trump others, no matter what. For making me believe that was what love looked like, how men should treat women and children. For not having the capacity to be what I needed when I needed it.

I have hatred toward my grandma for commenting on my body in a swimsuit when I was just a child. For making me believe we had a special connection. For telling me I killed my mom. For abandoning me right after I had just lost her. For making all the years since my mother's death about her. For never telling me about my step-grandfather dying, then lying to Molly about it. For not caring. For forgetting my existence completely since I was 16.

I have rage toward Susan for lying to my mom. For always playing the cool aunt while deceiving her. For Molly ending up with her dad. For me ending up where I did. For separating us. For standing me up when I tried to reconcile. For forgetting my existence completely since I was 16.

I have hatred toward Candy for always coming and going—choosing her own interests over everyone else's, even her daughters.' For trying to take advantage of Grandpa at the end of his life. For so easily washing me from hers.

I have anger toward Brandon for being cruel and selfish. For making me revolve my world around him. For criticizing and insulting me.

I have sadness toward Dane for not fighting for me harder.

I have anger toward Justin (the other guy from medical school)—for telling me to try with Carson before we could be together. For loving me so much, then allowing me to go down this road.

I have so much anger toward Carson. For being on that pedestal. For being judgmental and critical. For not having the capacity to actually love. For never trying to know or understand me. For making everything about him. For making me owe him from practically day one because of Justin, even though we weren't even together. For changing my entire career path rather than encouraging my dreams. For insulting my size—for weighing himself in front of me even when I asked him not to. For not wanting to know my story—because of his own fears—rather than supporting his wife. For never fighting for me. For throwing me under the bus. For isolating me. For making me move to his hometown. For his brain tumor. For never planning a date or doing something for me just because. For blaming it all on me. For only ever caring about himself first. For giving me pain meds after surgery so I could take care of four kids while he went to golf, rather than stay home. For not caring about my grandpa, yet expecting me to take care of his whole family. For forgetting the better years because of the last years. For dismissing me saving his life, more than once. For minimizing it all and calling it lies, it wasn't. For stealing my journals and other things. For freely sharing them with no regard for how it would impact not just me but our kids. For not owning that and, rather, blaming all of the gossip on my old *friends*. For misinterpreting the journals and spreading those misinterpretations. For saying only his parents and brothers knew the content. For naively believing that. For my kids having to care so much about whose week it is that they're afraid to sit by me on his week. For not being able to forgive me for the sake of our kids and for not accepting my apologies and attempts at having a conversation.

I have so much rage toward Jack. For abusing his wife and lying to his kids. For knowing my entire story and then using it against me to make everything worse. For using me for his own glory. For disposing of me when I was no longer useful. For lying on my applications—and then lying to my face. For trying to destroy me, my career—the very career that he rode to the top. For getting away with everything while continuing to defame me. For all the fake love, which now just feels like long-term betrayal. For being the worst "he" imaginable.

I have fury toward Alex for ruining me at age 16—at the worst time of my life—for taking advantage of that 16-year-old me. For doing it again several years later and manipulating and charming me for more than 20 years. For playing so many mind games that I questioned my own sanity for so long, even after it was legally over.

I have resentments toward big business and corporate medicine for not actually caring about patients—placing their greed and egos first. For being so fake and self-righteous—some claiming to be faith-based organizations that care about people, when in reality, they are like every other historically white male-dominated business that only cares about money and the good old boys' club. For making all of their employees just numbers, just as they do patients. For never investigating Jack's sexual assault but instead protecting their friend and dismissing me.

I have disappointment in what I thought was a women-led, empowering organization that also chose the easy way out—the male way out—believing only what they were told by Jack and never even asking questions to find the truth.

I have so much disappointment and sadness toward Emily and Jennifer—my two best friends—who completely backstabbed me, even though they knew the truth. For abandoning me like everyone else.

I have so much sadness toward my ex-in-law family for threatening me and using my kids to do so. For making me truly feel loved for so many years and yet forgetting all of it, never asking more questions. For not seeing me as the mother of Carson's kids for the rest of their lives.

I have so much anger at my mom for dying.

I have so much anger at my grandpa for dying.

I have so much anger at Nancy for dying.

I have so much anger at Anna for dying.

I have so much anger at God for taking all the good ones.

I have so much frustration, anger, resentment, and shame toward myself for all my bad choices—and for never seeing any of it until it was way too late.

I have so much sadness that I never could see my worth and value. That most of my anger at the "others" is because self-destruction is controllable, predictable, and known. That the resulting void and isolation are safe and comforting, so I never challenged others to value me or see my worth. That I was okay playing a part—until I wasn't. That somehow, staying in the toxic boat felt safer.

I also have sadness that I created a façade that felt safer than being alone—until it wasn't. I am sad that I didn't know. All I ever wanted in this world was to matter. To anyone, really.

To my dad—enough for him to never leave.

To my mom—enough for her to never die.

To my entire "family"—enough for them to understand that I actually needed people, not just for them to passively choose to acknowledge and decide, without my input, that I was fully capable of handling it all on my own. Although I appreciate the confidence, they were not wrong in their intent—but the feelings of rejection, isolation, and not having people were far more damaging to my soul.

To Alex—enough to be respected.

To Brandon—enough to never be called fat.

To Carson—enough to actually love me for me, to want to learn to love me for me. To be my person and my partner. To be willing to do anything and everything, including owning his actions—without always flipping it. I wanted him and us forever. I saw that it could have been possible. I just wish I mattered enough for him to try, rather than just expecting me to accept that he shouldn't have to try. Why did he not see the need to grow?

To bosses and the old white men who never took the time to just listen—to hear my passion and help guide and support that, rather than mute it.

To the ones who said they were my friends—to actually be friends, rather than jump ship at the first sign of adversity.

To Jack—enough so lives could be saved without mine being sacrificed by repeating Alex's cycle, Carson's cycle, my dad's cycle.

To those who were easily manipulated by Jack—for never being curious, for never asking questions, for falling for his ways.

To God—enough so that I didn't have to keep being tested, challenged, and forced to always be strong, resilient, and capable of handling everything.

So what do I wish for them?

I wish all of them peace, as they, too, find their way in this world. I wish no ill will. I hope they are all able to live and grow as people with good hearts and make a positive difference in this world. I wish from them forgiveness and an understanding that my apologies are genuine. Most importantly, though, I wish for them to know their worth and to have true and genuine love and safety.

I now understand capacity and how that was reflected in actions and behaviors. And in doing so, I can let go. I have freed myself of the pain. I have freed myself of the resentments. I forgave them all—for me—so I can be.

What I wish for myself?

All I want is to matter.

All I want is to be happy.

All I want is to be worth it.

I want someone to defend me, fight for me, and stand up for me.

I want to be worth the sacrifice, the time, the energy, the focus, the determination, the perseverance—the all of it.

I want to be shown, someday, that all of this has been worth it. The burning waves of chest pain that are so common and frequent. The feelings of hopelessness and unworthiness. The wanting to just give up, to tap out.

It's been a horrible, twisted game—some puppeteer playing master controller of my life, always keeping me on the fringe of having "it," only to pull me back. How much can a human take? Where is that ultimate breaking point?

It's a cruel, twisted joke—because on the surface, this puppeteer created a world in which the abandoned protagonist appears to be the crazy, selfish, too-high-standards, ungrateful antagonist.

And at times—when I've reached that breaking point—I have been just that.

It's the perfect setup, really.

No one would ever suspect it, so it will never end.

I'm too together.

Too strong.

Too resilient.

Too capable.

I can do it all.

And I'll still smile and be grateful. I'll advocate for the "others" whom the world left behind—because it all has to mean something.

And somehow—magically, without it even making sense—I'll be so damn good at it.

It's a gift—ha—no, it's personal experience.

I've mastered it.

They see and say- but you didn't use drugs, you didn't go through *all the things,* you had a great life. And YOU, Heather, CHOSE to ruin it. You chose it all—ahh, the concept of choice. The sick joke is on you—you did it to yourself.

Yes, sure, I did, in some ways, but not all. But they won't see that. And that is okay.

I will own every second of my truths—the ones tightly packaged and placed on the furthest shelf—buried deep in the most toxic barrels. The truth of what the master puppeteer has actually orchestrated. A truth no one would believe anyway. A truth this book only skimmed the surface of—because I've done the work to find the high road, to forgive and move on.

Who am I to be anything but Heather? I've created such an amazing Heather. She's so good, it's almost unbelievable. Which, ironically, she is just that—unbelievable.

She isn't who you see. She isn't who the world sees.

Heather is all the things—selfish, empathetic, smart, ungrateful, an advocate, a bitch, strong, resilient, a boundary-pusher, loud, chaotic yet together… She is the hurricane of order and handling.

She is who you want in chaos, at war, when any emergency happens.

But that Heather wasn't even real.

That Heather was skillfully, artfully, masterfully created—to protect the newborn, the three-year-old, the eleven-year-old, the sixteen-year-old, the twenty-two-year-old—the, the, the… the real Heather inside the layers of walls.

The outward Heather finally wanted a voice—and did it all wrong. She cracked and destroyed her perfect outer life in the process.

The real Heather remains, deep inside, and she is good.

She is survival. She just wants to finally breathe.

But breathing hurts. Breathing is the fire in the chest.

But breathing is leading to waking—to the growth of that inner Heather.

She is vulnerable and honest and raw and scared—yet still feels unworthy, unloved, and alone.

She was never worth the people—but she's starting to outgrow the plaster walls of the outward Heather.

The armor can't be rebuilt; it's now mere dust, being blown away by growth. It no longer has the ability to protect the Heather growing in honest, genuine, and true strength.

The emerging Heather doesn't want to create another shell, yet the desire to matter causes more anxious, burning pain. The rawness will evolve—but hopefully, it won't callous. She cannot go back there.

But, alas—and again—the puppeteer knows that even though it's terrifying, she will still survive. She will come out stronger, better, more resistant. But it will be real this time.

She doesn't want her kids—or anyone—to ever feel this same loss, this same abandonment, this same sense of unworthiness—the need to build a fortress of protection. She wants them to feel and be authentic.

She's fighting to avoid the scarring, but again, she can only take so much.

There will be a day when the stage lights turn on, and the puppeteer will emerge—declaring the results of what feels like the world's most twisted experiment.

My hope is that on that day, the real Heather will be there to see it, to feel it, to embrace the worth of it all. She will see her worth in it all—will feel the worth from it and for it all.

And 'the others'—the ones who questioned and doubted and ridiculed and abandoned and overlooked and chose not to love, the ones who said she wasn't worth it—will see she was there all along. Scared and crying and burning in the corner, just hoping to be found.

But she will have survived.

This Heather—she is here. She is strength, though sometimes she still burns. She will likely always burn at times, will always question at times.

She doesn't yet know the *why*. But does anyone ever really *know* their why until the very end? Like the saying:

The two most important days in your life are the day you are born and the day you figure out why.

But does anyone ever really *figure out* their *why* before the very end?

Each day, the *why* shifts. Even on days when it doesn't seem to. Even on days when it takes a step back. But regardless, each day is a small shift toward understanding—whatever that may be.

This Heather, though, has learned to trust the journey rather than always fight it or try to control it.

She has learned to embrace the small glimpses of sunlight that shine through the darkest and most painful moments—to see the joy and hope.

She knows her traumas. She has owned the actions she took as a result of—or in spite of—them.

She accepts where she came from, the road she's been on, and—more importantly—who she is now. Understanding, of course, that that is always evolving as well.

The most important thing about this Heather, though, is that despite it all—and not in spite of it all, as nuanced as that may seem—she does, in her soul, know her worth.

Her standards may seem high at times or in certain situations, but she is okay with that. She knows the traumas she survived made her worth it.

I forgive… all, even myself.

I choose to bless… all, even the naïve.

I have gratitude…

That I survived.

That I have the greatest gift in the universe because of it all—my kids.

That I found self-worth.

That it all made me stronger, even after it broke me to pieces.

I found my trauma's worth.

Epilogue

There is no epilogue yet.

But there will be—because my story isn't over. There will be more trials, more chaos, more moments of sadness and pain.

And yet…

There will also be more happiness, more joy, more peace, and more safety.

And in the end, it will all be worth it.

Made in the USA
Monee, IL
07 May 2025